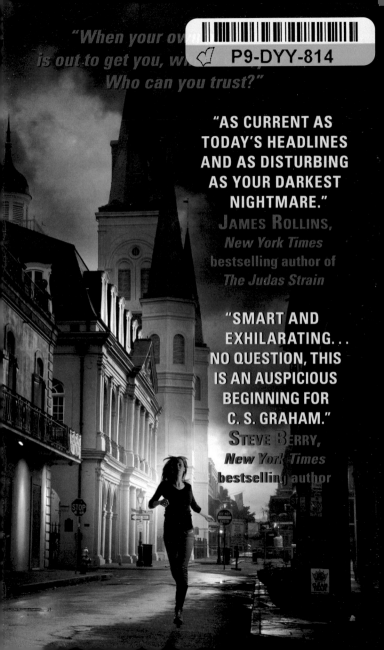

"When your own ___ is out to get you, wh___ Who can you trust?"

"AS CURRENT AS TODAY'S HEADLINES AND AS DISTURBING AS YOUR DARKEST NIGHTMARE."
JAMES ROLLINS,
New York Times
bestselling author of
The Judas Strain

"SMART AND EXHILARATING... NO QUESTION, THIS IS AN AUSPICIOUS BEGINNING FOR C. S. GRAHAM."
STEVE BERRY,
New York Times
bestselling author

P9-DYY-814

"Do you want to talk about why you joined the Navy?"

"That's easy. I joined the military so I'd have money to go back to college, and I chose the Navy because I didn't think they'd send me to Iraq."

"You didn't want to go to Iraq?"

"Are you kidding?"

"Did you like the military, Tobie?"

"No. I'm a lousy shot, I can't run, and I have trouble with authority. Or at least that's what the shrink in Wiesbaden told me. I don't like to take orders." Tobie figured the shrink's report was probably somewhere in the papers he was shuffling. That report and a lot of others. When you get a psychiatric discharge from the military, the process generates a slew of reports.

"Do you enjoy your work with Dr. Youngblood?"

"In some ways."

"In what ways don't you enjoy it?"

"I find it . . ." She hesitated, searching for the right word. "Disturbing."

"And why is that, Tobie?"

He was no longer smiling. And neither was she. "You know why."

By **C.S. Graham**

THE ARCHANGEL PROJECT

Forthcoming
THE DEADLIGHT CONNECTION

THE ARCHANGEL PROJECT

C.S. GRAHAM

HARPER

An Imprint of HarperCollinsPublishers

HARPER

An Imprint of HarperCollins*Publishers*
10 East 53rd Street
New York, New York 10022-5299

Copyright © 2008 by Two Talers LLC
ISBN 978-0-06-135120-4
Excerpt from *The Deadlight Connection* copyright © 2009 by Two Talers, LLC.

First Harper paperback printing: October 2008
First Harper special printing: May 2008

HarperCollins® and Harper® are registered trademarks of Harper-Collins Publishers.

Printed in the United States of America

Visit Harper paperbacks on the World Wide Web at www.harpercollins.com

10 9 8 7 6 5 4 3 2 1

To the people of New Orleans

AUTHOR'S NOTE

- The government remote viewing programs, their history, and the various historical incidents described in this story are real, as are the books mentioned in relation to them. These programs, known as Grill Flame, Sun Streak, Center Lane, and Star Gate (among others), were officially terminated in 1995-96 and some of their relevant material declassified. Only declassified information has been divulged in this story. For an entertaining look at the programs' history, we suggest *Men Who Stare at Goats,* by Jon Ronson.

- The declassified 1986 *Defense Intelligence Agency Training Manual for Remote Viewing* is real and is available on the Internet.

- The remote viewing sessions described in this book are as accurate as we can make them. For a more complete and authoritative analysis of the process, see Joseph McMoneagle's *Mind Trek.*

- The September 2000 policy document of the Project for the New American Century (PNAC) described in this book is real.

- The U.S. contingency plan herein referred to as "the Armageddon Plan" is also real, although it is not known by that name.

- Division Thirteen is a figment of the authors' imagination.

- The spelling "al-Qa'ida" is a more accurate transliteration of the Arabic word than the more familiar "Al Qaeda" typically seen in the Western press.

1

"Let me see the sketches."

Lance Palmer passed the folder to the elegant, Armani-clad woman who rode beside him in the limousine. He watched, silent, as she slipped on a pair of reading glasses and flipped through the folder's contents. She frowned at the crude representation of an encircled K emblazoned against a dark background, then paused again to stare at a vintage World War II C47 Skytrooper that seemed to soar through the air.

Hurriedly rendered in pencil on page after page of cheap loose-leaf, the drawings didn't look important. But these sketches—and the person who drew them—had the power to destroy some of the most important people in Washington and bring down a president.

Adelaide Meyer raised her gaze to Lance's face. "You're certain these sketches are from a remote viewing session and not the result of a security leak?"

"I'm certain." Remote viewing had been the object of intense scientific and governmental investigation for more than sixty years, but most people still had a hard time accepting it as real. Lance would probably have been suspicious himself if he hadn't worked with remote viewers in the Army.

Through the tinted, water-flecked window beside him, he caught a glimpse of the Lincoln Memorial as it swept past, its normal horde of tourists thinned by the storm lashing the city. Adelaide Meyer peeled the glasses off her face and rubbed the bridge of her nose. At fifty-three, she was CEO of one of the world's largest corporations, a sprawling conglomerate with interests in everything from the construction and defense industries to oil. She was also, through a series of subsidiaries and holding companies, Lance Palmer's boss.

"When you came to me with this proposal, I never expected it to turn into such a disaster."

Lance set his jaw. Thirteen years in Army Special Operations taught a man to accept responsibility for his mistakes. "It's a problem," he said, keeping his voice calm. "But it's not a disaster. It can be contained. Right now these sketches are meaningless."

Adelaide Meyer fit her reading glasses back on her face. She was slim and reasonably attractive for a woman her age, but in all other respects she was a woman cut in much the same mold as Madeline Albright and Maggie Thatcher: a hard-as-nails broad with the mind of a Rhodes scholar and the ethical standards of a serial killer.

"They won't be meaningless in forty-eight hours." Flipping back through the drawings, she paused again at the crude sketch of the old C47. Lance felt his ulcer burn. She looked up. "Who knows about this?"

"Henry Youngblood. The woman who did the remote viewing. I think that's all."

Adelaide Meyer kept her eyebrows plucked into razor thin, unnatural arcs. As Lance watched, one eyebrow arched even higher in a parody of a smile that had been known to make prime ministers ill. "You think? We don't pay you to think, Mr. Palmer. We pay you to know. And to do."

"If there's anyone else, we'll find them."

She closed the folder, drummed her fingers on the gold-embossed burgundy cover. "This woman; who is she?"

"Probably a student. We've pulled a list of the people who've been working with Youngblood from the university's records."

Her fingers stopped their drumming. "You don't know her name?"

"The only one who knows that is Youngblood. But he'll tell us. Don't worry." Lance's organization was very good at extracting information. They'd perfected their interrogation techniques at Guantanamo Bay and Abu Ghraib and a dozen other detention facilities the American people didn't want to hear about.

"See to it that he does." Adelaide Meyer punched the button on the limousine's intercom and spoke to her driver. "Mr. Palmer will be leaving us. There should be a taxi stand at the next corner." The limo slowed.

"I want this cleaned up." She reached for the morning copy of the *Wall Street Journal* and snapped it open. "I want it cleaned up and I want it cleaned up fast. Or

I'll have someone else do it. And I can guarantee you won't be happy with that." Over the top of the newspaper, her gaze met Lance's for one telling moment. "Understood?"

The limousine pulled in close to the curb, sending water from the gutter surging over the sidewalk. Lance opened the door. "Perfectly," he said, and stepped out into the lashing rain.

The rain beat against his shoulders, ran down his cheeks in cool rivulets. He stood and watched the limousine speed away toward Capitol Hill. Then he nodded to the nearest taxi driver. "Reagan Airport," he said, and slid into the backseat.

He put a call through to his wife, Jessica. "I'm afraid I'm going to be late tonight, honey. Tell Jason I'm sorry about missing his game." He listened to Jess make the requisite noises, then said, "I should be home by midnight. If not, I'll see you tomorrow morning."

Lance closed his phone. He had just over forty-eight hours, but he didn't expect this little clean-up operation to take anywhere near that long. He was very good at what he did.

2

"At the end of our last session, we explored the possibility that you might be setting extraordinarily high standards for yourself. Have you been thinking about that?"

October Guinness glanced at the psychiatrist seated on a gently worn leather chair beside the study's empty fireplace and laughed. "My sister's an electrical engineer making over a hundred thou a year, my brother has his own accounting firm, and I'm a college dropout. You're the only person I know who thinks I set unusually high standards for myself."

Colonel F. Scott McClintock had thick silver hair and kindly gray eyes set deep in a tanned face scored with lines left by years of smiling and squinting into the sun. But at the moment, he was not smiling. Templing his fingers, he tapped them against his lips before saying, "You compare yourself to your brother and sister?"

"Why wouldn't I? Everyone else does."

As soon as Tobie said it, she regretted it. It was exactly the kind of offhand remark McClintock picked up on. She watched him jot down a quick note, probably part of the growing itinerary for another session labeled "Family Issues" or something like that. After five months of coming here every other week, she was beginning to understand how the Colonel worked.

He was semiretired now, after nearly forty years as a clinical psychiatrist. Most of those years had been spent in the Army. He still worked with patients from the local VA hospital as a volunteer. Since Hurricane Katrina smashed the VA's facility on Perdido Street, he'd taken to seeing his few remaining patients here, in the study of his big old Victorian just off St. Charles.

"We haven't talked yet about the reason you dropped out of college," he said in that soft voice of his. "Maybe now would be a good time to touch on it."

Tobie shifted in her chair. "I don't want to talk about that."

There was a pause. He drew a deep breath and let it out slowly, a subtle sign that he was disappointed. While Colonel McClintock analyzed October Guinness, Tobie in turn analyzed the Colonel and his methods. She figured it was only fair.

"All right," he said. "Do you want to talk about why you joined the Navy?"

"That's easy. My stepdad told me that if I dropped out of college, he wouldn't pay for me to go back. I joined the military so I'd be able to get the GI Bill, and I chose the Navy because I didn't think they'd send me to Iraq."

It was the truth—as far as it went. But it also avoided

several key issues, including the fact that her real father, Patrick Guinness, had been in the Navy when he died. But Tobie didn't see any reason to give the Colonel more fodder for his Family Issues session than he already had.

"You didn't want to go to Iraq?" said the Colonel.

"Are you kidding? The only people who actually want to go to Iraq are either seriously delusional or very, very scary individuals."

"It didn't occur to you that your skills as a linguist might be found useful?"

Tobie laughed. As an expat's brat growing up around the world, she'd been fluent in Arabic by the age of eight. "Yeah. But I thought they'd assign me to the Pentagon, or to some nice safe ship parked out in the Persian Gulf. I didn't expect them to send me to Baghdad."

Sometimes she wondered what her life would be like if she'd been born and raised in one place rather than being yanked around the world by her parents. Any kid who grows up in Qatar and Frankfurt, Paris and Jakarta, is inevitably going to be strange—even when all their sensory input is firmly planted in the here and now.

But Tobie had spent her childhood bringing home report cards with teachers' notes that read, "October spends far too much of her time in class daydreaming . . . " Every year, her mother would sigh and get the same worried, baffled expression on her face. Meredith Guinness-Bennett's two oldest children were studious, hardworking, *normal*. But Tobie, by far the youngest, was always a problem, drawing strange pictures when she should have been studying, and running with the local kids rather than hanging out with the other expats' children. They were habits that left her with a passable drawing ability and a knack for picking up languages. But while her sister had been student body president and her brother captain of the football team, Tobie never quite fit in anywhere, even though she'd learned early to hide the things she saw, the things she knew.

She'd spent the first twenty years of her life trying very, very hard to convince herself it was all imagination, coincidence. But two experiences had ripped through that protective cloak of denial. Henry Youngblood called them "spontaneous remote viewing experiences," but Tobie hadn't known what they were at the time. The first was so traumatic that she'd dropped out of college. The second, in Iraq, nearly got her killed and helped earn her a psycho discharge.

She realized the Colonel was watching her closely. "Did you like the military, Tobie?"

"No," she said baldly, and saw a gleam of amusement light up his eyes.

"And why was that?"

"I'm a lousy shot, I can't run for shit, and I have trouble with authority. Or at least, that's what the shrink in Wiesbaden told me. I don't like to take orders."

Colonel McClintock shifted his papers but said nothing. Tobie figured the report from the shrink in Wiesbaden was probably somewhere in those papers. The Wiesbaden report, and a lot of others. When you get a psychiatric discharge from the military, the process generates a slew of reports.

"Post-traumatic stress syndrome," they'd called it. But October knew even that label had provoked dissension.

According to one psychiatrist at Bethesda, October Guinness was certifiably nuts and probably had been even before they'd made the mistake of letting her into the U.S. Navy.

"Do you enjoy your work with Dr. Youngblood?" asked the Colonel, surprising her by the shift in direction.

She relaxed a little. The Colonel was one of the few people with whom Tobie could discuss Youngblood's project. The other military psychologists she'd dealt with had all looked at her file and labeled her crazy. But McClintock had tapped his templed fingers against his lips and asked her questions about her daydreams as a child. He talked to her about what she'd seen in Iraq and how she'd seen it. Then he'd handed her a thick declassified Defense Intelligence Agency document called *Training Manual for Remote Viewing* and phoned his friend Dr. Youngblood at Tulane.

"I enjoy it in some ways," said Tobie. As a child, she'd eventually come to accept the idea that she was a bit weird. But between them, McClintock and Youngblood were working to convince her that she was neither weird nor crazy. She simply had a talent she could learn how to use—and control.

"In what ways don't you enjoy it?"

"I find it . . . " She hesitated, searching for the right word. " . . . disturbing."

"And why is that, Tobie?"

Their gazes met and held. He was no longer smiling, and neither was she. "You know why."

3

Once upon a time, Dr. Henry Youngblood had been considered a respected academic. Courted as a speaker at conferences, he'd been an easy favorite for grant money and was published regularly in all the right journals. Then he was sucked into a research program on remote viewing secretly funded by the United States government, and all that changed.

It had taken Henry a while to realize what his new interest was doing to his career. Scholarly journals started rejecting his articles. Colleagues snickered when the once esteemed Dr. Youngblood walked into a room. It was a career-wrecker, this kind of research. Not because of the involvement of the government— which was unknown—but because of the nature of the research itself. Yet Henry couldn't let it go. Even when he had to dig into his own pocket to continue financing his experiments. Even when the demands of operating without support kept him working in his office night after night, as he was now.

Casting a quick glance at the clock, he swiveled his chair toward his desk and flipped on his computer. The monitor stayed blank except for a bright yellow message that blinked out at him. *WARNING! WARNING! Unauthorized access to files detected.*

Henry huffed a short laugh. The warning system was the university's, not his. As far as he was concerned, the new hacker-protection program was just one more thing that could go wrong—and frequently did. He was a research psychologist, for Christ's sake, not a nuclear physicist. Why would anyone want to hack into his files?

Still smiling faintly, he typed in the password to clear the warning message and hit Enter. The message kept blinking.

His amusement sliding into annoyance, Henry glanced again at the clock. He was supposed to be meeting Elizabeth for dinner down in the Quarter at eight. Elizabeth Vu was thirty-nine years old, attractive, bright, and single; Henry was forty-eight, divorced for six long, lonely years, and carrying around a gut that spoke of an expanding love affair with New Orleans food. He was so preoccupied with his research that he rarely remembered he was supposed to have something called a life. He needed to get this data entered into the files before he quit for the night, but women like Elizabeth didn't come into Henry's orbit very often. The last thing he had time for was computer problems.

Rapidly pecking at the keyboard with two pointed

fingers, Henry punched in the password again. Then he paused and lifted his head when he heard the street door below open and close.

Tulane's psych department had relegated Henry to an office in the Psychology Research Annex, which was what they called the old two-story nineteenth-century white frame house on Freret Street that handled the department's overflow. The house had never been renovated to suit its new function, so what were once a dining room, parlors, and bedrooms had simply been pressed into service as offices and lab space. The place had been in bad shape even before Katrina; now it was a virtual death trap to anyone with mold allergies.

Being sent to the Annex was considered a state of exile: punishment for his determined pursuit of a project most academics considered absurd if not downright unscientific. But the Annex suited Henry just fine. He wasn't particularly troubled by mold. His office had once been a large corner bedroom at the back of the house, so it had the kind of nice architectural touches— like double hung windows and high ceilings and hardwood floors—that he loved about old New Orleans houses. True, the air conditioner was broken and the ceiling still showed an ugly brown water stain left from when Katrina took off most of the shingles on the roof. But he'd managed to scrounge up enough funds to have one of the unused rooms down the hall soundproofed for his research and training sessions. And because the Annex was on the edge of campus, people tended to leave him alone. Most of those with offices there were graduate students. The place was usually deserted by now.

Cocking his head, Henry listened to the footsteps coming up the uncarpeted stairs. Two men, or maybe three, he thought as the old wooden floorboards creaked. He glanced out the open side window to the driveway below. It was empty except for his ten-year-old Miata.

Henry sucked in a quick breath of hot air scented with jasmine and sun-baked asphalt. He'd been working in the field of parapsychology for almost twenty years, and never once in all that time had he himself experienced so much as a whisper of premonition, a hint of anything he might have termed extrasensory perception. Until now.

His heart hammering painfully in his chest, Henry turned toward the door. He'd pushed halfway up from his desk chair when a man's figure filled the open doorway.

The man paused, his pale blue eyes narrowing as the light from the overhead fluorescent fixture fell on the even, familiar features of his face. The two men behind him also hesitated. One was big and dark; the other more leanly muscled, with a pair of silver-rimmed glasses that lent an air of scholarly distinction to an otherwise military bearing.

"Lance." Awash in a giddy wave of relief that left him feeling vaguely silly, Henry sank back into his chair. "This is a surprise."

"Hey, Henry," said Lance Palmer, and smiled.

4

"Let me introduce you to my associates," said Palmer, one arm swinging around to indicate the men behind him. "Michael Hadley and Sal Lopez."

Henry returned the men's nods. He'd seen enough Navy SEALs and Army Rangers while working on government contracts out at Stanford to recognize the type immediately, with their tight jaws and fixed expressions and alert postures. The organization Lance Palmer worked for was full of such men. It never occurred to Henry to question why these two men were here, now.

"My boss was impressed with the results of your little demonstration," said Palmer, while Henry hurried to clear stacks of papers and books from the office's scattered, mismatched chairs. "Very impressed indeed."

Henry turned with a pile of books in his arms, his pulse thrumming with anticipation and hope. "It was accurate, was it?"

"Uncannily so. So accurate, in fact, I had a hard time

convincing my boss you hadn't found some way to fake the results." Both men laughed. It was a suspicion Henry had dealt with time and again when he'd been working on the Grill Flame Project for the Army.

"So are they interested?" asked Henry, trying hard to sound casual but not succeeding.

"The suits are drawing up the contracts even as we speak."

Henry shoved the books he'd been holding onto the top of the nearest filing cabinet, then just stood there, grinning like an idiot. Wait until Elizabeth and Tobie heard this!

"Where'd you find this remote viewer, anyway?" Palmer asked.

Henry felt his grin grow wider. "She's incredible, isn't she? A colleague of mine recommended her. She's the best viewer I've ever studied."

Palmer nodded. "Who is she, exactly?"

Henry gave a nervous laugh. From somewhere, unbidden, came a shadow of his earlier unease. "The identities of viewers are always kept secret. You know that, Lance."

Palmer leaned forward in his seat. He was no longer smiling. "But surely you can tell us now? After all, we're going to be funding this project."

Across the room, Sal Lopez sat with his hands loose at his sides, while Michael Hadley had taken up a position near the door. Neither man looked directly at Henry.

Henry had no illusions about the nature of the organization Lance Palmer now worked for. From the open window came the sound of the hot breeze shifting the leaves of a nearby oak and the blaring of a ship's horn from out on the Mississippi. Henry was suddenly, intensely aware of the stillness of the evening around them, of his own relative weakness compared to the strength and training of the three men ranged about his office. And he felt it again, that whisper of warning that spoke from across the eons. This time he listened.

He gave a shaky laugh. "I guess you're right." He turned toward the door. "Some of the things she's done are amazing. Let me get her file so I can show you. I'll be right back."

Henry hurried down the darkened hallway, his footsteps echoing hollowly in the old empty house. A slick layer of cold sweat lined his face, trickled down between his shoulder blades. He threw a wistful glance at the training room, with its reinforced walls and heavy, dead-bolted door. But the room was kept locked and he'd left the keys lying next to his computer. He thought about making a break down the stairs, then realized they'd hear and be after him in a minute.

His breath coming hot and fast in his throat, Henry ducked into one of the empty offices. He eased the door closed behind him, his cell phone already flipped open in his shaky hand.

His fingers were clumsy. He wasted precious seconds searching through the menu for Tobie's number. More time waiting for the call to go through. He kept his terrified gaze fixed on the panels of the closed door. His ears strained to catch the least hint of movement from the hall.

The phone began to ring.

"Come on, Tobie," he whispered as the it rang for the second, then the third time. "Answer."

It was possible he was wrong, of course. Maybe he was overreacting to the point of foolishness. He could deal with the embarrassment if it came to that. But if he were right—

A computer-generated voice said, "You have reached the mailbox of . . . *October Guinness*. At the tone, please record your message—"

"Damn," he swore, hitting the appropriate key and waiting for the requisite beep. "Come on." It finally sounded, high-pitched and long . . .

Just as a board creaked out in the hall.

5

Tobie was leaving Colonel McClintock's study when she felt her cell phone begin to vibrate in her messenger bag.

"Still going to therapy for your leg?" asked the Colonel, walking with her to his front door.

"I'm down to twice a week now," she said, ignoring the phone's gentle summons. The bullet she'd taken in her left thigh in the deserts of western Iraq had snapped the femur. That was bad, but the worst part was the way the subsequent weeks of immobility had aggravated an already bad knee. If she hadn't caught a psychiatric discharge, she would probably have been given a medical discharge. Although maybe not. The United States military was getting pretty desperate these days. "I've noticed lately it only tends to hurt when I run."

"Which you don't like to do anyway."

Tobie huffed a soft laugh. "Which I don't like to do anyway." She reached for the front door handle. "Tell Mrs. McClintock hello for me."

At the base of the porch's wide wooden steps, Tobie

paused. Her cell phone had quit vibrating. She fished it out of her bag and frowned at the sight of the message icon. Pressing Talk, she shifted the bag's strap on her shoulder and headed for her car.

Lance Palmer knew something was wrong.

The sudden stealth of Henry Youngblood's movements betrayed him. The Army had spent a lot of time and money teaching officers like Lance about people's behavior, about things like neurolinguistic programming and body language and voice patterns. But Lance didn't need anything more than common sense and a keen awareness to tell him that a man with nothing to hide walks with a firm, steady gait. He turns on lights. Makes noise.

Dr. Henry Youngblood moved furtively. Nervously. Like a man doing something on the sly. A man who is afraid.

Lance slipped his Glock 18 from its shoulder holster and motioned for Lopez and Hadley to follow him.

Hugging one wall to minimize the betraying creaks from the old floorboards, they crept toward the front of the house. The hall was lined with half a dozen closed doors. Lance resurrected the memory of Henry's careful footsteps, the distant click of a closing door, and focused on the two front rooms overlooking Freret Street.

Pausing at the end of the hall, Lance could hear the faint whisper of a man's voice coming from behind the door on their left. He settled into a balanced stance, the Glock extended in an easy, double-handed grip. His gaze met Lopez's and he nodded. Lopez pulled his own

pistol and with one powerful kick sent the door crashing open.

Henry Youngblood stood in the middle of the room,
his middle-aged body frozen in terror, his face a slack
oval in the early evening light. His hand jerked and the
dying sunlight streaming in through the front window
glinted on metal.

"He's got a gun!" shouted Lopez, squeezing his
Glock's trigger twice. The silenced percussion sounded
like pops in the small room.

It wasn't until two dark holes opened up between
Henry's eyes that Lance realized what the professor
held. Lance walked over to nudge the dead man's hand
with the toe of one shoe. "It was just a cell phone," he
said, giving Lopez a hard look.

Henry Youngblood was supposed to die, of course.
But not yet and not like this. Not with two bullets in
his head. And not before he'd told them everything
they needed to know. It was to prevent exactly this kind
of mistake that Lance had come down here and taken
charge of the operation himself.

"Shit," said Lopez.

Easing his Glock back into its holster, Lance bent to
lift the phone from Youngblood's lifeless grip.

If the professor had been talking to someone, he must
have ended the connection when he heard them in the
hall. Lance glanced at his watch, then flicked through
the menu to the list of outgoing numbers. Youngblood
had called someone named Tobie.

The name meant nothing to Lance. He hit redial,
his gaze traveling around the darkened room. It was
empty except for a dusty desk and an old wooden chair.

The office was obviously unused. Whatever Henry had come in here for, it wasn't to get a file.

The connection went through, going immediately to voice mail. "You have reached the mailbox of . . . *October Guinness*—"

An unusual name, Lance thought as he pressed End. He remembered seeing it on the university's pay list. He turned toward Michael Hadley and smiled.

"Got her."

6

Tourak Rahmadad snagged a bag of potato chips, popped open a beer, and wandered into the front room of the half-renovated cottage he and three fellow students rented in an area of New Orleans known as Gentilly. Unlike most of the other Middle Eastern students who formed Jamaat Noor Allah, the Light of God, Tourak actually liked America—which surprised him, because he had expected to hate it.

He'd been in the States for three years now, studying journalism and filmmaking at the University of New Orleans. After 9/11, when white Americans started treating people with dark skin and foreign-sounding names the way they used to treat American blacks, Tourak had begged his parents to let him study in Paris, or maybe London. But his mother insisted that he go to the States. She had a cousin, Kamal, who lived in New Orleans and promised to watch out for him. Actually, the desire to escape the watchful eye of cousin Kamal was one of the reasons Tourak wanted to go to Paris. But his mother was the one paying the tens of thousands of dollars it cost to send him overseas to study. And so he had come to America.

Life here had been difficult at first. So much was strange, different. But most of the people Tourak met in New Orleans were surprisingly friendly, and he had fallen in love with the city's moss-draped oaks and wide, slow moving river, with its platters of spicy crawfish and cold pitchers of beer. He liked Mardi Gras and shopping malls, cable TV and Baskin Robbins ice cream. But he still really, really hated the American government.

Flopping into a scruffy beanbag chair, Tourak pointed the remote control at the TV and flipped through the channels. He was restless tonight, unable to settle. In just forty-eight hours he would face the most important test of his life. Once, he had prayed to God to be given such an opportunity. Now he was nervous, afraid. His fear shamed him. What if he froze at the last moment? What if he couldn't do it? He would let everyone down.

He flipped through two more channels, then paused at what passed for an American "news" network. The network alternately amused and infuriated him. So much of what they broadcast was a tissue of lies and exaggerations, all carefully crafted to deceive and manipulate. In other countries, people were more cynical, more suspicious of those with the power and means to deceive. But Americans weren't like that. They were so credulous, so gullible. Even after Watergate and the Gulf of Tonkin, the Bay of Pigs and Iran-Contra, the American people still believed everything their government and news outlets told them. Tourak found that both incomprehensible and frightening.

He was about to switch the channel when a woman on the screen caught his eye. She appeared to be in her early thirties, dark and attractive in a way that reminded him of his sister Naji, who was a surgeon in Tehran.

The young woman was leaning forward in her seat, her face drawn and serious as she said, "We have to stop them, even if we have to kill them all to do it. If we don't, they'll destroy civilization and take over this country. I don't want my children to grow up in a world run by illiterate mullahs who rant about evil and preach holy war against infidels."

Practically choking on his beer, Tourak leaped from his chair and pointed the remote at the woman's face, zapping her out of existence. "You stupid, bigoted donkey!" he screamed at her. "We *started* civilization, remember? You're the ones who've been bombing the cradle of civilization back into the Stone Age. It's your politicians who rant about axis of evil and evildoers and preach crusades against anyone who isn't a Judeo-Christian. We don't want to take over your stupid country. We just want you to get out of our part of the world and stay out!"

One of Tourak's roommates, a physics student from Syria, called from upstairs in Arabic, "*Ya, habibi. Aish bi'dak?*"

"Nothing," Tourak shouted, then slammed out the door to go stand on the front stoop and look out over the ghostly dark neighborhoods of the ruined city.

He had come from Tehran to the States to study journalism because he'd believed in the power of the truth to overcome ignorance and prejudice. But over the course of the last three years it slowly dawned on him that he had been as naive as he accused the Americans of being. Because most people weren't swayed by words, particularly if those words were an uncomfortable truth.

Lately, Tourak had begun to believe the only truth Americans understood was the kind delivered by the barrel of a gun, or the explosive exit of a man driven to suicide by the grim realization that while he might be powerless in life, his death could change the world.

7

Most people who knew October Guinness looked upon her decision to move to post–Katrina New Orleans as proof-positive that the girl was certifiably crackers.

She had no previous connection to the city. Her father might have grown up in Louisiana, but he died when Tobie was only five years old and she'd never known his family. Her mother's people were from South Carolina and her stepdad from Oregon. His career as a petroleum engineer meant they'd lived in some far-flung places when Tobie was growing up, but Louisiana wasn't one of them.

She remembered calling her parents the night before her scheduled discharge from Bethesda. Her stepdad had retired to Colorado, and her mother had prattled on breathlessly about fixing up Tobie's old room and the looming deadline to register for next semester's classes at the University of Colorado—which was where Tobie had gone to school before dropping out just two months shy of graduation.

But she hadn't wanted to go home. Not as a twenty-four-year-old college dropout with a psycho discharge from the Navy. If she was going to start over, she wanted to do it someplace new. It seemed appropriate to rebuild her life in a city that was also struggling to rebuild itself.

"I'm not coming back to Colorado," she'd told her mother. "I've been accepted into Tulane. In New Orleans," she added into the stunned silence.

"Are you nuts?" her stepdad, Hank Bennett, had thundered on the other extension.

She'd leaned her forehead against the cold-frosted window of her hospital room and laughed. "That's what they're saying, isn't it?"

Hank didn't get the joke. He never did. "Do you have any idea what a mess things still are in New Orleans?"

"Yes."

"You'd qualify for in-state tuition here, you know. How much is Tulane?"

"A lot."

"I'm not paying for it."

"I'm not asking you to."

It was one of the reasons Tobie had agreed to start working for Henry Youngblood. He couldn't pay her much, but it helped supplement her GI Bill and the small disability payment she got from the Navy. Plus he'd arranged to give her three credits a semester. It was a deal she found impossible to refuse . . . even though it did require her to confront an aspect of herself she'd spent a lifetime avoiding. If Iraq had taught her one thing, it was that she couldn't continue to hide from the truth. Whether she was gifted or cursed, she had an unusual ability she needed to learn to understand and to control. Dr. Youngblood was teaching her to do both.

Now, sliding into the driver's seat of her 1979 yellow VW Beetle, Tobie rolled down the windows and opened the sunroof. Most people thought Tobie drove the old Bug because she liked vintage cars, but the truth was, she had bad luck with modern electrical products. She'd learned to buy the extended warranty on everything from computers and cell phones to DVD players and TVs because few lasted even a year. And she'd learned to buy cars too old to have a computerized anything.

According to Dr. Youngblood, good remote viewers frequently had an odd effect on electronics. At one time, he said, the CIA and NSA had actually tried to find some way to use the phenomenon to crash the Soviets' computers and weapons systems. But since the disturbances only affected electronics within a person's immediate vicinity, the government could never figure out how to use it against their enemy du jour. They'd just learned to keep remote viewers away from their own sensitive systems.

The inside of the car was still unbearably hot, so she left the door ajar to catch the evening breeze while she sat and listened to the message Dr. Youngblood had left on her voice mail. His voice sounded hushed, strained. "October? Henry Youngblood here. Listen . . . I'm afraid I might have made a terrible mistake. They came here, to my office. They don't know who you are, but these people are dangerous, Tobie. If they—"

The connection ended abruptly. Puzzled, she saved the message and was listening to it again when another call from Youngblood came through. But when she tried calling him back, she went straight to his voice mail.

Checking the time, Tobie shoved her phone into her bag and pulled away from the curb. If she knew Young-blood, he was probably still in his office. It would be easier to just swing by campus on her way home than to keep playing phone tag with him all evening.

She thought about his message as she drove toward the university. She didn't have a clue what the professor might have been talking about. In Youngblood's world, dangerous people killed tenure applications or cut off funding for projects. Was that it? Was someone threatening to close down Henry's program—and her job?

She could see a mass of heavy thunderheads building on the horizon, casting an eerie silver light over the scattered piles of building rubble and occasional squatty FEMA trailers that still dotted the streets. This part of town had stewed in Hurricane Katrina's floodwaters for less than a week. Not as long as other areas, but long enough to undermine a lot of aging foundations and wreck havoc with century-old floor joists and timber framing. The neighborhood was starting to come back, but she'd heard people saying it would probably be ten to fifteen years before the last of the FEMA trailers were gone.

By the time she turned onto Freret, thunder was rumbling in the distance and an early darkness had settled over the campus. She spotted Youngblood's little red Miata in the Annex's side yard. She thought about pulling in behind him, except she didn't have a parking sticker for this zone and the fines for violations were stiff. Turning onto Newcomb Boulevard, she had to

drive halfway down the block before she found a place
to pull her VW in close to the curb.

The evening was quiet, the stately old homes lining
the street somber behind their drawn curtains. She
walked back toward Freret, her footsteps echoing in
the stillness. A nearby stand of bamboo rustled faintly
in the suddenly cool breeze, and a dog began to bark.
Tobie ran one hand up her bare arm and wished she'd
thought to throw on a jacket over her T-shirt.

She was just stepping off the curb to cross Freret
when the Annex exploded.

A concussive blast of heat slammed into her, knocking her off her feet. She hit the ground hard, her ears
ringing, her arms coming up to wrap around her head
as jagged, flaming timbers rained down around her
and a roaring caldron of flames leaped high into the
stormy sky.

From the black Suburban parked around the corner,
Lance Palmer watched the dancing flames light up the
cloudy evening. The smell of smoke and burning timbers lay heavy in the sultry air.

A quick search of Youngblood's files had turned up
nothing they needed to worry about. They'd brought
the files away with them anyway, along with the professor's hard drive, just to be sure. It was to cover up
the missing files and dismantled computer that they'd
decided to torch the building.

An investigation might in time discover that the fire
had been caused not by some leaky gas line but by a
sophisticated incendiary device of the kind favored by
the U.S. military. An autopsy would definitely turn up

a couple of well-placed bullet holes in whatever the fire left of Henry Youngblood's head. But by then it would all be over. As soon as they took care of the girl, Lance thought, his embarrassing little problem would be solved. Even in the best of times, the NOPD hadn't exactly been known for their brains, and these were hardly the best of times. They'd never be able to connect the dots.

From somewhere in the distance came the screaming whine of an emergency vehicle's siren. Lance flipped open his phone. "Get me the address of a woman named October Guinness . . . That's right, October," he said again, when the voice at the other end of the line queried the name.

Lance leaned back in his seat and waited. With just a single phone call he could find out virtually anything he needed to know about anyone, from the most embarrassing details of their medical history to the brand of toilet paper they used. Within a minute he had the address.

"Number 5815 Patton Street?" he repeated. He nodded to Lopez. "Good. I want as much additional information on this woman as you can put together ASAP."

Lance slipped the phone into his pocket and smiled as the Suburban pulled away from the curb. Things hadn't exactly gone according to plan with Youngblood, but at least they had the girl's name. All they needed to do now was make sure she hadn't told anyone about what she'd seen, and then silence her. Permanently.

8

Fire engines and police cars clogged the street, their flashing blue and red lights reflecting off the water that pooled at Tobie's feet. She stood with her arms wrapped across her chest, her gaze fixed on the roaring inferno before her. Oh, God, Henry, she thought. Please tell me you weren't in there.

There were times when Tobie believed she probably deserved her psycho discharge. She still broke into a cold sweat when she heard the thump of a helicopter overhead, still awoke too often, screaming, in the middle of the night. And when Tulane's Psych Annex exploded in front of her, knocking her off her feet, for one hideous, heart-pounding moment, she'd actually thought she was back in Iraq.

When they sent Tobie to Iraq, they told her the linguist she was assigned to replace had been blown to pieces when his Humvee rolled over an IED. She always tried hard not to think about that when she went out into the field as an interpreter. She also tried not to think about the fact that the officers she was assigned to accompany were prime targets—which made her a prime target, too.

But it didn't take her long to realize that in Iraq, she was never safe. At any moment a mortar round could come smashing into their compound. Snipers might lurk behind any rock or ruined wall. Ambush potentially awaited every convoy that ventured out of the Green Zone. Every person she passed in the souk might be a suicide bomber.

Yet alternating with those intense moments of terror stretched vast hours of tedious boredom. Most of her days were spent at a scruffy desk in an airless room where she translated endless reports and transcriptions of intercepted telephone or radio conversations.

Then, in early September, her unit buzzed with the anticipation of a major coup. Telephone intercepts suggested a large gathering in the western desert, and some of the names bantered around in the intercepts seemed to be on their watch list. Satellite photos showed images of tents and white pickup trucks. The intel people went nuts. They were convinced they'd stumbled on a huge terrorist gathering. Tobie wasn't so sure. But she was just a linguist, an interpreter, not an intelligence analyst.

It was one afternoon when Tobie was looking at some low-level Predator reconnaissance photos Lieutenant Costello had stuck up on the wall, that the images first came to her, like a daydream or a memory she held in her mind. Flashes of sights and sounds and smells that had nothing to do with the airless office where she spent her days.

A laughing young woman braiding her hair. Gnarled hands kneading bread. A child spinning around, the gold coins on her ankle jangling as she danced before a Bedouin tent, its brown-striped camel hair sides stretched taut beneath the desert sky.

At first Tobie tried to ignore what she had "seen." She pushed it to the back of her mind, told herself it was just her overactive imagination. A daydream. But she knew it wasn't. Once before, during her senior year in college, she had ignored the images her mind somehow plucked from the ether. As a result, her best friend had died. The guilt she still carried from her inaction that day had driven her to drop out of college and, ultimately, hide in the Navy. She didn't understand why or how these images came to her, but they were powerful enough that she finally went to see Lieutenant Costello.

"This encampment," she said, standing nervously before his desk, "the one in the western desert you think is a terrorist gathering? It's not. It's just two tribes who've come together for a wedding. Those tents are full of women and children."

The Lieutenant looked up from the papers spread across his desk. He was a Marine, with a rawboned face and a pronounced disdain for Naval personnel—especially female Naval personnel. "You got that out of some intercept, Guinness?"

Tobie felt her cheeks heat. "No. I saw it."

His brows drew together in a frown. "Did we get some new photos?"

"No."

"Then where did you see this, Guinness?"

"I just . . . " She hesitated. "Sometimes I just know these things."

He stared at her for a long moment, his lips pressed together, not saying anything. Then he gave her a smile that wasn't really a smile at all. "You just 'know' these things, do you? We've been watching this buildup for weeks, Guinness. This is what we do, and we're good at it. There's been no indication of any wedding. It's a gathering of insurgents, and it's huge. You think it's something else, you'd better come to me with some solid evidence. This is an intel unit. We don't operate on feelings."

"But you're wrong. There are all these children—"

"That's the way these guys operate." Lieutenant Costello stood up and assembled the papers on his desk. "They hide in with women and kids, and then cry when they get them blown to smithereens."

"But—"

"There's no 'buts' about this, Guinness. A combined air strike and ground assault has already been called in for 0400 tomorrow morning." He hesitated, then added gruffly, "We've all been under a lot of strain here lately. Why don't you take the rest of the day off?"

He was being easy on her. She knew that. But she couldn't let it go. "If you let this happen, our forces will kill dozens and dozens of innocent women and children. They're—"

His jaw tightened. "Listen, Petty Officer—you're way out of line. I don't want to hear any more about this. Now just go to your quarters."

Tobie went to her quarters—for half an hour. Then she grabbed her helmet and flak jacket and headed for the helipad, where she talked her way onto a Black-hawk ferrying medical supplies out to forward head-quarters. She wasn't sure what she could do to stop the assault once she got there, but she knew she had to do *something*. She couldn't just pace up and down in her quarters while innocent people were massacred.

The Blackhawk crew put her in touch with a couple of Marine medics who let her perch on the outside of their Humvee as they headed out across the stony desert in the cold calm of predawn. The attack was scheduled for 0400, but as the Marines approached their unit, they could hear sporadic gunfire in the distance.

"Sounds like they've already started boogying," said the driver. "Our guys must have spooked someone."

A familiar thunder vibrated the air around them. Tobie leaned down to stick her head through the Hum-vee's open window. "Hear that chopper?"

The Humvee crested a rise and the driver screamed, "Jesus Christ!"

A white Toyota sped up the hill toward them, dust bil-lowing behind it into the night. Hot on its tail, a Kiowa helicopter materialized out of the dark sky, its whirling blades beating the crisp desert air, the insectlike spread of its landing gear and loaded pylons looming over them. Through the Toyota's grime-coated windows, Tobie caught a glimpse of a woman's covered head and half a dozen small, wide-eyed faces. Then the helicop-ter belched a missile and the Toyota exploded. Caught in the fireball, the Marine medics' Humvee flipped.

Tobie was thrown clear. She landed on her back, the impact driving the air from her chest. For what seemed an eternity all she could do was lay in a gasping agony, surrounded by the broken, burned bodies of the Iraqi family who'd tried to run in the Toyota. The Marine medics were dead, too.

But the guys in the Kiowa Warrior weren't through yet.

Pivoting at the top of the hill, the helicopter swooped back toward the wreckage, its machine guns spitting fire. Frantically scrambling for protection behind the upturned Humvee, Tobie felt a round tear through her thigh and heard the bone snap. She was lucky it was just a glancing blow; a direct hit would probably have taken off her leg.

Then all hell broke loose as the full-scale attack on the encampment below began. Pinned down by her broken leg, Tobie could only watch, helpless, as the tents below burst into flames. Screaming women erupted into the night, to be mowed down by withering machine-gun fire. Rockets shrieked, their explosions punctuating the endless rattle from the helicopters that filled the sky. The last thing she remembered was the sight of a crying child silhouetted, alone, against the fire's light.

The next thing Tobie knew, she was on a stretcher. She was babbling to anyone who'd listen about the wedding and what she'd "seen," until a nurse with a worried frown stuck a needle in her arm.

They flew her to Kuwait first, then to Germany. Whenever anyone asked her what in the hell she was doing out in the desert, she told them. A sad-eyed Air Force surgeon in Wiesbaden kindly suggested she might want to reconsider what she was saying, but Tobie refused to shut up. In the end, they gave her a psycho discharge.

She'd been lucky. Lieutenant Costello had tried to have her court-martialed.

"Excuse me, miss. You need to get back."

The crackling roar of the fire still loud in her ears, Tobie turned to find a short, squat policewoman studying her through narrowed eyes.

"I'm October Guinness. I'm the one who called 911."

The policewoman sniffed. She had peroxide hair and a broad, plain face prematurely hardened by overexposure to the ugly side of life. "Live around here, do you?"

"No. I was coming to see Dr. Youngblood."

"He's the guy you reported was in the building when it blew?"

"That's right. Dr. Henry Youngblood. He's a professor of psychology."

The policewoman fished a notebook out of her pocket. "And your name and address?" She wrote down the information, then said, "You his student?"

"No."

"Girlfriend?"

"No."

Tobie watched the policewoman's head come up and swore silently to herself. The tone of that last response had been all wrong and Tobie knew it. She didn't deal well with people in uniform—one of the many reasons she should never have gone into the military. "I work for him," she said, giving a half smile.

The smile was not returned. "Were you supposed to work for him tonight?"

"No."

"So what are you doing here?"

"He tried to call me about half an hour ago. I got the impression he was working late."

The policewoman lowered her notebook and looked pained. "So you don't actually know for sure that he was in the building?"

"That's his red Miata there, in the driveway." What was left of his Miata. Tobie stared at the blackened ruin of Youngblood's car and wondered how the policewoman would react to what she was planning to say next. "He left a strange message on my voice mail. Something about having made a mistake, and dangerous people. I thought he meant someone was threatening the funding for his research project, but now I wonder . . ."

The policewoman blinked. "Those were his exact words? 'Dangerous people'?"

"Yes."

The policewoman wrote it down. "You say this guy is a professor of psychology? Is he working on anything in particular?"

Tobie hesitated. *The giggle factor*, Youngblood called it. Tobie had learned to be careful about what she said about remote viewing and how she said it. "He was, um . . . He was looking into different forms of cognitive mental functioning. But I don't see how the project could have had anything to do with this."

The policewoman flipped her notebook closed. "Right. We've got your name and address. If we need anything more, we'll be in touch. In the meantime, I suggest you get out of the way and let these men do their work."

Tobie felt a pain pull across her chest. She drew in a

deep breath of smoke-tinged air to try to ease it. "But they're not even trying to rescue him. His office is in the back, on the left—"

"It'll be hours before anyone can get in to check and see if he really was here when the place blew. For all we know, this Dr. Youngblood of yours could be sitting in a coffee shop someplace sipping a latte."

"But—"

The policewoman took an aggressive step forward, one hand hovering suggestively near her hip. "Look, miss. I don't want to have to tell you again. Now get back."

Tobie clenched her jaw against an unwise response and swung away.

She walked across the street to Newcomb Boulevard, but she didn't go back to her car. Worried about Dr. Youngblood, frustrated by her inability to do anything, she stood on the sidewalk in front of the big brick bungalow on the corner until the lady who'd been hovering on the house's broad porch called her over.

Elegantly dressed in linen shorts and a silk blouse, the woman was excited and wanted someone to talk to. Tobie sat on the porch steps and let the woman rattle on about the rash of fires since Katrina and the continuing shortage of police. The flames from the fire felt hot against Tobie's face, but the damp chill from the bricks seeped up through the cotton of her skirt as she watched the Psych Annex burn.

9

Lance Palmer considered himself one of the good guys. As a kid he'd been Luke Skywalker, battling the forces of evil with a plastic light saber. He'd charged into imaginary jungles as a war-painted Rambo, rescuing anyone who needed it and killing as many gooks as he could. Later he'd been a star running back on his high school's football team in Lawton, Oklahoma, and joined the ROTC at Oklahoma State. He'd signed up with the Army right after graduation.

Lance loved the Army. He'd made it into the Rangers, then Special Forces. He'd spent thirteen years doing the kind of things he'd dreamed of doing as a kid, fighting America's enemies from Nicaragua to Afghanistan and advising U.S. allies on how to handle dissidents and other lowlifes.

But as much as he loved the Army and the action, Lance had eventually grown discontented with the money. The Army provided its officers with a comfortable, middle-class lifestyle, but he wanted more. He wanted a Beamer and a stock portfolio, while his wife Jess hungered for a beach house in Florida and skiing vacations with the kids in Aspen. Luxuries beyond the reach of an Army major.

But luckily for him, modern American warfare was changing. More and more, the United States was coming to rely on what they called private security firms—no one ever used the word "mercenaries," which was of course what they were. Some of the outfits the United States and Britain were sending to Iraq were full of crazy cowboys who'd as soon shoot a raghead as look at him. But Global Tactical Solutions was a professional organization. Yeah, they signed up some South Africans, but they drew the line at hiring the Pinochet-trained Chileans that some of the other firms were sending into Iraq.

After just one year at GTS, Lance had been appointed head of their Special Operations. He was a troubleshooter, the guy who handled their sticky stuff. Basically, he was doing exactly the same kinds of things he'd done as a major in the Army, only now he was getting paid a whole lot better.

"Hey, look at this," said Hadley. He was in the backseat, flipping through the stream of information coming in over their laptop as the Suburban headed toward the river. "Our girl was in the Navy. She's even an Iraq War vet." He let out a low whistle. "We're talking psycho discharge."

Lance twisted around in the seat. "Let me see that."

He'd handpicked the two men working most closely with him on this assignment. They made a complimentary pair: a former Navy SEAL, Michael Hadley was an expert on everything from computers and electronics to explosives, while Sal Lopez, an ex–Green Beret, was always handy to have around to do any necessary heavy lifting.

As Lance took the laptop from Hadley, Lopez turned down a narrow street crowded on both sides with lines of parked cars. He slapped the steering wheel with the flattened palm of his hand in frustration. "What the hell is going on around here?"

Looking up, Lance nodded toward the empty shell driveway of a darkened two-story on the corner of Patton and Nashville. "Just pull in there."

Lopez rolled the Suburban to a stop and killed the engine.

They were parked across the street from October Guinness's house. Lance had spent enough time in New Orleans to recognize the style. Shotgun doubles, they called them. A kind of duplex built without halls, each side of the house had one room opening right behind the other so that if you fired a shotgun in the front door, the blast could pass out the backdoor without hitting anything. Or so Lance had heard.

"Doesn't look like she's home yet," said Lopez. Both sides of the double lay dark and silent, the ornately turned wooden balustrades and colonnettes of the front gallery in deep shadow. "What's she do now that she's out of the Navy?"

Lance scrolled through the information. "She's a student. Tulane. Twenty-four. Single." They had photos from her passport, her driver's license, her old military ID. Not a bad looking woman, if you liked the type. Dark blond hair. Brown eyes. A square chin. He flipped through her Navy records and grunted. "Almost failed her PT twice. Can't run. Can't shoot. She was only in for two years."

"And the psycho discharge?" said Lopez.

"Post-traumatic stress syndrome. Iraq. Looks like something weird happened out in the desert when she was wounded." Lance glanced through her medical report, catching key phrases: "reported seeing visions . . . suffers from hallucinations . . . poor grasp of reality." He wanted to laugh. From the sound of things, the girl had reacted badly to a spontaneous viewing experience. The Navy, in its infinite wisdom, decided she was crazy and kicked her out.

"This is good," said Lance. "We'll set the death up to look like a suicide."

Lopez smiled. "She sounds easy."

Lance grunted. He had no qualms about what he was about to do, just as he had no regrets about what he had already done tonight. The girl had seen enough to be dangerous if she—or someone else—put it all together and started asking questions. Collateral damage, that's what the military called civilian deaths. There was always collateral damage in a war. Regrettable, but necessary.

And they were at war. The President was always telling them that. Lance was simply doing what needed to be done to protect his country. He was fighting for freedom and democracy and to make the world a better place. Henry Youngblood and October Guinness had become threats not just to the security of this country but to the future of the world. They had to be eliminated. Quickly.

With the air conditioner off, the interior of the Suburban was already heating up. Lance slid down the window, his trained gaze studying the neighborhood.

The shotgun double had a small side yard, dark now beneath the heavy shadows of the spreading oaks that lined the street. Beyond that stood an old corner grocery store that someone had turned into a combination nursery and florist shop. Two other houses faced the small, narrow street on this block, both shotgun doubles with camelback second floors. Only the house on the corner showed any lights.

"Who lives in the other half of our girl's double?" he asked.

"A guy by the name of King," said Hadley, back on the computer. "Ambrose King. A musician. Works at some club down in the Quarter."

"Which means he won't be home anytime soon." Lance opened the door. "Hadley, you stay here. Lopez, come with me. Let's take a look around before our girl gets home."

Silencing her was going to be a cakewalk, Lance thought as they crossed the darkening street. They just needed to make sure all knowledge of the results of her little session with Youngblood would die with her.

10

Pushing aside the memories of Iraq, Tobie got in her car
and headed home. She kept telling herself that maybe
the policewoman was right; maybe Henry had been sipping a latte in some local coffee shop when the Psych
Annex exploded into kindling. But every time she tried
to call him, she went straight to voice mail.

With a sigh, she flipped her phone closed and pulled
into the covered parking lot of the Whole Foods on
Arabella and Magazine. She could still smell the bitter
reek of smoke clinging to her clothes and hair, pinch-
ing at her nostrils. All she wanted was to go home and
stand under a hot shower. But she was out of cat food,
and while she wasn't the least bit hungry, she knew she
needed to eat.

Twenty minutes later, a bag of groceries on the seat
beside her, she pulled out onto Magazine. This was the
part of New Orleans near the river that hadn't flooded,

although the storm's winds had taken their toll on the neighborhood. The houses here were old, a mixture of stately Victorian mansions and tiny nineteenth-century cottages that all had one thing in common: a serious lack of off-street parking. Many of the narrowest streets—including hers—had been made one way, which meant she had to swing around in a wide loop in order to get home.

But even before she made the turn from Constance onto Eleanor, Tobie knew from the lines of cars on both sides of the street that parking, tonight, would be more difficult than normal. Glancing up the block, she caught sight of a stretch limo disgorging a white satin and tulle decked bride in front of the steps of St. Francis of Assisi, and groaned.

Oh, no. Not tonight. Weddings at one of the neighborhood's two churches were even worse than back-to-school nights at the nearby elementary. She'd be lucky if she could find a place to park for blocks.

One glance up Patton was enough to convince her not even to try her own street. She had to go down to Laurel and over another half block before she got lucky and was able to squeeze her little yellow Bug into the gap between an Explorer and a Lexus.

So far the rain had held off. But she could see lightning flickering in the distance as she shrugged into her cotton jacket, hefted the grocery bag, and set off walking. She smelled the coming rain in the air. Felt it. A clap of thunder exploded like an artillery shell, and she startled so badly she almost dropped her groceries.

She stopped, her arms clutching the bag, her heart pounding uncomfortably in her chest. She told herself she was being silly. The policewoman she'd spoken to at the fire didn't seem to attach much significance to the message Dr. Youngblood had left on her voice mail. The fire was probably due to a gas leak, she'd heard them say; the building was old, after all. They told her she was lucky she'd still been outside when the building blew. She had no reason to be acting like—well, like she deserved that psycho discharge from the Navy.

She quickened her step down Patton, her breath coming easier as she swung open her low gate and headed up the short brick walkway to her front gallery. An orange cat leaped over the edging of monkey grass and threaded through her legs, nearly tripping her. She laughed.

"Hello, Beauregard," she said, and fumbled for her keys. It was good to be home.

11

The rolling hills and gently wooded glens to the west of
Washington, D.C. sheltered an exclusive community
of sweeping country estates and genteel horse farms
known as Great Falls. There, in an imposing Tudor-style
building at the end of a long, private drive, lay the Fox
and Hound, an exquisite restaurant frequented by ambas-
sadors and ex-presidents and defense industry executives.
Lower level CIA officials and operational personnel like
Jax Alexander rarely saw the inside of places like the Fox
and Hound. But then, Jax wasn't a typical field agent. And
he wasn't the one paying.

He'd been named James Aiden Xavier Alexander, a
mouthful that just about everyone who knew him short-
ened to Jax. The only person who insisted on called
him "James" was his mother, and that was because she
refused to acknowledge the existence of his two middle
names, both of which were on his birth certificate at the
insistence of his father.

"I don't think it's too much to ask that my only child make an effort to attend his mother's wedding," said the elegant woman who sat across from him. Born Sophie Winston, she'd married Jax's father and become Sophie Alexander the same week she turned twenty-one. But in the decades since then she'd had so many different husbands and names, Jax wondered how she could remember what to sign on the bottom of her credit card slips.

Jax reached for his wineglass and decided, judiciously, to refrain from pointing out that he'd already attended six of her weddings. "I said I'll try. Matt is talking about sending me out to California next week."

"Really, James. I can understand how this job might have appealed to you when you were younger. But don't you think it's time you looked around for something more . . . " She hesitated.

"Respectable?"

"The word I was thinking of is lucrative."

Jax laughed and said, "I like my job," although that wasn't exactly true. He *had* liked his job until last winter, when a little run-in down in Colombia with the ambassador and some sociopaths in Special Operations had earned him a transfer to Division Thirteen, which was the CIA equivalent to being taken out to the woodshed.

"Dick was talking to me just the other day about a position he thought you might be interested in."

Senator Richard Talbot was the man scheduled to become Sophie's Husband Number Eight. Jax clenched his jaw, shook his head, and dredged up something he hoped would pass as a smile. "No thanks."

Softly pouting, Sophie stretched back in her seat and tossed her long, mahogany-colored hair away from her face in an innately feminine gesture that brought virtually every male head in the room around to stare at her.

Sophie had an undeniable gift, a gift she had long ago learned to use to her advantage. The candlelight was kind, but the fact remained that she still looked startlingly good for a woman in her forty-ninth year. She had been blessed with what she liked to call enduring bones. Of course, self-absorption, the regular expenditure of staggering amounts of money, and a little nip and tuck here and there all helped.

Most people considered Sophie a serial trophy wife, but in that they underestimated her—or gave her credit for too much guile, depending on one's point of view. Because the truth was that, at heart, Sophie believed in love and romance, in white lace and happily-ever-after. She honestly believed every time she married that she was in love with the man she'd chosen. More incredibly, she also believed each and every time that *this* marriage was going to be the one that would last.

Jax had stopped believing in anything by the age of seven.

Of course, Sophie might be a romantic, but she was also one smart lady. Every man she'd married—except for Jax's father—had had serious Money. And Sophie always managed to finagle prenuptial agreements that kept her own growing fortune safe while leaving the man's assets open to pillage and plunder.

But then, as far as Jax was concerned, any man stupid enough to marry a woman who'd already gone through that many husbands deserved to pay for his arrogance.

"You haven't even heard what the position is yet," said Sophie.

"It doesn't matter. I'm still not interested." Jax's phone began to vibrate in his pocket. He reached for it. "Excuse me a minute," he said, and slipped out of the dining room, to the foyer.

The call was from Matt von Moltke, head of Division Thirteen. "You need to come in right away," he said, his voice, as always, gruff and abrupt.

Jax looked at his watch. "Now?"

"Now. And bring a bag with you. You'll be flying out as soon as we're finished with the briefing."

"Flying where?"

"New Orleans," said Matt, and hung up.

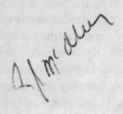

12

Clark Westlake took the steps to the Executive Office Building two at a time. It was late, even by Washington standards. But when he'd suggested to Vice President T. J. Beckham that they skip their weekly intelligence briefing, Beckham had pitched a fit. The VP didn't like being left out of the loop. So Clark was here to oblige.

Clark Westlake was forty-six years old, trim and good-looking, with a perpetual tan and only a touch of gray at his temples. Three terms in the House followed by a stint as CIA chief and his current role as Director of National Intelligence had brought him to first-name basis with that shadowy group of hyperrich, like-minded men who quietly ran the country. He confidently expected to be his party's candidate for vice president in the next election. Not only was he photogenic, but his intelligence background made him look satisfyingly tough on defense and homeland security without exposing him to the kind of nasty innuendos and smear campaigns that could derail the political aspirations of a real combat vet.

Passing through security, Westlake flashed one of his famous smiles at the comfortably middle-aged woman who occupied the desk just outside the VP's door. No hotties with implants for T. J. Beckham; the man was a poster child for solid middle-class values. "Hey, Susan. Shouldn't you be home by now?"

The Vice President's secretary returned his smile. "Shouldn't we all?" She hit the buzzer under her desk. "Go on in. He's waiting for you."

Westlake didn't like the sound of that. In addition to receiving a weekly intelligence briefing in person, the Vice President was also on the list of select officials who received the President's Daily Briefing, or PDB, as it was called. A slim booklet delivered daily, the PDB summarized current world threat intelligence. Presidents like Carter and Papa Bush faithfully read their PDBs every day. Most didn't. The current president was like Ronald Reagan: he rarely opened the thing. But newly appointed Vice President Beckham poured over his PDB like a schoolboy cramming for a quiz. Which meant he could sometimes ask Westlake some pretty embarrassing questions.

Westlake found Beckham standing in the center of his office, his hands wrapped in a near-professional grip around a putter, his concentration all for the ball he was about to tap into the cup.

"Clark," he said, not looking up. "Come on in. You don't mind if I keep practicing, do you? I've got a game with Bob tomorrow and I'm determined to be in top form."

"You beat him last time, didn't you?" said Westlake, going to lounge in a burgundy leather chair.

"Barely." T. J. Beckham eyed the shot, then gave the ball a quick tap that sent it straight home. "Ha!" He moved on to the next ball. "So. What dire threats are the folks over at ODNI fretting about these days?"

Westlake studied the tall, lanky man before him. Beckham habitually wore baggy gray trousers, red suspenders, and a red bow tie. He looked and sounded like a pharmacist from some old-fashioned corner drugstore in the wilds of Kentucky—which was exactly what he'd been when he ran for Congress nearly thirty years ago. Westlake had never understood how the man won his seat—or how he kept winning, year after year. It was a sad commentary on the state of the nation that such a man had been elevated to the position of vice president.

He hadn't been elected, of course. President Bob Randolph had chosen as his running mate Chuck Devine, an old-school party boss with the instincts and demeanor of a Soviet commissar. Then the unthinkable had happened: two years into his second term in office, Chuck Devine had dropped dead of a heart attack at the age of sixty-four.

The timing couldn't have been worse. The ongoing war in the Middle East combined with endless tax cuts for the rich had sent the deficit soaring and the economy tanking. Middle-class America was starting to feel the pinch, and the normally docile sheep on Capitol Hill

suddenly started worrying about how a too-close asso-
ciation with an increasingly unpopular lame duck president was going to hurt their chances for reelection.

And so they had rejected one after another of President Randolph's proposed nominees. Some were seen
as too cozy with the oil or defense industries; others
were described as too friendly with the likes of ex–
Enron chief Kenneth Lay or slimy lobbyists like Jack
Abramoff. In the end they had settled on T. J. Beckham
largely because they could choose no one else. Beckham was the Gerald Ford of the twenty-first century, an
easygoing, affable man who played golf with the press
corps, smiled a lot, and was confirmed as vice president largely because he had achieved the unimaginable:
over the course of a political career that spanned nearly
three decades, he had made no real enemies inside the
Beltway.

Clark Westlake cleared his throat. "There are a few
things we thought you should be aware of, sir," he said,
and launched into a discourse on the repercussions of
the rise in Chinese fuel consumption and the situation
in Somalia.

Beckham kept putting. He putted through Westlake's
witty retelling of the latest sex scandal to rock the British government. But when Westlake started talking
about a new Iranian missile test, Beckham looked up.

"What did you say this missile is called?"

"The Kowsar, sir. The Iranians are claiming it has a
new kind of guidance system that can't be scrambled.
And that it's invisible to radar."

"Is it?"

Westlake shrugged. "We don't know for sure yet. But

Iranian radar isn't particularly advanced. It's more likely the Kowsar can evade Iranian radar but not ours."

Beckham gave his golf ball a soft nudge that sent it rolling into the cup. "So what's the significance?"

"The Iranians are claiming the Kowsar as their own development. But sources suggest the missile is actually Russian-made. Acquired either from China or the former Soviet Republic of Kyrgyzstan."

"And?"

"The Revolutionary Guard is holding maneuvers this week. They've code named the exercise 'Great Prophet.'"

Beckham lined up another ball. "We hold maneuvers and test missiles all the time."

Westlake laughed. "Yeah. But we're the good guys."

"The Iranians might argue with that."

Westlake studied the VP's craggy, half-averted profile. It was the kind of stupid remark Beckham was always coming out with. How did you answer something like that? "Our concern is that the timing of the maneuvers and the missile test is not coincidental, sir. There are indications the mullahs are gearing up their defenses against a possible retaliatory strike."

Beckham slowly raised his head, his jaw going slack. "You mean, a strike from us? In retaliation for what?"

"A new terrorist attack on American soil."

Beckham went to stand before the window, the putter dangling forgotten from one hand. "Is there any indication such a terrorist attack is imminent?"

"I'm afraid so. There's been a lot of chatter lately."

"What kind of chatter?"

"Much of it's in code, sir. Plus we're still having problems getting good linguists. We know the Iranians are behind something that's going down soon; we just don't know what."

Beckham breathed a long sigh that came out sounding both worried and, oddly, annoyed. "These are dangerous allegations, Clark. Dangerous and troubling."

"Troubling, sir?"

The Vice President kept his gaze on the darkening scene outside the window. "My contacts in the intelligence community tell me you've been cherry picking high threat information. Creating the image of a threat that isn't really there."

Westlake was startled into giving a quick laugh. What the hell kind of contacts did T. J. Beckham have in the intelligence community?

Beckham kept his back to the room. "I still remember Colin Powell's speech before the UN. You remember the one, don't you? The irrefutable evidence of Iraqi weapons of mass destruction that weren't there, the meetings between Saddam Hussein's people and al-Qa'ida that never actually took place, the yellow cake from Niger that didn't exist outside of evidence forged by some murky foreign intelligence service. Like most of my fellow Americans, I sucked it all in. I believed it, and it was all lies. Lies, or a mistake. I'm not sure which is worse—or if it even makes much difference to the tens of thousands of young Americans who have been injured or died for it all. Not to mention the hundreds of thousands of Iraqi civilians."

Clark Westlake held himself very still. "What are you suggesting, sir?"

Beckham swung around. "I'm suggesting that there

are forces in this country that want war with Iran the same way they wanted war with Iraq, and for the same reasons. Not because either one of those half-assed desert states presents any real threat to this country, but because war is profitable, or because it fits in well with their own hidden agendas, or because they have some crazy idea that the end of the world is upon us and all they have to do to see God is ignite some final biblical confrontation in the Middle East."

"After what al-Qa'ida did to this country—"

"Al-Qa'ida?" The Vice President swiped one hand through the air. "Al-Qa'ida had nothing to do with Iraq, remember? Until we smashed the place and unleashed the fires of hell over there, Iraq was a secular state."

"But Iran—"

"Oh, yes; Iran is different. It definitely is run by a bunch of religious nuts. But they've never been allied with either al-Qa'ida, or the Taliban either. I wish we could say the same," he added dryly, "although everyone seems to have conveniently forgotten that shining example of American stupidity."

A heavy silence fell upon the room, broken only by the distant honking of traffic out on the street. Everyone knew the United States had supported the Taliban after the Russian invasion of Afghanistan, just like the CIA probably had more to do with the formation of al-Qa'ida than Osama bin Laden. But it was considered bad form in Washington to mention it. Clark rose slowly to his feet. "The threat of an Iranian-directed terrorist attack on this country is real, sir. Real, and imminent."

Beckham shook his head. "No. I don't believe it. Those Iranian mullahs might be a bunch of reactionary fundamentalist bastards, but they're not stupid. Any state that launches a terrorist attack on this country risks immediate destruction, and the Iranians know it. If we attack them, they'll hit back at us with everything they have. But they won't strike first. And you know it."

The two men faced each other across the length of the room. "What do you think this is? Deliberate scare mongering?"

"Actually, yes. You people fooled me once before, and a lot of innocent people are now dead because of it. I won't be fooled again." He raised one bony finger to point at Clark across the room. "And make no mistake about this: I'm prepared to go public with my concerns if need be."

It was no idle threat, and they both knew it. The idiot still had considerable influence on the Hill and with the press.

Clark Westlake held his jaw tight, his breath coming quick and fast. "If there's nothing more, sir, I'll excuse myself."

"Of course," said Beckham stiffly. "Thank you for the briefing."

"I'll make sure the President is aware of your concerns," said Westlake, and left.

The outer office was dark and quiet in the gathering gloom. Susan was no longer at her desk.

13

Tobie was spooning Pet Promise Wild Salmon Formula into Beauregard's bowl in the kitchen when the doorbell rang.

For an instant she froze. Beauregard meowed, weaving impatiently in and out through her legs. Food was very important to Beauregard. He'd been a scrawny stray when she found him, and he was determined never to be hungry again. She set the cat's food on the floor and hurried across the two front rooms to the door.

Through the tall windows opening onto the gallery she could see dark shapes silhouetted against the light cast by the street lamp. She flipped on the outside light and the shadows became three men neatly dressed in well-tailored suits, with short hair and cleanly shaven faces. Tobie slipped the security chain in place and opened the door.

"Miss Guinness?" A tall dark-haired man in his late thirties held up a badge he flipped open to show the

ID beneath. "FBI. We're investigating the death of Dr. Henry Youngblood. May we come in? We'd like to ask you some questions."

"Oh God," Tobie whispered. *"Henry."* She slipped off the chain and opened the door wider. "Are you sure he's dead?"

"I'm afraid so, miss."

The FBI agents were big, powerful men, all well over six feet tall, with broad shoulders and the kind of flat stomachs that spoke of a lifetime of crunches and bench presses. They filled her small living room of cottage-sized furniture in a way that made them seem out of place and vaguely intimidating.

"We understand you were working with Dr. Youngblood on his research project," said the man who had shown her his badge. Agent Lance Palmer, he said his name was.

"That's right. Since January. Why?"

It was one of the other agents who answered her, a lean, sandy-haired man with prominent cheekbones and wire-framed glasses. "We think this project he's been working on might have something to do with his death."

Tobie sank into the slat-backed rocking chair she kept beside the fireplace, her splayed fingers gripping the rocker's worn wooden arms. "The firemen found his body?"

"As soon as they were able to get into the building." Agent Palmer came to sit on the tattered camel-back sofa opposite her. "We're particularly interested in a session you did recently with Dr. Youngblood. A session that was used as a demonstration for a funding proposal."

"I'm not sure I know exactly which session you're

talking about. Dr. Youngblood was applying all over the place for funding, but I don't remember him saying any of the sessions we did were directly related to a proposal. Usually he thought the less I knew about the targets, the better."

Palmer leaned forward, his hands clasped loosely between his knees, his gaze hard on her face. "The target for this particular session was a room. An office, to be precise."

Tobie glanced down at the empty hearth and tried to remember. But all that came to her was the image of exploding light and the stink of wet burning timber. She shook her head. "I'm sorry. I don't remember."

The lean man with the glasses came to stand with one arm resting along the wooden mantel beside her. "During this particular session, you drew a picture of a plane. An old World War II transport called a Skytrooper."

Tobie was about to say *I'm sorry* again, then paused. "Wait. I think maybe I do remember that session. Was that for a funding proposal?"

The men exchanged quick glances. The older one, Palmer, the one Tobie had come to think of as being in charge, said, "Did you discuss the session with anyone else besides Dr. Youngblood?"

It struck Tobie as a peculiar question. "No. Why would I?"

"Did Dr. Youngblood ever discuss your session with anyone?"

"Not that I know of."

"Not with any of his colleagues? Or maybe a girl-friend?"

"No. I don't think he had one. Girlfriend, I mean."

"How about a boyfriend?" asked the third man, smirking. He was the tallest of the three, his arms thick with muscle, his eyes small and dark in a full-cheeked face.

Palmer didn't even turn to look at him. He just said, "Lopez," in a low, warning tone, and the big man closed his mouth.

Tobie glanced from one man to the next, and it was as if a canyon yawned in the pit of her stomach and ice water trickled slowly down her spine. For it had only just occurred to her to wonder how the FBI could have been brought into an investigation of Dr. Youngblood's death so quickly.

When she left Freret Street, the fire had still been smoldering. According to the policewoman, it would be hours before the firemen would be able to retrieve Youngblood's body. It would take more time still for anyone to decide his death was both suspicious and of a nature to require bringing in the FBI. She remembered Henry's quick, breathless message. *They came here, to my office . . . These people are dangerous . . .*

"We understand Dr. Youngblood called you tonight," said Palmer. "Right before he was shot."

Tobie opened her mouth to ask how he could possibly know so quickly that Henry had been shot. Then her instinct for self-preservation kicked in and she said instead, "That's right. He called about six-thirty and left a message." She stood up, her legs shaking so badly she wondered if she could walk. "Would you like to hear it? I think I left my phone in the kitchen. I'll get it."

Her hopes that the men would simply let her leave

the room were dashed when Palmer nodded to the scholarly-looking agent with the wire-framed glasses. "Go with her."

The agent at her side, she led the way through the darkened dining room to the kitchen. Her messenger bag lay where she had left it, on the counter beside the half-emptied grocery sack. "It's in my bag," she said, maneuvering to put some distance between herself and the man behind her as she reached for the bag's strap.

Tobie might not be able to run or shoot well enough to please the Navy, but she'd been only sixteen years old when she earned a black belt in tae kwon do. She'd blown out her knee working on her second degree while in college, but up until that fateful night in the deserts of Iraq, she had continued to train privately. Her love of martial arts was one of the things she had preferred the Navy not know about her.

Now, drawing a deep breath, she collected herself. Then she let out her breath in an explosive burst of energy and spun around, her left foot coming up in a high roundhouse kick that caught the man behind her on the side of the head.

Grunting, he dropped to his hands and knees. She kicked him again, her heel slamming into his forehead. He fell back, whacking his shoulders and head against the cabinet with a bang. As he slid to the floor, she heard Palmer shout, "Hadley?"

Someone at some time had added a utility porch onto the side of Tobie's kitchen, a small space just a few feet square, barely big enough for a washer and dryer and a door that opened into the side yard. Throwing her bag over one shoulder, she leaped for the door. With a howl,

Beauregard threaded himself through her legs as she fumbled with the dead bolt. "Hush, baby," she whispered, scooping him up under one arm.

The cat kicked and mewed. The lock was old and stiff, Tobie's fingers slippery with sweat. Panic rose thick and choking in her throat. Then the bolt shot back. She yanked the side door open, the night air cool against her hot face.

The wooden floorboards in the dining room creaked. Someone shouted, "Hey!" She heard the suppressed crack of a pistol shot as the window in the upper part of the door beside her exploded.

Tobie dove through the door. She heard a second shot, smelled the familiar stench of cordite as a bullet chewed through the wooden door frame beside her. Beauregard let out a howl and leaped from her arms.

Tobie jumped off the small concrete stoop and ran.

14

Tobie tore through the darkened, wind-tossed side garden.

She heard the big man behind her shout, "She's outside, headed for the street. Stop her!"

The front door banged open. Heavy feet thumped across the wooden gallery. "What the fuck?" Palmer's angry voice cut through the night. "Where is she?"

Her heart pounding, Tobie veered toward the corrugated iron fence separating her yard from the florist on the corner. The fence was a good eight feet high and thickly overgrown with jasmine and honeysuckle, but there was a gap where two lengths of the fencing didn't quite meet. She squeezed through the narrow opening just as Palmer shouted, "There she is!"

Tripping over garden hoses and flowerpots, Tobie dodged between the nursery's long rows of raised garden beds to yank open the heavy wooden gate at the far end. She stumbled out onto the broad, lamplit expanse of Nashville Avenue and knew she'd made a mistake. The instant those men rounded the corner, she'd be an easy target.

"Jesus." She swerved sideways, down the narrow, darkly shadowed opening between two houses. A dank, tomblike smell of wet earth and cold brick enveloped her. She could see a low chain-link fence stretching across the rear garden in front of her. She leaped it without breaking stride and felt her knee almost give way beneath her.

Limping badly across someone's darkened backyard, she darted up their driveway to the broken brick sidewalk and saw the shadow of a man silhouetted against the streetlight on the corner. "There!" he cried, and ran toward her.

Her messenger bag thumping against her hip, Tobie sprinted across the street. Dodging the jutting fender of a parked Mercedes, she hit the muddy strip of half gravel, half grass on the far side of the pavement and her feet slid, her arms windmilling as she tried to keep her balance.

Breathing hard now, her lungs straining to draw in air, she ran along a row of rusting tin sheds backed by a cinder-block wall that rose up to engulf her in shadow. She could hear a dog barking from somewhere close at hand. A lamp in the house beside her flicked on to throw a square of light across her face and shoulders as she ran past. She shied away, but it was too late. She heard the men shout again.

A flash of lightning veined the dark clouds overhead. She ran on, her bad knee exploding in fire with each step. A cool wind lifted the damp hair from her forehead and flattened the thin cotton of her skirt against her thighs. She smelled rain and heard the rumble of thunder mingling with the sweet chiming of church bells ringing out over the tops of trees bending restlessly with the wind. The wedding was ending.

Throwing a quick glance over her shoulder, she dashed toward the narrow, car-lined street and the low-slung, modern brick sprawl of St. Francis of Assisi Elementary School beyond it. She could hear the sound of car engines gunning to life, see the stab of headlights piercing the darkness. There were people here, but not many. All were in a rush to get to their cars before the storm broke. She wasn't safe yet.

She was conscious of people turning their heads to stare at her. Crossing the parking lot, she slowed to a trot, her lungs straining, her chest jerking with each breath. She dodged down the walkway that ran along the high walls of the old brick church and felt the wind gust up stronger. A fine mist hit her face, blessedly cool against her hot sweaty skin.

She could see more people, spilling down the church steps, milling about on the wide swath of paving that stretched to the curb. Throwing another glance over her shoulder, she saw Lance Palmer, his hand held significantly beneath the front of his suit jacket. She broke into a run again.

Heedless of the startled expressions and indignant exclamations she provoked, Tobie pushed her way through the laughing, talking crowd that filled the open space before the church. A row of shuttle buses stood lined up at the curb, ready to ferry the wedding guests to some distant reception site.

The first bus was almost filled. She leaped onto the

steps just as the doors snapped closed and the bus
lurched away from the curb.

She swung around, one hand flinging out to grasp
the nearby chrome bar as the bus swayed and picked
up speed. Through the glass doors she could see Lance
Palmer start forward through the crowd. Then he disappeared into the night.

15

Jax Alexander lived in a narrow brick town house over-
looking the Potomac. He had inherited the house from
Sophie's father, the late Senator James Herman Winston. It was Senator Winston who had paid to send him
to a string of expensive East Coast boarding schools—
he kept getting kicked out—and, ultimately, to Yale.
The Winstons were a venerable old Connecticut family
who could trace their ponderous wealth and prestige
back three centuries. It always grieved the senator that
Jax took after his father, who was neither venerable nor
ponderously wealthy.

The mist was drifting in off the water as Jax let himself into the town house's paneled entry hall. Through
the French doors in the living room, the river showed
as a sheet of moon-struck silver that rippled lazily with
the flow of the current. He could see the red message
light blinking on the answering machine in the kitchen.

Hitting the Play button, he headed up the stairs to pull an overnight bag from the closet.

"Hey, Jax." Sibel Montana's low, husky voice drifted up the stairs after him. "I got your call about the tickets to *Turandot*. I'll be free tomorrow after four-thirty."

Jax squeezed his eyes shut and swore under his breath. Sibel Montana was a brilliant, funny, long-legged lawyer with Williams and Connolly. It had been nearly four years since he'd met a woman who connected with him the way she did. But in the past three months he'd already had to cancel two dinner dates, a weekend in the Hamptons, and a trip to Barbados with her. Opening his suit pack on the bed, he punched in Sibel's number on his phone and went to yank open the top drawer of the antique mahogany dresser that stood in an alcove overlooking the river.

Sibel's voice was a warm contralto. "Hi, Jax."

"I got your message," he said, tossing boxers and socks into his bag. "I've got the opera tickets and reservations at the Old Ebbitt Grill. There's just one potential problem. I need to go out of town. But I should be back by tomorrow night."

There was a long silence at the other end of the phone. "That's what you said the last time, Jax. You didn't come back for two weeks."

Jax retrieved his toilet kit from the bathroom. "I know. I'm sorry, Sibel."

Sibel was a smart lady, and she had lived in Washington, D.C., for six years. It had taken her only two dates before she added Jax's evasiveness together with a few other clues and figured out exactly what he did for a living. Now, she let out her breath in a long sigh. "You know, Jax . . . I don't think this is going to work."

He heard the break in her voice and stopped packing. "Don't do this, Sibel."

"I'm sorry, Jax. For a while I thought maybe I'd get used to it. But the closer we get, the more it bothers me. We all have jobs that require us to keep business out of our private lives, but with you, it's so much worse. What kind of relationship can I have with someone who is constantly being sent out of town on a moment's notice and who can't even tell me where he's going or what he'll be doing?"

"Sibel—"

"I like you, Jax. I like you a lot. I think we could have had something special together. If you ever decide to change jobs, give me a call."

"Sibel, please listen—"

"'Bye, Jax." The connection ended.

"Son of a bitch." He snapped his cell phone closed and tossed it on the bed beside his half-packed suitcase and the holster for his Beretta.

16

Division Thirteen had its offices deep in the bowels of the CIA's sprawling headquarters at Langley. You couldn't sink much lower at the Company, either literally or figuratively. The head of the division, Matt von Moltke, had been relegated to a cubbyhole near the maintenance department, his cramped office barely big enough for a beat-up gray metal desk, a couple of filing cabinets, and a Formica-topped conference table that looked like a sturdier version of something salvaged from a 1950s-era diner.

Jax arrived at the office to find Matt sitting at his desk, his forehead furrowing as he studied a series of spreadsheets while wolfing down a triple-decker club sandwich.

"You haven't been home yet, have you?" said Jax.

A 250-pound giant of a man with wild, silver-laced black hair and a thick beard, Matt shoved the rest of his sandwich into his mouth, drained the can of generic diet cola that was never far from his reach, and swallowed. "Hell. It's early yet."

He pushed back his chair and stood up, lurching awkwardly when his weight came down on the leg that had been mangled by a run-in with a Bouncing Betty on a rain-slicked jungle path in the Mekong Delta. He'd had a wife, once—or so Jax had heard. He still had a daughter, Gabrielle, who lived near her mother somewhere in the Midwest. But since the breakup of Matt's marriage, the Company had become his life. He'd been sidelined here, to the division, way back in the eighties as punishment for kicking up a fuss over the U.S. funding of death squads in El Salvador. For some reason Jax had never quite figured out, the division had suited Matt von Moltke just fine. Twenty-odd years later, he was still here.

Matt limped over to an ominous-looking pile of books and files stacked at one end of the Formica and chrome table. "You need to find out what you can about the death of this man," he said, flipping open one of the files to extract a large black and white photo.

Jax stared down at a picture of a balding, overweight man with gentle eyes and a pleasant smile. "Who was he?"

"A guy by the name of Dr. Henry Youngblood. Professor of psychology at Tulane University. His name came up in a police report tonight. He's on our watch list."

"What's the Company's interest in him?"

"He worked on a project for us back in the late eighties and early nineties. We need to make sure nothing that's happening in New Orleans now involves us. And that nothing's going to come out that might embarrass us."

Jax looked up. "Why 'embarrass'? What was this guy doing?"

"Remote viewing."

Jax kept his gaze on Matt's plump, hairy face. "What the hell is that?"

Matt cleared his throat. "It's a term developed about thirty years ago by a couple of physicists out at Stanford Research Institute in California. Basically it's just an academically sanitized label for the ability to observe distant places and events through alternate channels of perception."

"You're not saying what I think you're saying, are you?"

The skin beside Matt's dark brown eyes creased into a smile. "Ooohhh, yeah. Clairvoyance, telekinesis, precognition . . . you name it, the U.S. government has studied it at one time or another."

"Please tell me this is a joke."

Matt reached for another one of the fat files and held it out. "Nope. It started at the end of World War II, when we captured some reports on the Nazis' parapsychology experiments that interested our guys—not as much as the Germans' work on the A-bomb and jet engines, of course, but it was intriguing. Things really picked up in the seventies, when George H. W. Bush was Director of the CIA. Most of the programs back then were run through the Stanford Research Institute, but not all of them."

Jax perched on one end of the table and started thumbing through the file.

"You remember the Iranian hostage crisis?" said Matt.

"I've read about it."

Matt sighed. "You're such an infant. Anyway, they had the Army's remote viewers from Fort Meade working twenty-four hours a day during the rescue mission."

Jax looked up. "You mean the Army had a hand in this, too?"

"The Army, the Navy, NASA, the NSA—you name it. Everybody had projects going on this at one time or another."

"NASA?" Jax laughed. "What for?"

"They had the idea maybe astronauts could be trained to use telepathy. It's the same reason the Navy was interested. They wanted to find a way to stay in touch with their submarines when traditional communications technology failed . . . and maybe follow the movement of the Soviets' boats at the same time."

"And the National Security Agency?"

"They were worried about Soviet remote viewers being able to access our top secret files. Maybe even use telekinesis to mess with our computers."

"You mean to tell me the Soviets were fooling around with this, too?"

"That's right. At one point there was a real psi arms race going on."

"You mean, as in psychological warfare?"

"No, I mean psi as in 'psychic.' "

Jax groaned.

"We had film clips of Soviet sessions that showed their group moving objects, even killing. We had no way to verify any of it, but it was worrisome, to say the least. Once Reagan was elected, we got into the psi business big time. The White House started consulting astrologers and fortune-tellers, and things really went off the deep end. There was talk about shit like a Photonic Barrier Modulator to induce death telepathically, and a Hyperspatial Nuclear Howitzer, which was supposed to use thought waves to send a nuclear explosion from the deserts of Nevada to the corridors of the Kremlin."

"Jesus." Jax snapped the file closed. "And this is still going on?"

"All psi-related projects were supposedly terminated in 1995."

Jax raised one eyebrow. "Supposedly?"

Matt shrugged. "It's hard to tell with these things. You know that. It was a Special Access Program from the very beginning."

"Of course," said Jax. Anything sensitive, nasty, or just plain stupid was usually made into a Special Access Program, or SAP, as they were known in the business. SAPs were black operations, kept hidden from both the public and Congressional oversight by a procedure that allowed access only by those personnel specifically cleared by the program's manager. The Iran-Contra deal had been an SAP; so had the development of the Stealth aircraft. Setting aside the file folder, Jax leaned over to study the title of the book at the top of the nearest stack: *Mind Wars: The True Story of Secret Government Research into the Military Potential of Psychic Weapons*. He wanted to laugh, except this wasn't a joke. "Well, I can certainly see why they'd want to keep this a secret."

"It's not exactly a secret anymore. In 1995 the Company hired a private think tank to evaluate the entire history of remote viewing. Some of the guys I know who were in the program say the deck was stacked against them—the civilian scientists doing the review didn't have top secret clearance, and the Government refused to declassify some of their most spectacular successes. They say the CIA wanted a negative review and only released the data that would give them that conclusion."

"Is that true?"

"Hell, I don't know. But have you ever known the Company to commission a review that didn't bring in the result they wanted? The review board found that remote viewing failed to produce the kind of specific information required for intelligence work, and all remote viewing projects were shut down."

Jax eyed the piles of paperbacks and hardcovers. There was even a dog-eared Defense Intelligence Agency manual. "So where do I start? It's not that long a flight."

"This is probably the best of them." Matt lifted a slim volume from one of the stacks. "It's written by a career Army sergeant named McMoneagle. Some of his remote viewing episodes are incredible. He talks about remote viewing Soviet subs hidden inside huge warehouses, and locating a lost airplane loaded with nuclear weapons that went down over Africa."

"You don't actually believe in this, do you?"

Jax watched, bemused, as Matt's gaze slid away to focus on something across the room. "Read up on it. I think you might be surprised."

"Right." Jax slid off the edge of the table. There was a flight leaving in forty-five minutes to take him to New Orleans. "So if these programs were all shut down back in 'ninety-five, then what's this Tulane professor been up to?"

"As I understand it, he's had a small program going at the university down there for the past year, training remote viewers and trying to identify criteria that can be used to select the most promising candidates. That was one of the main problems all the old programs faced: they were never able to find a way to predict who would be reliably successful."

"Who's been funding him?"

"He'd cobbled together some grant money here and there, but I gather he was struggling to keep the program going. He put in a proposal to us a few months ago."

"And?"

"We turned him down . . . at least, as far as I know."

"Ah. But how much do you know?"

Matt met Jax's gaze, the big man's eyes dark and troubled. "That's the problem, isn't it?"

Jax frowned down at the stacks of books with titles like *Mind Race* and *Using Your Psychic Abilities* and sighed. "This is going to sink what's left of my career if it ever gets out. You know that, don't you?"

"Chandler personally requested you be the one assigned to it."

Jax laughed. Gordon Chandler had been ambassador to Colombia at the time of his little episode last winter. And then, three months ago, the asshole had been appointed the new head of the CIA when former head

Clark Westlake was elevated to the position of intelligence czar. Chandler had been doing his best ever since to get Jax fired from the Company. A different kind of man would have quit; Jax Alexander was biding his time, waiting for the chance to get even.

But Chandler was no fool. He knew Jax. He knew, too, that the future of his own career depended on getting Jax before Jax got him.

"Then I'm fucked," said Jax.

Matt balanced the file back on top of the stacks of books and shoved them toward Jax. "I think that's the general idea."

17

"Hey, lady! This is a private bus."

Her face hot and wet with mingling sweat and rain, Tobie turned toward the bus driver and found rows of exquisitely dressed wedding guests staring at her. "Sorry." She flashed what she hoped was an apologetic grin. "Could you just let me out at the corner of Calhoun?"

"Some people," muttered the driver, and swung onto Magazine.

The instant the bus swooped in close to the curb, Tobie leaped out. It was raining hard now, great, wind-gusted sheets of water that fell in waves from a lightning-torn sky. She hurried down Calhoun, her shoulders hunched and head bent against the downpour, her hair hanging in a wet curtain beside her face. A car splashed past and she spun around, heart pounding, adrenaline pumping, ready to run. The car disappeared around the corner.

By the time her Bug appeared as a yellow blur through the falling rain, she was drenched. Her skirt clung to her thighs, her cotton jacket hanging heavy and wet. Jerking open the door, she tossed her bag onto the far seat and slid in.

Rain drummed on the metal roof, cascaded in sheets down the windshield. She was shaking so badly she had a hard time fitting the key into the ignition. The engine sputtered to life and the voice of Lee Ann Womack blared out incongruously from the radio. Tobie punched the power button, turning it off. She wrapped her hands around the steering wheel, her breath soughing hot in her throat. Then she threw the car into first and hit the gas.

Turning onto Tchoupitoulas, she tore upriver toward Audubon Park. She had no thought in mind beyond putting as much distance as possible between herself and the men chasing her. But at the corner of Tchoupitoulas and Henry Clay, the light turned red and she had to stop. She watched the overhead traffic signal shudder in the wind, watched her windshield wiper blades beat back and forth, and tried to figure out what the hell she should do.

She didn't dare go to the police, she realized; not when the men chasing her carried FBI badges. So where could she go? She tried to think of someone—anyone she could turn to. She'd made friends since moving here to New Orleans, good friends. But what would a couple of eccentric artists and a French Quarter musician know about dealing with the kind of men who flashed FBI badges and fired guns equipped with suppressors?

And then she thought about Colonel McClintock.

She'd never been clear on exactly what the Colonel had done during his many years in the Army. But she knew he'd spent two tours in Vietnam, and she'd seen pictures in his study, curious old photographs that hinted at colorful adventures involving far more than the kind of calm therapy sessions he'd had with her. Plus, he knew about Henry's project. If anyone could help her make sense of what was going on, it was the Colonel.

Reaching over to the seat beside her, she fumbled around in her messenger bag for her cell phone. Her hand closed around it just as the traffic light changed, painting the rain-slicked black streets with a vivid wash of green.

The guy behind her in a white pickup decorated with two American flags leaned on his horn. Tobie dropped her phone on top of her bag and took off.

Lance Palmer closed his cell phone and held it in a tightened fist, his gaze fixed on the rain-flecked window and distant white lights that flickered past in the darkness. They were on the I-10 heading west out of the city toward the suburbs and Metairie Country Club, the destination of the wedding reception shuttle bus. He'd had a car with four men at the club waiting when the shuttle arrived. Except that according to the shuttle driver, October Guinness had hopped off the bus back on Magazine Street.

"Take the next exit and turn around," said Lance.

Lopez glanced over at him. "We lost her?"

"We lost her." Lance swiveled sideways in his seat

and flipped the phone open again. "Let me see what else we've got on this girl," he said to Hadley as he punched his own home number on the phone's auto dial.

Hadley was a mess; his swollen left eye was turning blue and purple, and blood still oozed from a cut on the back of his head. There was obviously more to this girl than any of them had figured.

"Hey, Jess," said Lance, his head tipped at an awkward angle to cradle the phone between his ear and shoulder as he reached to take the laptop from Hadley. "Looks like I'm not going to make it home tonight after all."

Lance paused, his gaze scanning the directory of files while he listened to Jess's soft expressions of disappointment. "What?" he said a minute later, his attention jerked back to the phone. "Sure I'll tell them good-night. Put them on."

His ten-year-old, Jason, was watching TV and could barely spare him a quick "'Night, Dad." But the little one, six-year-old Missy, recited a long and tangled tale about her cat, Barney.

"That's nice, honey," he said finally. "I love you, too. Now let me talk to Mommy again for a minute, would you?"

"I should be home tomorrow morning," he told Jessica when she came back on. "'Night, darling."

He dropped the phone into his pocket and started flipping through the files on October Guinness. "Get onto headquarters," he told Hadley. "Tell them I want to know everything there is to know about this woman. I want her license number and the kind of car she's driving. I want to know who her friends are and where they live. I want the activity on her bank and credit cards monitored. And I want someone assigned to do absolutely nothing except wait for her to turn on her cell phone."

Hadley shook his head. "She's not going to be stupid enough to use it."

"Are you kidding? So someone taught her how to kick. Big deal. She's a lousy college dropout who couldn't even make it in the Navy, for Christ's sake. What does she know?" Lance glanced out the window again. The rain had slowed to a drizzle, more like a fine mist that swirled around the car. "She'll use it."

18

Halfway down the block, Tobie pulled in close to the curb and parked. A drop of cold water from her wet hair rolled down her cheek, and she swiped at it absently with the back of one hand as she reached for her phone. She had the phone open and was about to punch in Colonel McClintock's number when she froze.

She had a friend, Gunner Eriksson, who kept a little shop on Magazine Street where he worked restoring antiques. Gunner had three passions in his life: woodworking, his wife Pia, and political activism. A true conspiracy nut, he'd tell anyone who'd listen that the government was covering up everything from who really shot JFK to the truth behind 9/11. He was always going on about the Patriot Act and something he called TIP. She remembered one rant he'd gone off on, about how the government had set up a program to record and monitor the cell phone calls of everyone in the United States.

Tobie closed her phone and set it aside, then stared at

it as if it were a false friend. She didn't believe a fraction
of the nonsense Gunner was always rambling on about.
But what if that part of it were true? And if it were true,
how many people had access to that computer system?
The FBI, surely. And what about the private companies
that ran the system? Everything in the government was
privatized these days, wasn't it?

She realized she was shaking, and pressed both hands
to her face, squeezing her eyes shut. Her breath came in
quick short pants that felt hot against her palms. Then
another thought occurred to her. Her eyes flew open
and she reached out quickly to turn off the phone and
yank out its battery, terrified it might act like a homing
beacon that could lead Dr. Youngblood's killers to her.
That was possible, too, wasn't it, using global position-
ing coordinates?

Oh, God. What else didn't she know? She felt hopelessly lost and afraid, alone and totally out of her element. Yet she couldn't afford to make any mistakes.
Not one.

She became aware of a scraping sound and realized
the rubber blades of her windshield wipers were drag-
ging across dry glass. It had stopped raining. Sitting
forward, she switched off the wipers, put the car in gear
and eased out into traffic.

She might be ignorant and inexperienced, she told
herself, but she was smart and she could learn. All she
needed was a teacher.

"I can do that myself, you know," said Tobie, then
sucked her breath through her teeth in a hiss when
Colonel McClintock touched an alcohol-saturated pad

to a jagged cut on her calf. The pungent scent of the alcohol pinched at her nose and she sneezed.

"You just sit there and drink your tea and concentrate on warming up," said the Colonel. "You're shaking so hard your teeth are chattering."

"It's June in New Orleans. My teeth are chattering because I'm scared."

They were sitting in the Colonel's book-lined study, Tobie on the somewhat threadbare sofa, the Colonel on the old trunk he used as a coffee table, a first aid kit open on the floor at his feet. Outside, the rain had started up again, but softer now, a gentle scattering of drops that pattered on the windowpanes and the broad leaves of the elephants ears and banana trees in the garden outside.

He spread antiseptic ointment on a bandage and pressed it into place. "I hope your tetanus shot is up to date."

"It is." Tobie held the bandage in place with her fingertips while the Colonel tore off a strip of adhesive. "What am I going to do?"

He kept his head bowed, his lips together, his attention seemingly on the task of bandaging her leg. Tobie felt a welling of impatience but curbed it. After all these months of mutual analysis, she had come to know his ways. He was a brilliant man, but patient and unhurried in his thinking. He never said or did anything without thoroughly considering all possible options and their consequences.

After a moment he said, "These men who came to your house . . . you realize that you can't be sure they're FBI, simply because they had badges?"

"Yes. Except that they didn't just flash some badge

at me. They had ID cards. I know what they look like. Those suckers were real."

He pressed the last strip of adhesive into place and leaned over to gather his first aid kit together. "There are other organizations in the government that have been known to carry FBI badges. The FBI doesn't like it and it's not supposed to be done anymore, but I suspect it still happens."

"Other organizations like—what?" Tobie kept her eyes on his lined face as he stood and walked across the room to tuck his first aid kit into a drawer of his desk. "Oh God. Don't tell me the CIA." He was starting to remind her of her friend Gunner. "The CIA isn't allowed to operate inside the U.S., remember?"

"I'm afraid you're a few years out of date, Tobie. The government has used their so-called War on Terror to start doing a lot of things Americans would never have tolerated if we weren't so scared."

"I don't think they make it a habit of going around rubbing out innocent, law-abiding citizens."

"The government does kill people. They do it all the time in the interest of national security—or what they tell themselves is national security."

From overhead came a thump and a woman's gentle voice; the sounds of the Colonel's maid, LaToya, settling Mary McClintock into bed for the night. Soon, Colonel McClintock would go up to read to his wife as she drifted off to sleep.

Tobie kept her gaze on the Colonel's face, lit now with a soft light cast by the green glass shade of the banker's lamp on the corner of the desk. "Why would the CIA be interested in Henry Youngblood?"

"We don't know for certain you're dealing with the CIA. It's just one possibility out of several. Except . . . you said they were asking about Henry's remote viewing program? That they were particularly interested in some session you did for Henry that he was using as a demonstration for a funding proposal?"

"What are you suggesting? That Dr. Youngblood was applying to the CIA for funding?"

He didn't answer her. Instead, he walked over to where LaToya had set the tea tray. "How much do you know about the history of remote viewing?"

"I know the Army had a unit back in the seventies and eighties that developed a lot of the techniques Dr. Youngblood was teaching me. He talked a fair amount about the work he did with them when he was out at Stanford. He used to joke about the CIA a lot, but he never said anything about them being involved in RV."

"I suspect that over the years a good half of the funding for the program came from the CIA through one conduit or another."

Tobie felt a strange, almost numbing sense of unreality creep over her. "Oh, Jesus."

"What exactly was the target in this demonstration you did? Do you remember?"

She ran her splayed fingers through her hair, still damp from the rain and hanging in untidy clumps around her face. "A building. An office. Nothing unusual."

"You need to try to remember everything you can about it."

"I've tried. I can't. It was weeks ago. And it didn't seem important at the time. Do you have any idea how many sessions Youngblood and I did over the last four or five months?"

He lifted the quilted cover off the teapot and carried it over to where she sat clutching her empty teacup in both hands. "It will come. It's not easy to think clearly when you're scared."

"I'm okay," she said.

"I know you are. You're a lot stronger than you give yourself credit for sometimes." He poured the steaming tea into her cup. "The most important thing right now is for you to keep yourself safe."

He put the teapot on the table at her elbow and came to perch again on the edge of the trunk before her. "Here's what you need to do . . ."

19

Deep within the shadows of a spreading oak tree, Tobie rolled her VW to a stop and cut the engine. The rain had tapered off again but the sky was still black with clouds, the pavement sheened with wet.

Ignoring the PERMITS ONLY sign, she'd turned into the narrow road winding around Loyola University's athletic center, to the one-way street that ran behind the parking garage. It was late now and the rain had driven most of the students indoors. But the garage was still filled with cars.

Following the Colonel's instructions, she'd carefully gone over her own VW before leaving his house. "They might have put a tracking device on it," he'd warned her, telling her exactly where to look and how. But she hadn't found anything. And so now, for the first time in her adult life, she was about to steal something.

"You do realize," McClintock had told her, "that they could have put out an APB on your car?"

Tobie had stared at him. "What are you saying? That I could have the police chasing me, too?"

He shrugged. "Until we know who you're dealing with, it's better to be safe and assume the worst. Even if these people haven't brought the police in on this, it's not that hard to get someone's license plate number. And that car of yours is like a yellow beacon."

"So what am I supposed to do? Steal another car?"

He'd laughed. "Now that would get the police after you. You don't need a new car, Tobie; all you need is a new license plate."

Tobie took a deep breath and opened her car door. In the stillness of the night the clicking latch sounded dangerously loud. Now that the worst of the storm had passed, the temperature was rising again. The smell of wet earth and leaves hung heavy in the air, mingling with the sweet scent of a mimosa blooming unseen somewhere in the darkness.

With a quick glance up and down the street, she went to crouch at the back of her car and slip the Colonel's screwdriver from her pocket. "How often do you look at your license plate?" he'd told her. "You'd be surprised how many people don't even know what their own license plate number is."

She hadn't said anything, but she was one of those people. Whenever anyone asked for her license number, she always had to go look at it.

The two screws holding the metal plate came off easily. She dropped them into her pocket and stood up, the license plate tucked out of sight beneath the inside of her still damp jacket, her heart pounding uncomfortably at the thought of what she was about to do.

There were people, she knew, who did memorize their license plate number. Her own stepfather, Hank Bennett, could rattle off the license plates of every car he'd ever owned. What if she made a mistake and picked a car belonging to someone like him?

The first floor of the parking garage was separated from the street by no more than a low wall, easily stepped over. She walked up the ramp, her footsteps echoing eerily in the low-ceilinged, deserted space. What she needed, she decided, was a car that obviously belonged to a girl, the kind of girl unlikely to obsess about things like license plate numbers.

It didn't take her long to find what she was looking for: a silver Honda Civic with a pair of miniature pink ballet slippers hanging from the rearview mirror, an ALPHA LAMBDA DELTA decal in the back window and a MOUNT CARMEL VOLLEYBALL sticker on the bumper.

With another quick glance around, Tobie hunkered down at the Honda's rear bumper. She kept expecting to feel the clamp of a heavy hand on her shoulder or hear a shout from across the garage. Setting aside the Honda's plate, she fit her own license in its place . . .

And felt one of the screws slip from her fingers to roll away into the darkness.

Easing her weight down on her good knee, she skimmed her hands in ever-widening, panicked circles across the pavement. Just when she thought she wasn't going to find it, she felt the screw roll beneath her palm.

She sat back on her heel, her lower lip held tight between her teeth, and carefully twisted the screws into place. Sweat dampened her forehead, plastered her

T-shirt to her body. Hiding the Honda's license plate beneath her jacket, she stood up and walked away.

Her legs were shaking, but she was breathing easier now. Moving quickly, she fit the purloined plate onto the rear of her car, then slipped behind the wheel and turned the key. The engine roared to life and she felt a zing of elation run through her so powerful it left her fingers tingling.

I did it. Ha!

Smiling, almost giddy with relief, she slipped the car into reverse, backed onto the street, and took off toward Tulane's Student Union, where she knew she'd be able to find a twenty-four-hour ATM. She was going to need cash.

The Colonel had wanted her to spend what was left of the night at his house, but she'd refused. She knew from an incident last Easter, when one of Mary McClintock's nieces came to visit, that it confused Mary, having people in the house overnight.

Tobie had seen snapshots of Mary McClintock in the Colonel's study, photographs of her as a beautiful woman with thick hair the color of sunsets and a wide smile. After years of casually forgetting things, she'd now slipped so far into the fogs of Alzheimer's that she no longer recognized her husband, although she still loved to listen to his voice reading to her.

But it wasn't only a desire to avoid confusing Mrs. McClintock that had stopped Tobie. She also realized, belatedly, that she'd already put the Colonel and his wife in serious danger simply by coming to him.

He'd tried to argue with her, of course. When he realized he wasn't going to change her mind, he warned her not to use her credit card to pay for a hotel. But he hadn't told her not to use an ATM, and she hadn't thought to ask.

She knew she was running a risk, using one. But did it really matter, she reasoned, if some computer in Maryland or Virginia flagged her withdrawal? She'd be gone before anyone could possibly show up to check it out.

Lance was going through a stack of printouts when Michael Hadley stuck his head around the door frame. "Our girl just hit an ATM at Tulane, near the Union. Withdrew two hundred dollars."

Lance looked up. They'd taken a suite at the Sheraton for the night, although he had started to worry that their quarry might already have headed out of town. "Good. That means she's still here in New Orleans."

He pushed to his feet. They had men at the airport and at the bus and train stations, but there was always the possibility she'd simply driven out of town. He'd alerted their people in Colorado to tap her parents' phone and keep an eye on their house. He glanced at his watch. "What do you suppose she's been up to for the past couple of hours?"

Hadley shrugged. "If she used a Tulane ATM, it means she's staying close to the familiar."

"We need a list of all the hotels in that area." Lance stretched. "With any luck, we might get out of here before morning after all."

20

Barid Hafezi stood in the doorway to his daughter's darkened room and watched her sleep.

Yasmina was eight years old, a small, wiry tomboy with laughing brown eyes and a mischievous grin. Her ten-year-old brother Faraj was the serious one. He was probably reading a book with a flashlight under the covers in his room down the hall. But Yasmina was like her mother, a carefree spirit who drew like an angel and could charm the squirrels out of the trees.

Barid sucked in a deep breath, but it did nothing to ease the tight pain in his chest. Twenty-five years. It had been twenty-five years since he'd fled the turmoil of Iran for the United States. He'd built a new life for himself here, a safe life for his wife and children. It hadn't been easy, but he'd managed to get a Ph.D. in journalism from NYU while his wife, Nadia, earned her Ph.D. in microbiology from Columbia. Now he was a professor at the University of New Orleans, while Nadia had just earned tenure at Loyola. They owned a graceful old cottage in the Broadmoor neighborhood of New Orleans. Hurricane Katrina had made them refugees again for a while, but now they were back home and soon, Inshallah, the repairs on the house would finally be finished. Only, he was very much afraid he wouldn't be here to see that happen.

It had been four months now since the man he called "the Scorpion" had first come to him. Barid had never learned the man's real name. The man wore cowboy boots and a Stetson, and had a tattoo high on his bulging bicep—a tattoo of a scorpion superimposed on two crossed arrows with the words DE OPPRESSO LIBER beneath. Barid had looked it up on the Internet. It was a United States Special Forces tattoo.

At first the Scorpion had smiled and talked pleasantly, although even then the man made Barid nervous. He had known men like the Scorpion before, in Tehran. In Tehran, such men had been agents of the SAVAK, the Shah's old secret police. The SAVAK might not have worn Stetsons and cowboy boots, but at heart such men were all the same. Perhaps such men had believed in something, once. But soon they believed only in their own power.

Like the agents of the SAVAK, the Scorpion was well versed in the use of fear and intimidation to control men. He showed Barid pictures of his children: candid shots of Yasmina at school; of Faraj walking down the street; of brother and sister at play with their white bunny, Cupcake, in the backyard. The message was implicit: *Your children are not safe from me. I can get at them anytime, anywhere.*

Then Cupcake disappeared and the Scorpion had shown Barid more photos—ghastly, sick images that haunted his dreams. This time the message was explicit: *Follow instructions or what was done to your children's bunny rabbit will be done to your children.*

At first the Scorpion's orders were simple. Barid was to form a small group of Islamic students who would meet once a week to study the Koran. Jamaat Noor Allah, they were called: the Light of God. Some of the students were politically moderate, others more angry. Did that matter? Barid had no way to know.

Then he was told to assign certain journalism students to certain projects. Again he reluctantly complied. Surely no harm could come from that? But the requests soon became more ominous. He was given the funds to buy a derelict house in the Lower Ninth Ward. Then he was told to rent another house, this one in the Irish Channel in the unflooded part of the city near the river. Because of the way the Scorpion phrased his instructions, Barid knew there were more men than the Scorpion involved. "This is the house we want you to buy," the Scorpion would say. Or, "Here are the Korans for the group's meetings. We want you to make certain each student has one."

Barid never asked why he was being made to do all these things. At first he hoped that if he did as he was told and kept his nose out of it, the men might spare him. But eventually he'd had to admit that he was only fooling himself. He might not know what these men were doing, or why. But he knew too much to be allowed to live.

At one point he'd given some thought to going to the American authorities, but the memory of that Special

Forces tattoo always stopped him. He had no way of knowing whom the Scorpion worked for, and so he knew there was no one he could trust. Ever since 9/11, too many Americans treated Muslim citizens the way the Nazis had started treating Jews in 1930s Germany. If the Americans locked him up as a suspected "enemy combatant," his family would be left completely vulnerable. And so for the sake of his children, he continued to cooperate. And he kept his mouth shut.

"Barid?"

He felt his wife's hand touch his shoulder, slide down his arm in a gentle caress. "You're doing it again. Watching them. Why?"

He turned to enfold her in his arms and draw her close so she couldn't see his face. He longed to tell her the truth, to say, *I watch them because there are evil men out there who have threatened to kill my children if I don't do what they say. And even though I have done all that they have asked, I know it won't be enough. I know that one day they will kill me, if for no other reason than to keep me silent. And so I watch my children because I know that someday, soon, I will never see them again.*

Except of course he couldn't say any of that to Nadia, because when he was gone, his children would need their mother, and he couldn't do anything that might put her life in danger, too. So all he said was, "I watch them because it brings me peace."

And even though he knew she didn't believe him, she said no more.

21

The Coliseum Street Guest House lay on a narrow, cobble-lined block of Coliseum, across from Trinity Church and just half a block down from the official boundary of the Garden District. A narrow, two-story galleried building with thick brick pillars and transomed French doors, it had once served as the *garçonnière* and kitchen of a Creole plantation. The plantation house and its sprawling acres had long since disappeared, leaving the *garçonnière* looking like a bit of French Quarter archi-tecture that had somehow strayed into a neighborhood of Yankee-built Greek Revival and Queen Anne–style mansions.

The current owners had grandiose plans for someday turning the ancient building into an upscale bed and breakfast. But at the moment the place was still seedy enough that they had no problem taking in a guest who chose to pay cash, carried no luggage, and had a streak of dirt across her nose.

Tobie was given a room on the second floor overlooking the deep backyard where a giant sycamore rubbed against the double hung window with every gust of wind. Dropping her messenger bag on the wicker chair that stood beside a chipped, white-painted iron bed frame with a sagging mattress, she caught sight of her reflection in an age-spotted mirror hanging above the empty fireplace and said out loud, "Oh, Jesus."

Her eyes were wide and dilated, her face white, her hair hanging in damp, stringy clumps. The wet vines and shrubs she'd run through had left green stains across the front of her white T-shirt and skirt, and her calves and sandaled feet were flecked with drying mud. She looked like a wino just coming off a three-day binge.

The room had a compact bath carved from one corner near the fireplace. Stripping off her clothes, she turned on the shower and stood beneath it, letting the hot water cascade over her head and shoulders. The backs of her legs were still trembling, and it was a minute or two before she could set to work washing her hair with the bar of soap she found wrapped up beside the sink.

It was such a wonderfully mundane task, washing her hair, a touchstone of normalcy in a life careening suddenly, wildly, off track. For one moment she closed her mind to everything that had happened in the last hours, to the whirlwind of confusion and suffocating fears, and simply concentrated on the sensation of wet hair gliding through fingers and the familiar comfort of hot steam filling her lungs.

The room had an air-conditioning unit built high up in the wall, but she couldn't get it to work and finally just gave up and opened a window. The last thing she wanted to do was call attention to herself by complaining about it. She washed her T-shirt, skirt, and underclothes as best she could in the sink and spread them out near the open window. She wasn't sure the clothes would even dry in the moist, hot night air, but hotels like this one didn't furnish their guests with hair dryers.

Wearing nothing but a towel, she sank down on the edge of the bed and attacked the wet, snarled mess that was her hair. The sultry breeze pushing through the screen of the open window brought with it the pungent aroma of wet earth and sweet jasmine underlain by the subtle, pervasive hint of decay that was ever-present in New Orleans.

Once, when Tobie was seven or eight years old, her family had passed through New Orleans on their way to visit her mother's people in South Carolina. Like most of the Bennett-Guinness family's vacations, it had been a tumultuous two weeks of her stepfather barking orders and her mother softly pleading as Tobie and her brother and sister squabbled in the backseat. But the three days they'd stopped in New Orleans had been pure magic. She remembered hours spent in the dusty wonder of the Cabildo; hours more exploring the tangled batture that stretched between the levee and the Mississippi, with Hank yelling, "If you get bit by a snake, I'm going to make you pay the hospital bill." Tobie smiled at the memory. Then her smile slipped. The urge to call Colorado, to hear her mother's soft drawl and her stepfather's flat, calm tones, was so overwhelming it brought the sting of tears to her eyes. But she knew better than to give in to the urge to call anyone close to her.

For hours, her focus had been on survival, the need

to escape, to find a safe refuge for the night. Now came time for reflection, and with it, anger. A man she'd both liked and respected had been brutally murdered. She'd been shot at and chased through a driving rainstorm by three men who claimed to work for her own government, whether they actually did or not. Because of them, she was alone in a cheap hotel room, without a change of clothes or even a toothbrush. She was worried about her cat. She had classes in the morning she didn't dare go to. She couldn't use her cell phone or her credit cards. She couldn't even talk to her own mother and stepfather.

Raising her head, Tobie pushed her hair out of her face, her hands clenching together behind her neck as her anger hardened slowly into determination.

That viewing session had obviously been a success. *What had she seen*?

She and Henry had done dozens of sessions—perhaps as many as a hundred or more, many of them with buildings as targets. How was she supposed to remember the details of one seemingly insignificant session?

She shoved away from the edge of the bed to stand beside the open window and draw the warm air deep into her lungs. *Calm down,* she told herself. *Think.*

Henry had designed a special soundproofed room in the Annex, with heavy curtains at the windows, thick carpet on the floor, and a comfortable reclining chair. In the beginning, when he first introduced her to the phenomenon he called remote viewing, he used to have her listen to a series of tapes—soothing tones that were fed to her through earphones and were designed to help her sink down into what he called "the zone." But it hadn't taken her long to learn to reach the zone herself, once she understood what was required. She simply needed to put herself in a state of pure relaxation. When she was ready, Henry would start the remote viewing session.

At first they used live targets. Henry would have another student or associate drive to an unknown location at a preappointed time. He'd say to Tobie, "Elizabeth is at the target," and she would close her eyes and focus on that person. Gently at first, like a feather brushing across the mind, the images and impressions of the target's location would come to her.

The first time Tobie tried it, she didn't expect it to work. She'd drawn pictures of a stone-walled, castle-like structure and the sun gleaming off huge sheets of looming glass. She was a good enough artist that her sketches were easily recognizable. When she finished, Henry called in the student and Tobie learned the target location: the tiny, castlelike Confederate Museum, now virtually engulfed by the modern Ogden Art Museum.

As she gained experience, the targets had grown more sophisticated. Sometimes the target was a photograph, double-wrapped in an opaque envelope that Henry laid on the table before him. Often the target was described simply by its geographical coordinates. And still the images would come to her, like a memory of something glimpsed in a dream.

She couldn't be sure but she thought the demonstration session had used geographical coordinates.

Closing her eyes, she let the humid breeze from the open window bathe her cheeks and lift the drying hair from her forehead as she fought to remember that one session.

It had begun like all the others. As always, the first impressions of the target had come in quick, fragmented flashes. *A tall building outlined against a blue, cloudless sky. Sunlight glinting on a glass and steel facade. A small patch of grass. The splash of a fountain. A pile of sand with orange cones.* She tried to recapture those images now, but they were too generic, too overlaid with memories of hundreds of such buildings seen over the years. It could have been any modern office building or hotel in any city.

At the time, Henry hadn't seemed particularly interested in the building itself. "That's good, Tobie," he'd said. "Now go into the building."

And so her focus had narrowed, honing in quickly on one particular office. *A large office richly furnished with an Oriental carpet and oxblood leather sofas. An American flag in a brass stand strategically placed behind a broad mahogany desk.* She remembered a file on the desk, a burgundy-colored file labeled THE ARCHANGEL PROJECT. For some reason she couldn't explain, the file had drawn her, so that she'd described it in great detail, lingering even when Henry tried to get her to move on.

He had told her that happened sometimes with remote viewing: the viewer would become obsessed with an object that was more interesting or seemed somehow more powerful, often to the point of veering away from the actual intended target to something more remarkable or fascinating nearby. However much Henry tried to get her to shift her focus, she hadn't been able to tear her attention away from that file.

The file had been closed, but that didn't make any

difference. She'd still been able to describe what it contained. In some of the early experiments Henry told her about, remote viewers were able to accurately describe small objects inside closed metal film cans.

She remembered seeing documents: pages of text along with maps and diagrams and photos. She'd sketched some of the images, including an old World War II plane.

One of the men who'd come to her house had said something about a plane, a vintage C47 Skytrooper.

But however hard she tried, she couldn't remember anything else in the file. Only the gold emblem embossed on the front of the folder stood out clear in her mind: a K enclosed in a circle, like a cattle brand from the old West.

Tobie opened her eyes, her lungs emptying on a slow, shaky exhalation. It was an emblem she'd seen constantly during her year in Iraq: the Circle K of Keefe Corporation. Keefe was all over the place in Iraq, supplying the military with everything from oil to food. One of their subsidiaries, Jones & Bearde, was building the huge permanent bases the United States was putting in there. Another subsidiary, Meyer Oil, had managed to secure a virtual monopoly over the Iraqi oil fields. Their contracts with the Defense Department were said to be worth tens of billions of dollars. She thought there'd been some kind of stink about it at the time the contracts were renewed. She couldn't remember exactly what it was about.

But Gunner Eriksson would know.

22

The man Barid Hafezi knew only as "the Scorpion" parked his Mercedes GL450 SUV in his wide faux-stone driveway and killed the engine. His name was Paul Fitzgerald, and he paused for a moment, as he often did, to admire his house's soaring Palladian windows and travertine steps. The place had cost him close to $800,000, and he was damned proud of it. It was ridiculously big for one guy, but his boys always came to stay with him for a month in the summer and a week at Christmas. It didn't feel too big then.

He opened the car door, the noise carrying in the dry Texas air. The streets were deserted at this hour, although the subdivision was always like this, at any time of day or night. When he'd been a kid growing up in a two-bedroom bungalow in Minneapolis, he and his three brothers spent virtually every waking minute outside, even in the middle of winter. But kids didn't play outside anymore. They spent all their time inside, surfing the 'Net and playing video games. Even his own boys. He tried to interest them in fishing and camping and hunting, the things he'd learned to love growing up. But he could tell they weren't really interested.

Paul Fitzgerald let himself in the oak and leaded glass door that had cost him a cool ten grand, then paused to punch in the security system's code. He was aware of a heaviness deep within him, a kind of sadness that he couldn't seem to shake even though it made no sense and wasn't like him. The job was almost finished. He was set to fly into New Orleans for the last time tomorrow. He shrugged his shoulders. Maybe that was it. New Orleans. The place was damned depressing, ever since the storm.

Tossing his Stetson on a chair, Fitzgerald opened the fridge for a beer. He stood for a time sucking on the bottle and looking out at his backyard, with its high, gleaming white vinyl fence and in-ground pool. His latest bank statement lay open on the counter. He picked it up and smiled. Last year he'd taken the boys to Disney World for a week, but this year . . . this year he'd be able to take them anywhere they wanted to go.

McLean, Virginia: 5 June, 12:10 A.M. Eastern time

Adelaide Meyer kicked off her crocodile pumps, poured herself an icy margarita from the pitcher her maid, Maria, had left in the fridge, and went to sink into the down-wrapped cushions of the white sectional sofa at one end of her living room.

In her youth, Adelaide hadn't been a particularly attractive woman. But she'd always been tall and thin, and by the time a woman hit her fifties, being tall and thin and having the time and money for self-indulgence was what really counted. Adelaide had more than enough money to pamper herself, and money buys time.

Reaching for the remote, she switched on a Bach CD and closed her eyes as the music surrounded her. She lived alone in a 10,000-square-foot house in one of Virginia's most exclusive areas; the help had their own quarters in a separate small cottage at the end of the garden. She had no children and had never married. She had, on occasion, taken lovers, but men for the most part bored her. Adelaide's passion was for money and power.

The daughter of a Texas oilman, she had been born to money. But while her fellow debs focused on marrying lawyers and money market managers, Adelaide focused on petroleum engineering. Graduating from Texas A&M, she went to work for her father's company just a week after turning twenty-two. It wasn't easy being a woman in the oil industry, driving out to rigs at the crack of dawn and dealing with roughnecks, or maneuvering around the good old boys in the boardroom. But Adelaide was smart, and she was determined. When her father dropped dead at the age of fifty-five, no one questioned her move to take over his company. And when she sold her company three years later to Keefe Corporation, they took her on as a vice president.

Now CEO of Keefe, she was one of the wealthiest and most powerful women in the country. She had helped put the President in the White House, and he repaid her by funneling billions of dollars' worth of no-bid war contracts in her direction—and making sure no one audited the books too closely.

The sound of the doorbell brought her head around. She heard voices in the foyer, Maria's softly accented tones mingling with the unmistakable New England vowels of Clark Westlake.

Adelaide took another sip of her drink as Maria led him into the room. "So what's so important you couldn't tell me about it on the phone, Clark? There's a pitcher of margaritas in the fridge. Want Maria to get you one?"

Clark didn't want a margarita. He waited until the maid had withdrawn, then said, "I've just come from T. J. Beckham's office. He's threatening to publicly accuse the President and the intelligence community of sexing up the threat from Iran."

Adelaide shifted her weight against the sofa's plump cushions. "He can't go public with that kind of charge. He has nothing to back it up."

"He said something about 'contacts' in the intelligence community."

Adelaide arched an eyebrow. "And you believed him?"

Clark walked to the French doors overlooking the floodlit outdoor pool. "You don't?"

"There are still some disloyal discontents, particularly in the CIA. But most have been squeezed out and the few that are left have been discredited. They're nothing to worry about."

Clark gave a soft laugh. "I'm not so sure it's a good idea to piss off a bunch of spooks. They were mad as hell about being made to look like they were to blame for the fiasco we walked into in Iraq."

"And what did they do about that?"

He cast her a wry smile. "Nothing."

Adelaide took another slow sip of her drink, her gaze on the man pacing restlessly up and down her living room. He was an extraordinarily good-looking man, tall and fit, with a wonderful smile. But he was obviously weak. Funny she had never realized that about him before. When he'd called to tell her he was on his way over, she considered telling him about that troublesome remote viewing session. Now she was glad she hadn't. The last thing he needed was one more thing to make him goosey. Besides, that little hiccup would be dealt with soon.

A sudden thought occurred to her and she frowned. "Have you told the President about this?"

Clark swung around to look at her, his eyes widened in a way that made him look considerably less attractive. "Are you kidding? Of course not."

She nodded. No one told the President bad news, or even potentially bad news. Bob Randolph could be very nasty to anyone unwise enough to threaten the presidential image of perfection and invincibility. The man believed all his own sound bites.

Clark came to sink into a nearby chair. "I probably shouldn't have included the CIA's report on the Iranian chatter in Beckham's briefing."

"No. You needed to give him a full briefing. The last thing you want to do is arouse suspicion by deviating from normal procedures."

"But if he suspects—"

Adelaide laughed and stood up. "Relax, Clark, and have a margarita. We won't have to put up with him much longer."

23

The next morning, the sun came up like a big orange ball in a clear blue sky, and the city of New Orleans steamed.

Jax pulled his rented Pontiac G6 in close to the curb and parked. Beside him, what was left of Tulane University's Psych Annex smoldered behind lines of yellow crime scene tape that flapped lazily in the warm breeze coming off the river.

Jax opened his car door. Crime scene tape meant crime. Maybe this wasn't going to be a simple case of gas explosion—accidental death—investigation closed after all. So much for his tickets to tonight's performance of *Turandot* at the Kennedy Center's Opera House—and any hope of changing Sibel's mind about the future of their relationship.

A New Orleans city cop with the massive jowls and ponderous belly of a dedicated beer lover reluctantly left the steps he'd been leaning against and ambled over. "I'm sorry, sir. There's no parking here. You're gonna have to move your car."

Jax flashed the man a friendly smile and held up an Alcohol, Tobacco, and Firearms badge. The badge looked real because it was—just like the ones from the FBI and the Office of Homeland Security, and the press corps card Jax also carried. He even had an IRS ID he used when he really wanted to scare people.

"Agent Jason Aldrich, ATF." He nodded to the fire-scorched pile beside them. "What can you tell me about this?"

The patrolman stood up straighter and stuck his thumbs in his waistband to hitch up blue trousers pulled low by the combined weight of holster, handcuff case, ammunition pouch, radio, and collapsible combat baton. "You'll want to be talking to Lieutenant Ahearn. He can tell ya what you need to know." He turned his head and yelled, "Hey, Lieutenant. We got the ATF here."

A lean, small-framed man with sandy hair and a sprinkling of freckles across a sunburned nose had been standing beside the blackened remnants of what had once been a red Miata. He now turned, pale eyes squinting against the brightness of the sun as he waited for Jax to come up to him.

Lieutenant Ahearn was not as impressed with Jax's ATF badge as the patrolman had been, although he was careful to veil his hostility and surprise behind a show of cooperation. "Everything's preliminary at this point, I'm afraid," he said in the crisp, peculiarly cropped

New Orleans accent that sounded more like the Bronx
or Jersey than the mint-julep-sippin' South.

"I understand that," said Jax. "And I don't want you
thinking we've any interest in taking over your investigation, because that's not the way it is. We're just wondering what you've found about this fire that makes you
think it's suspicious."

"Suspicious?" The lieutenant blinked. His short
blond eyelashes and eyebrows were so fair they virtually disappeared against his white skin. "Well, I don't
know how things are up in Washington, D.C., but down
here, we find a man with a couple of bullet holes in his
head in a burned-out building, and we tend get suspicious."

A comedian, thought Jax, still smiling. "Any leads?"

The detective met his smile with a steely glare. "I
think you'll need to go through channels to get that
kind of information, Mr. Aldrich."

Jax sighed. It was too hot for this. "Let me explain
something to you . . . "

Half an hour later, having invoked the specter of
six hundred incompetent idiots from Homeland Security descending on Ahearn's investigation, Jax sat in
the G6 with the air conditioner running full blast and
put a call through to Matt. "See what you've got on a
woman named October Guinness . . . That's right, the
lady listed in the police report as having called in the
fire. Lives at 5815 Patton." Jax glanced across the street
at the brick house with Italianate arches on the corner
where a middle-aged woman with madras shorts, long
skinny legs, and a straw hat was setting a flat of bego-
nias along the front edge of the shrubbery.

He heard Matt von Moltke's breath ease out in a long, troubled sigh. Matt always took this stuff way too personally. "Found something, did you?" he asked.

"'Fraid so." Jax straightened his tie and thumbed through his wallet to find his press card. In his experience, middle-aged women who lived in big expensive houses were far more forthcoming with journalists than with ATF agents. "Looks like your man Youngblood ended up with a couple of bullets in his head."

"And this woman? This October Guinness?"

Jax shut off the engine again and opened the door. "She was here when the building blew. According to the cops, she was working with him. Which may or may not mean anything. I'll let you know."

Jax's conversation with the Uptown lady who lived in the raised cottage across from the Psych Annex was only vaguely informative.

She'd been in the back room watching television when the place blew, although she stood out on her front porch for a good forty-five minutes and watched the Annex burn. For much of that time she'd had company in the form of a young, pale-faced girl with big eyes and a tendency to start violently at loud noises. October, the girl had said her name was.

Jax gave the Uptown lady a business card that read: JACOB ANDERSON, ASSOCIATED PRESS. Then he went looking for October Guinness.

24

"You're not going to like this," said Hadley, tossing a copy of that morning's *Times-Picayune* onto the table.

Lance flipped open the newspaper and found himself staring at a headline that screamed, TULANE PROFESSOR SHOT DEAD. There was even a photo of the blackened ruins of the Psych Annex with the caption, *Police suspect fire linked to murder.*

He muttered a crude expletive, then said it again when his cell phone rang. He flipped it open. "Palmer here."

Adelaide Meyer's voice came through low and lethal. "Half the state of Louisiana consists of nice, out-of-the-way lakes and swamps filled with obligingly hungry alligators, yet you decide to turn this guy into a torch?"

Lance leaned back in his chair, his gaze meeting Hadley's. Hadley drew a pointed finger across his neck in a slicing motion and grinned.

"There've been some unexpected developments," said Lance. "But it's nothing we can't handle."

"Unexpected developments? You mean, as in arson and murder? You have less than thirty-six hours. Or have you forgotten?"

"It'll be over by nightfall," said Lance.

He pushed up from the table and went to stand beside the hotel room's wide window overlooking the city. "Our girl's obviously smarter than we gave her credit for," he said to Hadley. "Get on to headquarters. We're going to need some more backup down here. I want to see a copy of the last six months of her cell phone usage; let's get taps put on anyone and everyone she calls regularly. And run her credit card bills for the same period. I want to know where she shops, where she likes to eat. Let's see if we can find some kind of a pattern."

Hadley started to turn away but stopped when Lance added, "And start looking at hotels in the city that take cash. She spent last night someplace. I want to know where."

"I'll get on it," said Hadley.

Lance leaned his hands on the windowsill and stared out over the sprawl of the half-ruined city. From here he could see the wide brown coil of the Mississippi River winding its way between the levees. He opened his cell phone and punched in a number.

"Fitzgerald? . . . Lance here. I'm in New Orleans. When were you planning to fly in?"

Paul Fitzgerald might dress like a Texan, but his voice still carried the flat intonations of his northern childhood. "This afternoon. Why?"

"Better make it this morning. I'll explain when you get here."

"Trouble?"

"Maybe."

Lance hung up, then put in another call to his wife. "Hi, honey; it's me. Looks like I might not make it home for another twenty-four hours. Tell the kids I miss them, would you?"

Tobie was the first customer through the door of her bank when it opened at nine o'clock that morning. She filled out forms to withdraw $650 from her savings account—which essentially cleaned it out—and another hundred dollars from her checking account. Then she waited in line, her throat constricted with anxiety, until a bored teller with ebony skin and bright red hair called out, "Next."

Tobie stood with her hands gripping the edge of the counter, her gaze darting warily about the bank lobby while the teller typed the account information into her terminal. Tobie half expected the woman to look up and say, "I'm sorry, your accounts have been closed," or to see burly men with ominous bulges under their coats advancing toward her.

But then the woman was counting out the bills and stuffing them into a long white envelope. It wasn't until Tobie felt her breath gusting out in a long sigh that she even realized she'd been holding it. She shoved the envelope into her bag, said, "Thank you," and walked rapidly toward the door.

A minute and a half after October Guinness walked out the double glass doors into the bright sunshine of a cloudless morning, the bank manager received a directive from Washington, D.C., freezing both her accounts.

Hoarding her resources, Tobie bought a bare minimum of toiletries and other necessities from the Rite Aid down the street, then headed for her friend Gunner Eriksson's antiques store near the corner of Magazine and Felicity.

Gunner called it an antiques store, but most of his business came from his furniture restoration business. The grime of centuries obscured the shop's front windows, nothing on the floor had prices, and half the stuff piled inside looked as if it'd been picked up off the curb when people were gutting their houses after the hurricane. Tobie had to lean her shoulder into the heavy old timber door and push hard even to get it to open.

A cowbell attached to the top of the door let out a melodious jingle. But the shop was empty.

"Hello?" she called, her voice echoing in the dusty stillness.

Gunner's El Salvadorian wife, Pia, appeared at the top of a long flight of stairs leading to their second-floor living quarters overhead. An artist, Pia also used the big open space as a potter's studio.

"Tobie! Thank God!" She clambered down the steps, a small, lithe woman with straight black hair that brushed against her slim shoulders. "We've been so worried about you, and you haven't been answering your phone. Are you all right? The FBI were here this morning looking for you. They said you were missing."

"They were here?" Tobie spun toward the dusty window, her gaze darting up and down the street, panic clawing at her. *How had they known to look for her here?*

Pia came up beside her. "They're gone now. Tobie, what's going on?"

Tobie's breath was coming in quick little pants. She rubbed her hands against her face, trying to calm down, trying to think. *If they knew who her friends were, where could she go?* "I don't know what's going on," she said to Pia. "Some men came to my house last night claiming to be from the FBI and asking questions about Henry Youngbood. Then they tried to shoot me."

Anyone else might have thought she had finally cracked. But Pia had grown up in a country were people frequently "disappeared" into government prisons, never to be seen again. "*Madre de Dios,*" she whispered.

"I need to talk to Gunner," said Tobie. "Is he here?"

"No. He's at the Save Our Heritage demonstration in the French Quarter—"

"Where in the French Quarter?"

"Jackson Square. It's one of the few places in the Quarter you can plug in a PA system." If there was a demonstration in New Orleans about anything, from the latest genocide in sub-Saharan Africa to the recent push to require all purveyors of liquor in the Quarter to put in bathrooms, Gunner was sure to be there with his public address system.

"If anyone else comes looking for me," said Tobie, turning toward the door, "tell them you haven't seen me."

Pia snagged her arm. "Tobie, wait. I don't understand. Why would the FBI want to kill you?"

"I don't know if they're really the FBI or not. It all has something to do with Dr. Youngblood."

"You think these are the men who killed him?"

"Yes."

Pia fumbled in her pocket for her cell phone. "Let me call Gunner. He can leave the—"

Tobie touched her friend's hand, stopping her. "No. I'll go there."

Pia looked up, her straight brows twitching together, her soft dark eyes haunted by memories of the war-torn land of her childhood. "Don't you think you should stay here? If those men are out there looking for you—"

Tobie shook her head. "If they've been here once, they could come back."

Pia reached up to wrap her arm around Tobie's neck in a quick hug. Tobie had never been hugged much as a child. Her mother was too nondemonstrative, too German. But Pia was always hugging her friends. She held Tobie close in a rush of warmth and affection. "Be careful. You know we're your friends," she said. "If there's anything we can do . . . "

Tobie's arms tightened convulsively around her, then let her go. "I know. Thank you, Pia."

25

Michael Hadley was in a foul mood. His eye hurt. His head hurt. His shoulder was stiff. But more than anything, last night's debacle had stung his pride. He was a Navy SEAL, for Christ's sake. He'd been trained to kill. Had killed, more times than he could remember. And a pathetic, psycho loser of a girl had beat the shit out of him.

He pecked at the keys of his laptop, then let out his breath in an explosive sound that brought Palmer's head around.

"What is it?"

"She cleaned out her bank accounts this morning as soon as the bank opened."

Palmer stood up so fast he knocked his chair over. "What the hell? Those accounts were supposed to be frozen."

"It took a while to get through to our contacts. The directive reached the bank about a minute too late."

Palmer swore long and hard. "And the taps on her friends' phones?"

"They should be in place by noon."

Lance came to drum his fingers on the edge of the table. "It shouldn't take long now."

Hadley wasn't so sure. "She seems to be playing it smart. She hasn't called anyone."

"She will. So far she's been lucky. But she's going to make a mistake, sooner or later. And when she does, we'll nail her."

Leaving her Bug in a lot at the edge of the Quarter, Tobie pushed her way through the crowds toward Jackson Square.

With each step, she penetrated deeper into a different world, a world of narrow shady streets and Creole buildings of worn brick and crumbling plaster, where banana trees were draped over iron gates and fountains whispered unseen from hidden courtyards.

As she neared the leafy outlines of the square, she could hear a speaker's voice coming loud and clear over Gunner's PA system. "The ancient buildings of this city are a priceless heritage that the people who run New Orleans are willing to squander in the name of greed," said a woman, her voice throbbing with indignation. "They say it's the only way to get this city back on its feet, to prevent the blight left by the storm from becoming permanent, and to provide our people with jobs. But who's going to want to visit New Orleans once the very buildings that make this city unique have been knocked down to make way for some tacky casino and another dozen high-rise hotels that could be anywhere? Where will the jobs be then?"

A rousing cheer rippled through the growing crowd.

Squinting against the morning sun, Tobie was about to cross the street when she saw a sign propped in the dusty window of a shop near the corner: PREPAID CELL PHONES. NO CREDIT CHECKS. NO HASSLES.

Changing direction, she ducked into the store and bought one.

Tobie circled the square, her gaze scanning the crowd. She could see Gunner Eriksson fiddling with the wiring of his PA system at the edge of the square. She sometimes wondered what the activists and agitators of New Orleans would do without Gunner Eriksson and the PA system he carted around in his old Chevy van. She made sure no one was watching him before she approached and said quietly, "Gunner, I need to talk to you."

He swung around, his mouth going slack. A tall, tow-headed Swede originally from Minnesota, he looked like he'd be more at home at the helm of a Viking ship cutting through iceberg-filled northern seas than in the steamy heat of New Orleans. "Tobie!"

"Not so loud." She threw a quick glance at the people milling about them. "Can we go someplace quieter?"

"Come over here." Taking her arm, he drew her out the gates to the narrow alley that ran alongside the cathedral. "Pia called me," he said, swinging to face her. "She said you're running from the FBI."

"They could be FBI. I don't know." Tobie shivered and clutched her arms across her chest. It was cooler in the alley, the air scented by the ancient dank stones of the old Spanish buildings around them. "I need you to tell me what you know about Keefe Corporation."

His blue eyes opened wide. "Keefe? You think Keefe has something to do with this?"

"I'm not sure. Their name was on some documents I saw. What can you tell me about them?"

"Jeez. Where do you start? They're in everything from oil exploration and drilling to every kind of big-time construction project you can think of. Airports. Chemical plants. Dams. You name it."

"Ever hear of something called the Archangel Project?"

He thought a moment, then shook his head. "I know Keefe was in with Halliburton on that oil pipeline project the Taliban refused to let them build in Afghanistan. Maybe it has something to do with that. Now that we've taken out the Taliban, the pipeline project's a go."

"Gunner, we hit Afghanistan because of 9/11."

"You think it's all just a coincidence?"

Tobie stared off across the square, to the Moon Walk and the tops of the ships just visible over the looming mass of the levee holding back the river. She'd learned a long time ago not to try to argue with Gunner's conspiracy theories.

"I know Keefe was providing a lot of the logistical support in Iraq when I was there," she said.

Gunner nodded. "There was a big stink when they were awarded that contract. It was never put up for public bid, and the President's brother sits on their board of directors. Some senator tried calling for an investigation, but the Administration kept saying the criticism was just politically motivated, and the guy couldn't seem to get the press interested."

"So he dropped it?"

"No. He was killed in a private plane crash." Gunner watched a group of tourists in shorts and tank tops stroll past, their shoulders fiery red with sunburn. Tobie could see his eyes were troubled. "Have you thought about going to the police?"

"And tell them what? That the FBI is trying to kill me? You know they'll think I'm crazy."

Gunner nodded. He knew about her psychiatric discharge from the Navy, and he knew how people treated her when they heard about it. "Where are you staying?"

"I've got a hotel."

"You know Pia and I would be glad to have you come—"

"No," said Tobie quickly. "I don't want to put you in any more danger than I already have."

"Don't worry about—"

"Gunner, these men are killing people."

He was silent for a moment. A hot breeze picked up, heavy with the smell of the river and crab boil from the restaurant on the corner. In the square, a new speaker had taken the mike.

Gunner said, "We should be finished here by noon. If you want, I can look into Keefe, see what I turn up. I'll give you a call if I find something, but it would be better if we prearranged a meeting spot."

"A meeting spot?"

"Yeah. Say, City Park? Maybe at Bayou St. John, near the stables?"

"Why the park?"

"It's a nice open space. If they have either one of us under surveillance, we'll know it. And laser and infrared microphones require a line of sight they won't have among the trees."

Once, Tobie might have laughed. Instead, she dug a notebook and pen from her bag and jotted down her new number. "I bought one of those prepaid phones so no one can trace it."

He gave her a lopsided grin. "I thought I was the paranoid conspiracy nut."

She punched him lightly on the shoulder and smiled. "Where do you think I learned this stuff?"

26

Jax found the house at 5815 Patton Street silent and baking in the hot morning sun. It stood on short piers, its weatherboard siding painted yellow with white trim and black shutters.

Pushing open the low gate, he walked up a path edged with liriope and white four o'clocks closed tight against the light. The neighborhood was quiet and smelled faintly of the dampness left by last night's rain. His footsteps echoed dully as he climbed the two wooden steps to the front porch. He was about to knock, then noticed the door stood slightly ajar. When he touched his knuckles to the panel, the door creaked open about half a foot.

"Hello?" he called, not expecting an answer. Young women living alone in cities with New Orleans's crime rate didn't leave their doors unlatched.

He glanced around the covered porch, with its fanciful gingerbread trim and white rocking chairs, to the street beyond. A black Suburban parked at the corner had its windows up and the engine running, probably for the air conditioner. The windows were tinted, so he couldn't see the driver, and from this angle he couldn't get the license number. It probably meant nothing. Just some soccer mom waiting for her kid to finish his piano lesson.

Jax put one hand on the Beretta Cougar he wore shoved in a waistband holster at the small of his back. "Miss Guinness?"

There was no answer. He pushed open the door and went inside.

The house had been efficiently but thoroughly ransacked. Walking through the living and dining rooms into the kitchen beyond, Jax studied the half-emptied grocery bag with an overturned tub of Ben and Jerry's ice cream that had melted and run down the counter. Across the room, a neat bullet hole showed in the fractured glass of the utility porch door. The door was still open, and the bullet had obviously been fired from the inside.

He made a quick search of the bedroom, then moved to the small side garden. He was expecting a body. He didn't find one.

Wandering back inside, he put in a call to Matt. "Looks like whoever got your Dr. Youngblood might have also taken out the girl."

There was a silence at the other end of the phone. Then Matt said, "She's dead?"

"I don't know. Someone's torn her house apart and shot up her side door. There's a blood smear on one of the kitchen cabinets, but it's not much. Looks like she ran. She could have got away."

"Any idea yet who's doing this?"

"No. But I don't see anything that links back to the Company." Jax hesitated. "Although there is a black Suburban parked down the street."

Matt grunted. "Everyone drives SUVs down there. They need them to evacuate for hurricanes."

"Do you want me to come in?"

"Not yet. Something is obviously going on. I've got some info on the girl I'll be sending you."

Jax gazed out the open door at a swaying clump of butterfly iris in the side garden. "I have tickets to the Opera House tonight. *Turandot.*"

Matt laughed and hung up.

Stepping carefully around a pool of melted ice cream on the floor, Jax walked over to inspect the scarred wood of the back door frame. A bullet had buried itself in the wood. He was fingering the gouge when he heard a soft meow.

He swung around. An orange and white cat stood before the refrigerator, shifting restlessly from one front paw to the other.

"Hey there." Crouching down, he scratched behind the cat's ears and smiled as the cat closed its eyes in purring bliss. "Where is she? Hmmm? Do you know?"

From where he was parked down the street, Sal Lopez put in a call to Palmer.

"Our girl's got company. Some dude in a G6. Late twenties, early thirties."

"Is he in the house?"

"Affirmative. Want me to check him out?"

"Negative. Get out of there. He's probably calling the cops."

Lopez jotted down the G6's license number. Then he threw the Suburban into gear and hit the gas.

27

In Jax's experience, if you wanted to know what was really going on someplace, you talked to the secretary.

The secretary of Tulane's psych department was a fleshy woman named Chantal LeBlanc. She wore a lime green and aqua striped shirt, inch-long false fingernails, and enormous gold hoop earrings that bounced against the ebony skin of her neck when she moved her head. At the sight of Jax's press card, her eyes widened and a big smile spread across her face.

"You want to know about Dr. Youngblood, you've come to the right place," she said, leaning forward and dropping her voice.

Jax settled himself in the chair beside her desk. "You know about the project he was working on?"

She huffed a laugh. "'Course I know. Who you think typed up all them funding proposals?"

"He was having a hard time finding funding?"

"Wasn't he just. He got a bit of money from the university, but that ran out months ago." She dropped her voice even lower. "They didn't believe none of it."

"Really?"

"Nope. Called it voodoo and hoodoo and just plain hooey."

Jax laughed. "In those words?"

She grinned. "Not exactly. But it's what they think, believe me."

"Yet he did get funding from someone."

She shook her head, the big hoops swinging. "Lately, he was paying people outta his own pocket."

"Where was he applying for funding?"

Chantal's face fell and she glanced away. "I don't know. He always did the cover letters himself."

"Was there anyone in the department here working with him?"

"Are you kidding? He got a few undergraduates through work study and by offering them credit, but no one in the department here would touch that stuff—not even the grad students. I think the only reason he got Dr. Vu to agree to help him was because she was kinda sweet on him."

"Dr. Vu?"

"Elizabeth Vu. She's a statistician with the math department. Their offices are in Gibson Hall."

Tobie sat in her car with the windows down and the sunroof open, letting out some of the heat. She wanted to call her next door neighbor and ask him to lock up her house and check on Beauregard, but when she glanced at her watch, it was barely eleven. Ambrose King never got up before noon. He could be really, really cranky if anyone woke him before that.

She called the Colonel instead.

His voice was reassuringly calm. "Tobie. You're not using your cell phone, are you?"

She stared off across the heat-shimmered, black-topped parking lot to where a tour bus was disgorging a load of middle-aged women all wearing identical bright yellow fanny packs. "No."

"Good. I've been worried about you. Remember anything yet?"

"A little. I need to talk to you."

"I'm just getting ready to take Whiskey for a walk along St. Charles." Whiskey was the McClintocks' arthritic old yellow lab. "Why don't you come join me?"

She turned the ignition and rolled up the windows. "I'll be right there."

By the time Tobie pulled in next to the curb on St. Charles and parked, the morning's blue sky had faded to a white heat haze, and puffs of clouds were beginning to appear on the horizon.

After Katrina, the floodwaters from the collapsed levees had reached as far as St. Charles. She'd seen pictures of survivors paddling pirogues down the venerable avenue. But unlike some sections of the city where the water had reached depths of twelve feet and more, the ground here was higher; the gracious old mansions that stood on brick piers on either side of the street were little touched.

As she got out of her VW, a streetcar clanged past on its newly rebuilt tracks, the green metal of its side dull in the heat. She could see the Colonel coming up the neutral ground toward her, the old yellow dog padding happily at his heels. Tobie waited for a lull in the traffic, then crossed over to meet them.

"I've been thinking about your visitors," he said as she fell into step beside him. "I still have a few friends in Washington. If you like, I could give them a call. Put out a few feelers and see what I touch."

Whiskey came up to sniff Tobie's hand, and she stooped to pet the old dog. "You think those men really are linked to the government in some way?"

"FBI badges are one thing; IDs are something else. I think we might be looking at some kind of a linkage, yes. But not necessarily. All you need is an organization with good graphics capability."

"I've remembered the viewing session they were interested in."

He glanced over at her. "And?"

"The target was an office in some large modern building. I'm not sure exactly where, but it didn't look like anything in New Orleans. There was a file on the desk, labeled the Archangel Project. It contained photographs, including one of an old airplane. I recognized the logo on the file. It was the Keefe Corporation."

He was silent for a moment, his lips pursed. "This isn't good, Tobie. Keefe has a lot of ties to the Administration. To everything. Hell, they're in something like two hundred countries. They're everywhere."

"My friend Gunner says the President's brother sits on their board of directors."

"Your friend Gunner is right."

They watched Whiskey frisk on ahead, his tail wagging, his nose to the grass, sniffing. McClintock said, "There was a time when the lines between business and government were clearly drawn. That's not true anymore. Now we have a vice president meeting with energy representatives to help draft the Administration's energy program, and pharmaceutical companies helping draft legislation for prescription drug benefits. The military doesn't even have its own mess halls and laundries and motor pools anymore; all that's let out to private contractors for big bucks. Hell, we even hire private companies to come into our prisons and torture people."

"You're starting to sound like Gunner."

McClintock didn't smile. "The way I see it, either you know something these men want to know, or you know something they don't want anyone else to find out about. They took the time to talk to you, which means they want something from you, some kind of information. But I suspect they're willing not to get it in order to shut you up." He glanced over at her. His gray eyes were hard. "You need to figure out what that something is."

"I've tried. I can't."

"Until you do, Tobie, you can't trust anyone. Anyone. If you let these people get you boxed in, you're dead."

Tobie felt a chill tingle around the juncture of her shoulder blades. "What do you mean, 'boxed in'?"

"I mean you can't let the police bring you in. Even just for questioning."

A BMW convertible overflowing with college students cruised by, the top down, music blaring, a blond girl in a halter top hanging out the back and laughing. A shriveled black man with a plastic bag bulging with aluminum cans was working the trash receptacles in the neutral ground. As they drove past, the girl lobbed her beer can at him and shouted something.

"Could they do that?" Tobie asked. "Take me away from the police?"

"With FBI credentials? In a heartbeat."

McClintock watched the old man stoop to pick up the girl's beer can. "I think maybe you should consider getting out of town. Finding someplace to hide."

"With my mother?"

"No. Not there. Not anyplace familiar."

"For how long?"

He gazed off across the broad, leafy avenue.

"You mean forever, don't you?" She swung to face him. "I'm not doing that."

"October—"

"No. I'm just starting to get my life back together. I'm not going to let some jerks with guns and ties to a bunch of money-grubbing politicians come along and destroy it. These people think I know something that can hurt them. Well, you know what? I'm going to remember what that something is, and I am going to hurt them. I'm going to destroy them, before they can hurt me or anyone else again."

28

Bob Randolph was the kind of man who was born to be president. Tall, athletic, and good-looking, with a shock of gently graying blond hair and a boyish smile, he came from a family that had already produced one president, some half a dozen U.S. senators, and a raft of governors, representatives, and federal judges. True, he'd never done anything productive in his life, but he'd managed to steer clear of any scandals that couldn't be either covered up or just flatly denied.

He also played a mean game of golf.

T. J. Beckham had grown up hunting coons and fishing for bass rather than playing tennis at the club, sailing off Cape Cod, and dallying with pretty girls on all the most prestigious golf courses in the country. But everyone who was anyone in Washington played golf, so he had set himself to learn, and succeeded pretty darn well. T. J. Beckham tried not to be a prideful man, but he did pride himself on his determination, just as he prided himself on his loyalty. When he was selected as vice president after the death of Chuck Devine, Beckham set himself to be a faithful veep. He knew the office of vice president carried no authority and that his role was to serve. Yet his role was to serve not only his president and his party, but also his country. And lately he'd begun to realize that there were times when a man had to choose where his ultimate loyalty lay.

Trailed by a gaggle of Secret Service men, they were walking toward the third green of the Army and Navy Country Club when Beckham said suddenly, "I've tried, Mr. President, but I just can't keep my mouth shut any longer on how I feel about what you're doing."

Bob Randolph glanced over at him. Randolph was neither the most brilliant nor the best educated man to sit in the White House, but he was an expert on reading and manipulating people. He was also sly and self-centered to the point of being amoral—a combination Beckham had always found both vicious and dangerous. "What's the matter, T.J.? You don't like the way I'm swinging my nine iron?"

Randolph's smile was a winning one, and he used it now. Beckham resisted the urge to smile back and simply let the moment slip away. He shook his head. "It's my job to support you, and I have tried. But I don't think what you're doing is right. and I'm being pushed real hard by my conscience to stand up and speak out before it's too late."

"You going to join the long list of people telling me how *not* to fight the war in the Middle East, T.J.? Is that it?"

"No, Mr. President. I think you're trying to ma-nipulate this country into another war. You've moved a second carrier group into the Persian Gulf. You've got the Secretary of State and Secretary of Defense out there rattling their sabers on everything from Fox News to *Larry King Live,* and it seems like every time I pick up the *Wall Street Journal* or turn on the TV, there's some hysterical new piece about Iran. Now, I may be from Kentucky, but I'm not naive enough to think all these people aren't pushing your agenda."

Bob Randolph kept his smile in place, but his blue eyes were snapping. "What do you want me to do, T.J.? Let those crazy mullahs go nuclear?"

"The Iranians haven't done anything they're not al-lowed to do under the Nuclear Nonproliferation Treaty," Beckham reminded him. "At least they signed the treaty—unlike some of our allies. And if they wanted to, they could back out of it. Just like we backed out of the ABM Treaty."

Randolph thrust his head forward in a way that made him look considerably less presidential. "What? You saying you trust them? We're talking about *Arabs* here, T.J. Those people learn to lie and cheat before they learn to walk."

"Actually, Mr. President, the Iranians are Persians, not Arabs. And after spending thirty years on the Hill, I'd say neither the Arabs nor the Persians have cornered the market on lying and cheating."

"I'm afraid you're forgetting what's at stake here, T.J. I'm not going to have another 9/11. Not on my watch. These are evil men we're talking about, and if we don't fight them over there, we're going to be fighting them here. Better Tehran than Topeka, I say."

"Mr. President, Iran had nothing to do with 9/11. It's been thirty years since the Iranian Republic came into being after the fall of the Shah, and they've never attacked anyone. How many countries have we attacked in the last thirty years?"

Randolph swung to face him. "What's that supposed to mean, T.J.? It's a heavy responsibility this country bears, and I'll be the first to admit it. But we bear it with pride. It's our moral obligation to keep the light of freedom alive—not just for ourselves, but for the world. We can't turn our backs on the struggles of the people in the Middle East, just like we can't ignore the threat these mullahs pose to us. And we certainly can't show weakness by backing down from evil regimes that—"

Beckham swiped one hand through the air with a grunt of disgust. "For Pete's sake, Bob. You're not on a stump making a speech. This is me you're talking to, and you won't get me to shut up by mouthing the same old easy platitudes about freedom and democracy. I've seen those two words used to justify the killing of far too many innocent people in my life. Freedom and democracy have nothing to do with your plans for Iran and we both know it."

The President's affable charm slipped away, leaving in its place something that was no longer genial and no longer attractive. "You want reality, T.J.? I'll tell you what's reality. Twenty years ago this world was divided between us and the Soviets. Well, we whipped their sorry Commie asses, and now we're not just top dog, we're the only dog on the block. The world is ours. Ours, and ours alone. The empires of the past were nothing compared to what we have. The United States was ordained by God to rule the world, and I'm not about to let Him down."

T.J. studied the younger man's face. "God told you that, did he?"

"As a matter of fact, yes. He did."

"You scare me," said Beckham, and he turned and walked off the green without looking back.

29

Paul Fitzgerald walked out of the New Orleans Armstrong Airport into a blast of muggy heat. He was wearing a leather-banded Stetson and a custom-made pair of alligator boots, and within ten seconds of stepping into the muggy heat, he could already feel himself start to sweat.

New Orleans was not one of his favorite places. It was a great town for partying, for getting drunk and getting some ass. But the place had been a mess even before Katrina, full of homosexuals and liberals and welfare cheats with way too much 'tude. Now the people in this place were just plain nuts. He supposed watching your house, your friends and family, your entire *city* drown, could do that to you. They were putting the place back together, slowly. But Fitzgerald knew from the trips he'd made down here recently that huge swaths of the city were still virtual ghost

towns, full of stray dogs and cats and eerily dark at
night. He would be glad when this assignment was
finished.

"Hey, man," said Michael Hadley, popping the hatch
on the dark Suburban.

The guy was a mess, the side of his face swollen and
discolored. "What the hell happened to you?" said
Fitzgerald. He tossed his bag in the back, slammed the
hatch, and slid into the front seat. "What's going on
down here?"

Hadley hit the gas. "I'm going to let Palmer explain
that to you."

Jax thumbed through his various forms of credentials
and decided to approach Dr. Elizabeth Vu with a version
of the truth. He told her that he worked for the U.S. government and was looking into Youngblood's murder.

She stared at him for a moment with the slow, silent
assessment of an intelligent woman. "What can I do
for you, Mr. Alexander?" she said, settling back in her
desk chair and inviting him to sit.

Jax took the seat opposite hers. "We're investigating the
possibility that Dr. Youngblood's project on remote viewing might have had something to do with his death."

She was an attractive woman in her late thirties or
early forties: small and fine-boned and slim, with long
black hair and striking Asian features. But her face was
pale, her eyes swollen and red. Jax remembered what
Chantal over at the psych department had said about
Dr. Vu being "sweet" on Youngblood.

"How much do you know about remote viewing, Mr.
Alexander?"

"I've read some of the literature."

"And you think it's all either a delusion or one big fraud. Don't you?"

Jax smiled. "And you don't?"

"I was skeptical, at first. Who wouldn't be? I was sure the stats would prove Henry wrong, that the results of what he called 'successful viewing' were no more accurate than random coincidence."

"And?"

"The stats proved me wrong." She brought up her hands to lace them together before her. "I know why you're smiling. You think the experimental procedure must be sloppy. That it's all pseudoscience. It's not. It's a carefully defined technique. Some of the first people who worked on this for the government were a couple of physicists. *Physicists.* How much more scientific can you get than that? One was a specialist in nanotechnology, the other in lasers and infrared. Remote viewing works. I don't know how or why, but it does."

"Have you ever tried it?"

She leaned forward. "As a matter of fact, yes. When Henry's research funding started running low, I volunteered to do some sessions with him."

"And?"

"For his training sessions, Henry used the standard technique with a pool of local sites—things like the Superdome, the Huey P. Long Bridge, the sea lions at Audubon Zoo—specific, easily identifiable sites each written down on a separate five-by-seven-inch card and sealed inside double envelopes. One person would be designated the target, a second person the viewer."

Jax nodded. He'd glanced through some of the books Matt had given him.

"Henry and the viewer would go into his sound-proofed room, while the person selected as the target would randomly pick one of the sealed envelopes, open it, and drive out to the designated site. At a prearranged time, the viewer would start the session."

She paused, a faint tinge of color touching her pale cheeks. "I know what you're imagining. Crystal balls and Ouija boards and all that nonsense. But it wasn't like that at all. I simply sat in that room, went through a series of relaxation techniques, and then closed my eyes and let the images come."

"So what did you see?"

"The first time? Flashing lights. A whirling circle. What I imagined were pistons going up and down. I described it. Sketched it out. It made no sense to me."

"What was it supposed to be?"

"The carousel in City Park—what they call 'the Flying Horses' down here."

Jax was silent a moment. "A coincidence?"

"Mr. Alexander, I'm a statistician." She picked up a pen from her desktop and began fiddling with it. "The problem most people have when attempting remote viewing is what Henry called 'imagination overlay.' They try to interpret what they're seeing—like I did. I saw the poles of the horses going up and down and decided they must be pistons. That's where most people get it wrong. But with proper training that can be mini-mized. Anyone can do it."

"Anyone?"

The corners of her eyes crinkled into a smile. "That's right. Even Doubting Thomas CIA agents."

"I never said I was with the CIA."

"You didn't need to. Henry told me once that the only people who go around saying they work for the U.S. government are CIA agents. Just like if someone says they work for the Department of Defense it usually means they're with NSA."

Jax kept a straight face. "Really?"

"Yes. He also said the CIA never really lets anyone go. That's why you're here, isn't it?" She stood up and walked to the window overlooking the long expanse of lawn stretching out to St. Charles Avenue. "Who killed him, Mr. Alexander?"

Jax shifted in his chair, watching her. "I don't know. It would help if we knew who was funding his research."

Turning, she leaned back against the window. "For the last month, Henry was funding his own research. He was scrounging around trying to find sponsors, putting in proposals all over the place. He had a few people interested, but nothing had come through yet."

"Who was interested?"

"I'm not sure. He was trying both government and private corporations. But even companies that were receptive preferred that he keep quiet about it. Henry called it the giggle factor. People are embarrassed to admit they're interested in something that seems to veer outside the normal bounds of science." She gave a wry smile. "Did you know that Church's Chicken funded some of the original remote viewing research back in the seventies?"

"You're kidding. Why?"

"Pure interest on the part of Mr. Church. But most people are motivated by greed. There's been some speculation that RV can be used for geological exploration."

"How?"

"The technique with the index cards and local sites I described is used for training, or to accumulate a pool of results easily subjected to statistical analysis. Remote viewing can get much more sophisticated."

"Yet you say anyone can do it?"

"With proper training and guidance, yes. But the results from most people are not reliable. They get some things right, other things wrong. Sometimes they miss entirely." She shrugged her shoulders. "It's a talent. Just as certain people have better eyesight or hearing, certain people seem to have a gift for . . . " She hesitated.

"The paranormal?"

"That's a word I don't like to use. It's become too associated with the occult and the lunatic fringe. Henry liked the term 'cognitive talent.' "

"How much of a difference are we talking about here?"

"When using the card target technique, a good, trained viewer is about sixty-five percent successful—considerably better than a guess but still not reliable enough to be useful. It's why the government abandoned the project back in the mid-nineties. The first people they had working in the project—people like Pat Price and Joseph McMoneagle—were very good. But then they found themselves being forced to use people like a senator's girlfriend and some Israeli charlatan who passed himself off as psychic. Their success rate went way down. Henry was trying to identify criteria for selecting reliable remote viewers. He found one girl who's incredible."

"She's reliably accurate?"

"Not entirely. No one is. But her success rate is very high. The images come to her quite clearly and with amazing detail. She has the ability to simply allow the information to flow in without any imagination overlay or attempted analysis. Sometimes she can even read words or numbers, which is something most people who try remote viewing can't do. Henry said it probably has something to do with the way our minds process information."

"She was one of his students here at Tulane?"

"She's a student, yes, but not in Henry's department. She was actually recommended to him by someone at the VA hospital."

"She's a veteran?"

Dr. Vu nodded. "She was wounded in some incident that occurred in the western deserts of Iraq. Friendly fire."

"Do you remember her name?"

The woman gave him a long, penetrating look. "I'm not sure I should tell you that."

"It was October Guinness, wasn't it?"

The statistician didn't say anything, but Jax knew by the widening of her eyes that he had guessed right.

He knew a deep level of disquiet. "Have you heard from her since Youngblood's death?"

"No. Why would she contact me?"

"Because she's in danger and she's running scared." Jax pushed back his chair and stood. "We need to bring her in. But that's not going to be an easy thing to do without spooking her. She doesn't know she can trust us. So if you do hear from her, will you contact me?"

Elizabeth Vu stayed where she was, her arms crossed at her chest. "How do I know she can trust you?"

Jax took out one of his cards—one of the ones that actually said *James A. X. Alexander* on it—and laid it on her desk. "You don't."

30

At twelve-thirty, Tobie called her next door neighbor, Ambrose King.

"Jesus Christ, October." He yawned into the phone. "What time is it?"

"It's lunchtime for most of us, Ambrose. Listen, I've had to go out of town for a few days. Do you think you could check on Beauregard and see that he has enough to eat, and give him some fresh water?"

"Sure. When you think you'll be back?"

"Hopefully in a day or two. Thanks Ambrose."

"Bingo," said Hadley, sticking his head around the corner.

Lance looked up from the city map he and Paul Fitzgerald had spread across the table.

"We got her," said Hadley. "She called her next door neighbor to ask him to take care of her cat."

"From a pay phone?"

"Nope. From a prepaid cell."

"Huh. So she's being clever. Just not clever enough."

"Our boys sent us something else, too," said Hadley. "Dr. Elizabeth Vu from the math department just tried to call the girl's old cell phone."

Lance frowned. "Vu? Isn't she the statistician who was working with Youngblood?"

"You got it."

"Maybe we should have paid more attention to her. Have Ross and O'Meara go check her out." Lance pushed back his chair and stood up. It was about time they got a break. "In the meantime, pull the records on our girl's new cell phone. Lets see who she's talked to in the last twenty-four hours. And get the GPS coordinates. If she leaves it on, it'll work like a homing beacon and lead us right to her."

Jax opened the door to let the G6 air out and leaned against the side. He was parked in the shade, but it was still hot. A light breeze had kicked up, smelling of sun-baked river silt, long-growing grass, and hot asphalt. He loosened his tie and tried for the fifth time that day to call Sibel. She wasn't answering.

Frustrated, he punched in Matt's number.

"Where's that information you said you were sending on the girl?"

"It's coming. We should be able to get it out to you in a few minutes. We've been busy. There's been a lot of chatter floating around the last few days, but it's strangely hard to pin down."

Jax grunted. "Tell me about October Guinness."

There was a pause filled with the tapping of computer keys. Matt let out a low whistle. "She was in the Navy.

A linguist. Speaks something like a dozen languages. Her stepfather's a petroleum engineer and worked all over the place. Even did a stint in the Persian Gulf, which is where our girl learned her Arabic. The Navy sent her to Baghdad."

That must have been a surprise. "She was wounded?"

"Yeah. How'd you know?"

"Someone mentioned the VA hospital."

"She caught a round in the leg. Laid her up for some time, mainly because it complicated an earlier knee injury. But that's not the main reason she's still going to the VA. They have her in therapy. And I don't mean just physical therapy."

Jax squinted up at the spreading branches of the oak over his head, where a blue jay had started making an angry racket. "I don't like the sound of this, Matt. Spit it out."

"She got a psycho discharge."

Jax slapped his hand against the roof of the car. "Oh, great." He climbed in and slammed the door. "That's just what I need."

Tobie had never tried remote viewing on her own.

Several times in the past she'd had what she now understood were spontaneous viewing experiences. But even after she started working with Youngblood, she'd shied away from attempting on her own to duplicate the procedure he'd taught her. With his help, she'd been slowly coming to see her remote viewing ability as a talent rather than a curse. But the idea of deliberately doing it on her own still scared her.

Now she had no choice.

She drove to the zoo, found a place in the shade to leave the Bug, and walked through the trees toward the levee. The river breeze was kicking up, rustling the leaves of the live oaks overhead. A woman and two kids had spread a picnic blanket in the shade. Tobie could smell the sharp scent of their fried chicken, hear the children's laughter, the mother's soft voice. The woman glanced up, her gaze following Tobie as she kept walking.

She found a hollow place behind the broad, twisted trunk of an oak that looked as if it had been there since the days of Lafitte and General Jackson and the War of 1812. She sat on the grass with a pad of paper and a pen beside her, crossed her legs like a Buddhist monk, and tried to relax.

She drew in a deep breath and let it out slowly, keeping her spine straight. When she'd done sessions with Youngblood, he always gave her the targets. At first she would just focus on whoever had been sent to the target site. Then he started giving her more distant targets, designated by geographical coordinates. Once, he had a friend in Hawaii put a photograph in a sealed envelope and set it on his desk, and had her view that.

Even Youngblood admitted he didn't understand how it all worked. But Tobie knew the link between the target, the tasker, and the viewer was always there. Neither the tasker nor the viewer ever knew what the target was—that was important, so that the tasker wouldn't inadvertently influence or coax the viewer's report of what she or he was seeing. But the tasker had to be *aware* of the selected target, in the sense that he had to be able to say to the viewer, "Elizabeth is at the target site," or, "The target is shown in the photograph sealed in an envelope and lying on a desk in Hawaii." Lately he'd started simply giving her coordinates, saying things like, "Focus your attention on forty-five degrees, twenty-five minutes, fifty-two seconds North, and eighty-six degrees, fifteen minutes, twenty-two seconds West."

Would it work if she tried to set her own target?

She knew the target she was seeking: the same office that had served as the target for Henry's funding proposal. So how could she be sure she was really "seeing" it and not simply imagining it?

A bubble of panic rose within her. She pushed it down. She needed to be receptive, to believe in herself, otherwise this wasn't going to work. She closed her eyes, concentrated on the gentle touch of the wind against her face. But all she could see was flames dancing against a night sky. The dark vibrating shadow of helicopter gunships looming overhead. A little girl screaming and a mother's frantic face as she ran—

Tobie opened her eyes, her breath coming hard and fast, fingers raking her hair back from her hot forehead. She stared up the slope of the river levee, where the mother was now playing Frisbee with her children.

It wasn't going to work, October thought, her panic in full flight. She couldn't do this. She couldn't remote view that office again. Not reliably. She couldn't even remember what else she'd drawn in those quick, largely unintelligible sketches she made during her session with Youngblood. So what was she supposed to do now?

She was just pushing to her feet when the phone in her bag began to ring.

31

Tobie flipped open her phone and heard Gunner's voice.

"Don't say my name."

She took a moment to digest this. "All right. But why?"

"I think it's better. I'm calling from a pay phone."

She leaned back against the rough tree trunk. "Why?"

"It occurred to me they might have pulled your old phone records. If they look at who you've called in the past, they could tap my phone."

"That's against the law."

"Nothing's against the law anymore, Tobie. Not if you're the Administration—or close to them. And Keefe is very close to the Administration. These people are scary, Tobie. I've got some stuff you need to see. Do you remember where to meet?"

"Yes."

"Can you make it for two o'clock?"

She glanced at her watch. She could grab something

for lunch and still make it to City Park in plenty of time. "I'll be there," she said, and hung up."

Homicide Detective William P. Ahearn of the New Orleans Police Department stood in the middle of Dr. Henry Youngblood's living room and shook his head. File cabinets had been yanked open and searched, but the twenty dollar bill tucked beneath a bowl on the entrance table hadn't been touched. The professor's computer hard drive was gone, but his DVD player was still there, as was a nice little Yamaha CD player.

"I don't like this case," Ahearn said to his partner, Sergeant Trish Pullman. "Nothing makes any sense."

Trish reached out to straighten one of the pictures on the wall, the kind of automatic gesture typical of a woman used to picking up behind three teenage sons, but stopped herself when Ahearn said quietly, "Crime scene, Trish."

She flashed him a wry grin. "Sorry."

He went to stand beside a pile of jumbled books. "What were they looking for?"

"It obviously wasn't money."

"No. And it's not a coincidence either," said Ahearn as his phone began to ring. He flipped it open. "What you got?"

"I thought you might be interested in this one, Lieutenant. A report just came in on a burglary on Patton Street, off Nashville."

"And why did you think that might interest me, exactly?"

"The house belongs to October Guinness, the woman

who witnessed last night's explosion. From what I hear, the place has been ransacked."

Ahearn's gaze met his partner's. "We'll be there in ten minutes."

Lance frowned down at the computer printout in his hands. The Pontiac G6 had been rented to someone named Jason Aldrich from Virginia. Only, Jason Aldrich didn't exist.

"Who is this guy? And what's his interest in October Guinness?"

"We're still checking," said Hadley.

Fitzgerald stuck his head around the doorway from the other room. "A call just came through from Lopez. He spotted the girl at a Lebanese restaurant. Uptown."

Lance stood up and grabbed his suit jacket. "Tell him to keep her in sight but not to approach her yet. I'm on my way."

32

Byblos Restaurant on Magazine was one of Tobie's favorite
cafés, a quirky Lebanese place with a tin ceiling and
wooden floors that looked as if it might once have been a
dime store. She ate an eggplant and crab cake, then ordered
baklava to go, since City Park was on the other side of New
Orleans near the lake and she was running out of time.

Leaving Byblos, she drove up Magazine to Louisiana
Avenue, planning to take Claiborne over to Carrollton.
She didn't notice the black Suburban until she was half-
way between Camp and Chestnut.

She wasn't sure how long the Suburban had been
behind her. She only spotted it because she was nervous enough about her stolen plates that she kept glancing in her rearview mirror, looking for cops. At first
she thought she was just being paranoid. The Suburban wasn't exactly on her tail; it was just there, holding
steady some two or three cars back.

She eased up on the gas. The red pickup that had been right behind her moved over into the left hand lane and passed her, followed by a white Toyota.

The Suburban hung back.

Tobie pressed on the accelerator and wove in and out of traffic for one block, two. The Suburban kept pace with her, never edging up too close, but not falling behind either.

"Shit," she whispered, her hands tightening on the wheel.

At the corner of Washington and Magnolia she hung a quick right, drove a block, then darted left. She zig-zagged across Broad and under the Pontchartrain Expressway, hoping to lose her shadow at a light. But the guys in the Suburban were good.

She fought back the urge to floor the accelerator and try to outrun them. The last thing she needed was to bring the police down on her. *If you let these people get you boxed in*, the Colonel had told her, *you're dead*.

So what the hell was she supposed to do?

Her throat dry, her breath coming in quick little pants, Tobie forced herself to hold to the speed limit. She wound through streets of ghostly abandoned houses that still bore faint, ugly brown waterlines and the orange spray-painted markings of the rescue teams. By now she was hopelessly lost. Most of the city's street signs had been lost in the storm and many of them were still down.

She turned left and right and then right again, suddenly emerging onto a broad, tree-lined avenue she didn't even recognize. It wasn't until she heard a clang and looked up to see a red streetcar rolling down the center of the street that she realized she was on Canal. Inadvertently, she was leading her shadow dangerously close to City Park.

Throwing a glance in her rearview mirror, she hit the gas, edging up until she was just past the streetcar. She swung a quick left, bumped over the tracks onto Cortez, and heard the shriek of metal brakes as the Suburban tried to follow her.

The streetcar slammed into him broadside, pushing him some twenty feet up the neutral ground before they came to a shuddering, screeching halt.

"Ha! Take that, you bastard," she cried, her pulse thrumming with elation. Then another black Suburban darted from around the wreckage and she went, "Holy shit."

She hit the gas, her rear tires jackknifing as she tore up the street. The guy in the second Suburban was on her ass in an instant. She tried to pull away but this dude wasn't in the mood to play nice and follow along behind her at a cozy distance. He was obviously pissed. He edged right up behind her, close enough to tap her rear bumper once, twice.

By now she was on Moss, winding along Bayou St. John. She managed to put about five or six feet between her VW and the guy behind her, but the road here was treacherous. There was one spot opposite Cabrini High School where both the bayou and the road beside it took a sharp curve to the right. Someone had put up a row of crosses, one for each of the speeding motorists who had drowned here in the last ten years. Seeing the crosses,

Tobie hit the brakes and spun her wheel. Behind her, the Suburban accelerated.

She heard the squeal of tires and glanced back to see the Suburban soar off the road. For one glorious moment the sonofabitch was airborne. He hit the water with a teeth-jarring splash.

She floored her accelerator and didn't look back.

33

"How did they find me?" Tobie asked Gunner.

They were walking through the long grass of City Park, deep in the area beyond the stables where the trees were thick and the leafy canopy overhead whispered relentlessly with the early afternoon breeze. Gunner squinted up at the sunlight filtering down through the moss-draped live oaks. "You say you noticed them after you left Byblos?"

"Yes." She crossed her arms at her chest and hugged herself. There was a fine trembling going on inside her that wouldn't seem to stop. Even her voice was shaky. "Why?"

"Do you eat there much?"

"Yes. But how could they know that?"

"It wouldn't be hard if they ran your credit card records."

"How could they get that kind of information?"

"Depending on who they are, they either hacked into

your credit card company's records or they simply ordered the company to turn them over."

Tobie was silent for a moment. "Can the Government do that?"

"Are you kidding? With the Patriot Act, they can do anything they want. As long as they say it's for national security reasons, no one is going to complain or try to stop them. In fact, it's a federal offense even to tell anyone the Government requested the information."

Tobie watched the oak leaves flutter in the breeze, watched a white ibis take off from the calm green water of the bayou. She'd known that, of course, but it hadn't particularly worried her. She was a good, law-abiding American citizen; how could she ever imagine someone might use those Draconian powers against *her*?

"Of course, it doesn't even have to be the Government doing this," Gunner was saying. "All that information collection has been contracted out to private companies."

"Do you know who?"

"I think Keefe is one of them. There are supposed to be safeguards, but, well, you know how that goes."

"Oh, God. How do you fight someone who has the power to lay their hands on every little detail of your life?" she asked, her voice a whisper.

"You can't. Not openly. And not by yourself. Maybe if you find out what's behind all of this, you can go to someone in Congress."

"Oh, right. Someone like that congressman you were telling me about? The one who ended up dead in a plane crash?"

Gunner held out a thick manila envelope. "I looked up the Keefe Corporation on the Internet. You wouldn't believe the shit they're into. And God knows what they're up to that isn't public information. Especially these days."

Tobie took the envelope and shoved it in her messenger bag. "Thanks, Gunner. I never should have contacted you. I'm sorry. I didn't mean to put you in danger."

"I just wish there was more I could do to help. There didn't seem to be anything on an Archangel Project. If I find something, I'll call you." He hesitated, then said, "Have you thought about getting out of New Orleans?"

"You're the second person who's suggested that to me. The trouble is . . . where am I supposed to go?"

Gunner stared off across the treetops, toward the shattered neighborhoods that stretched between the park and the grassy levees of the lake. Afternoon thunderheads were starting to build, although here in the park the sun still blazed down bright and hot. "I don't know. But you need to stay away from anything and anyone familiar." Bringing his gaze back to hers, he put his hand on her shoulder and squeezed. "I'm worried about you, October."

She gave him a wry smile. "I'm worried about myself."

Hadley was on his laptop at the Sheraton, trying to run down some nonexistent guy named Jason Aldrich, when the call came in from Lance Palmer.

"Our girl has a new license plate," said Palmer, giving him the number.

"You lost her?"

"That's right." Palmer's voice was tight. "Along with two of the Suburbans."

Hadley glanced over at Fitzgerald, who just shrugged.

"Where are you?" Hadley asked.

"Emergency room. Lopez had a slight run-in with a streetcar. They think he's going to be all right, but they want to keep him under observation for a few hours."

"You all right?"

"Me? Yeah. I just need to change into some dry clothes."

"Dry clothes?"

"Don't ask."

"And the girl?"

"She'll surface again," said Palmer. "And when she does, we take her out. Forget about trying to make it look like a suicide or an accident. I just want this girl dead. Understood?"

"Got it."

34

Tobie considered herself a typical all-American chicken-shit. She was not hero material. She'd survived the terror of being in Iraq largely by playing mind games with herself. In Iraq, when she thought about where she was and what could happen to her there, she froze up. So she learned not to think about it.

Colonel McClintock had all kinds of terms for it, like "sublimation" and "suppression," words she vaguely remembered from Psych 101. He said sublimation of fear was the reason at least half of all vets suffered from post-traumatic stress syndrome. People can only repress so much for so long, he said; then it starts bubbling up.

She didn't think she deserved her psycho discharge from the Navy, but she figured she probably did have PTSS. Most sane vets did. Hell, half the people in New Orleans were suffering from PTSS, although their demons had been unleashed by Katrina rather than Iraq.

She figured maybe, in some way, what she'd been

through in Iraq had prepared her for what she was going through now. People had been trying to kill her there, and people were trying to kill her now. There were differences, of course. In Iraq, none of it had been personal. She'd been a target not because she was October Guinness, but because she was a member of an occupying military. Now the people trying to kill her were after her and her alone. She wasn't sure if that was better or worse. At least it removed that element of randomness.

But there was another difference, one that she knew did make her present situation worse. In Iraq she'd had over a hundred thousand guys on her side. She always knew there was someone watching her back—lots of guys watching her back. Here, she was on her own. Every time she contacted one of her friends, she put them in danger.

After leaving Gunner, she went to sit in the Fair Grinds Coffee Shop, just off Esplanade Avenue. Like almost everything else in that part of New Orleans, the coffee shop had flooded after the storm. But it had been one of the first places to reopen, and continued to serve as a rallying point for a neighborhood determined to rebuild itself.

Fishing the envelope from her bag, she drew out a thick sheaf of Internet printouts. She found herself staring at an article concerning a study advocating the military destruction of Iran, published by a Washington think tank called the Freedom Institute for Democracy. At first she thought Gunner had included the site by accident; then she noticed Keefe Corporation listed as one of the study's sponsors.

She glanced through it in a hurry. It was pretty alarming stuff, reminding her of the policy document produced by the Project for the New American Century—PNAC—back in September of 2000. In a Mein Kampfesque call for world domination, PNAC had advocated rallying the people of the United States to attack Iraq in the wake of a Pearl Harbor–like disaster. Gunner was always using it as evidence to support one of his crazier conspiracy theories, that the U.S. government was covering up something about 9/11. She shifted the article to the bottom of the pile.

The rest of the printouts dealt mainly with Keefe Corporation's various projects. There were articles about Keefe's involvement in building American bases and military installations everywhere from Iraq to Uzbekistan to Pakistan; about their contract to supply the U.S. military; about legal suits against various chemical factories built by Keefe. There were several articles on the proposed pipeline through Afghanistan, oil exploration in Arctic wildlife refuges, and, buried amidst reports on the buildup of mercury around Keefe's offshore drilling platforms, a brief mention of the corporation's funding of a study on the use of psychics in the exploration for mineral deposits.

Tobie pulled out the page and stared at it.

Here, it seemed, was the source of Keefe's interest in remote viewing. Had Henry Youngblood put in a funding proposal to Keefe Corporation? A proposal that included a trial remote viewing session? A session in which she had seen something no one was supposed to see?

She dug her prepaid phone out of her purse. About

the only person she knew at the university who'd been associated with Youngblood's research was a statistician from the math department, Dr. Elizabeth Vu.

Tobie was about to punch in the woman's number when she hesitated, remembering Gunner's warning. What if the bad guys were monitoring Vu's phone? She knew she was probably being paranoid, but she turned off the phone again, and then, for good measure, pulled out the battery. Pushing back her chair, she went to use the coffee shop's pay phone.

Dr. Vu answered on the second ring. "Hello?"

"Dr. Vu? This is October Guinness. I was wondering if I could come by your office this afternoon?"

"Oh, hi, October. I'm about to leave my office for the day. I need to do some work on my boat this afternoon—I'm taking my brother and his family out this weekend. Why don't you come to the marina? I'd like to talk to you myself. The boat's at the Orleans Marina, slip 23, Pier 4. Say in about an hour?"

"I'll be right there," said Tobie, and hung up.

Jax was on his laptop, flipping through Matt's information on October Guinness, when the call came through from Dr. Elizabeth Vu.

"I just heard from October. She's coming to see me."

Jax looked at his watch. "Now?"

"In an hour. At the Orleans Marina." There was a pause. "I hope I'm not making a mistake telling you this."

"You're not."

He hung up the phone, then sat staring at the photograph on his computer screen, a photograph of an unexpectedly fresh-faced young woman with brown eyes and shoulder length, honey-colored hair. She didn't look crazy. But he had read her medical reports.

He slipped his Beretta into the waistband of his slacks and reached for the city map.

Detective William P. Ahearn fingered the bullet-scarred wood of October Guinness's kitchen door frame. This investigation just kept going from bad to worse.

He glanced over at the lowlife with long scraggly hair and ragged jeans who stood in the middle of the kitchen floor. Ambrose King, he said he was; played the sax at some tourist trap down in the Quarter. The guy might have called the cops, but he wasn't exactly being cooperative.

"You say she contacted you? Where is she?"

The lowlife stuck his hands in the pockets of his jeans and looked blank. "She didn't say. She just said she had to leave town for a few days."

"In the middle of a murder investigation?"

Ambrose King rolled his shoulders in an exaggerated shrug. "She didn't say nothing about that."

Ahearn met his partner's gaze. She raised her eyebrows and turned away to hide a half smile.

He walked back toward the living room, his gaze sweeping the ransacked house. "I see DVDs, but no DVD player or computer. What else do you think is missing?"

King ambled behind him. "Tobie has a laptop, but I think she took it in to get fixed last week. Her DVD player died a month or so ago. I don't think she's replaced it."

Ahearn turned to give the guy a hard look.

King stared back at him. "What? What you thinking? That I lifted her stuff? Man, you'd have to be nuts to want any of Tobie's electrical shit. It's like she generates this electromagnetic field or something. If she walks up next to you when you're on your computer, it freezes. I've never seen anything like it."

Ahearn pushed out his breath through pursed lips and swung back to the kitchen. "Let's get that bullet to ballistics," he said to Trish. "See what they can tell us about it. And I think maybe we ought to find this Guinness woman. She has some serious explaining to do."

35

The Orleans Marina lay in that part of the city known as the West End, on the shores of Lake Pontchartrain just north of the Old Hammond Highway. Hurricane Katrina had devastated this part of the city. Many of the houses here were still derelict; others had already been bulldozed, leaving empty lots of rutted mud. But some houses had FEMA trailers in their yards, with olive-skinned crews hanging Sheetrock or hammering on roofs.

Leaving her car parked on Lake Marina Drive, Tobie passed through the gate in the high seawall that effectively hid the marina from the street. The sheltering boathouses and the small park beyond them had saved the Orleans Marina—and its boats—from the worst of Katrina's storm surge. In contrast, the sailboats and yachts docked at the Municipal Marina on the lake's edge had been smashed into a tangle of nearly unrecognizable wood, fiberglass, and metal.

Walking through the gate, she found herself in a broad basin a quarter of a mile wide and filled with pier after pier of dazzling white sailboats and cabin cruisers that lolled lazily in the protected surge of the tide. Sunlight glittered on the open expanses of water between the piers. Thunderheads still hung dark and heavy over the north of the lake, but here the sun beat down golden and hot.

At mid-afternoon on a weekday, the place was virtually deserted. She found the fourth pier and hurried down the rough steps to the graying wooden dock, her gaze scanning the numbers on the slips. A woman called her name.

"October?"

Tobie turned toward a large fiberglass cabin cruiser. Dressed in a white T-shirt, denim capris, and boat shoes, Dr. Vu was at the stern coiling up a line. "October," she said, drying her hands on the seat of her pants as she moved toward the bow. "Please, come aboard. How are you?"

Tobie scrambled over the cruiser's side. She knew the question wasn't meant to be funny, so she was careful not to laugh. She'd always had a bad tendency to laugh at what most people considered inappropriate times. It had frequently landed her in trouble during her school days—and later in the Navy. She had no doubt it contributed to her psycho discharge.

"I'm okay," she said. "But I think the people who killed Dr. Youngblood are now trying to kill me."

Dr. Vu's mouth went slack. "But . . . why?"

"I don't know. I was hoping you might."

"Me?"

"Do you know if Dr. Youngblood was applying to Keefe for funding?"

"The Keefe Corporation? I suppose it's possible, but he kept that sort of thing confidential even from me."

"He didn't say anything to you at all about where he was applying?"

Dr. Vu turned away to dump out an ice chest. She was quiet for a moment, thoughtful. Then she said, "I remember, about a month or two ago, he told me he'd run into someone he knew. Someone he'd met while working on a remote viewing project he did for the government."

A flock of sea gulls wheeled overhead, their harsh cries drifting on the breeze. Dr. Vu squinted up at them, a sad, soft smile lighting her face. "Henry was excited about it. Whoever this person was, he was familiar with RV and knew it worked. Henry was hoping the guy would convince his boss to consider a funding proposal."

"Was this guy still with the government?"

"I don't think so, no. Although I could be wrong."

"Do you remember his name?"

"I think it was something like Lance, but I'm not sure."

The sound of a car door slamming cut through the rhythms of the wind whispering through the rigging and the gentle lapping of the waves. Tobie stared off across the bobbing boats to the long narrow parking lot near the seawall. Two men in khaki slacks were approaching the pier, their polo shirts flapping loose in the breeze. Tobie watched them clamber down the steps. They were unfamiliar to her.

She brought her gaze back to Dr. Vu's face. "You say

Dr. Youngblood ran into this man? You mean here, in New Orleans?"

"Yes. On Canal."

"What was he doing here? Did Youngblood say?"

"I believe he was doing some kind of recruiting."

The men in polo shirts had paused at the cruiser's bow. Tobie watched them, her heart beginning to beat hard and fast. Both were tall and broad-shouldered, with narrow hips and short cropped hair and the kind of military bearing that reminded her of the men who'd come to her house last night. It might not mean anything, she reminded herself. People with enough money to buy forty- to fifty-foot boats and keep them in a marina like this usually had the spare time to stay slim and toned. But still . . .

One of the men, in his mid-thirties, with a tanned, handsome face and heavy dark brows, squinted into the sun and smiled. "You're Dr. Vu, aren't you?"

Dr. Vu turned. "Yes. May I help you?"

"I'm Stuart Ross." He came along the short length of dock that divided the slips and stepped aboard, the other man close behind him. The second man was fairer skinned, with a redhead's sprinkling of freckles across his nose. As Tobie watched, the redhead reached behind his back and pulled out a black Glock. He shoved the gun in her face.

"Don't make a sound."

Sucking in a quick breath, Tobie glanced toward Dr. Vu. The woman stood with her eyes wide, her arm gripped tight in Stuart Ross's big tanned hand. The semiautomatic he held was outfitted with a suppressor, just like the Glock in Tobie's face.

"We're going for a little boat ride." Ross threw a quick glance around the cockpit and shoved Dr. Vu toward the helm. "Take her out."

Dr. Vu stumbled. "And if I refuse?"

"Believe me, you don't want to do that."

Dr. Vu's hands closed on the wheel. Tobie could see the woman was obviously shaken, but she didn't look to be in danger of falling apart.

Tobie remembered the stories Dr. Youngblood had told her about Dr. Vu, about how her village was flattened by American B-52s during the Vietnam War. About how she'd seen her mother blown to pieces, her brother turned into a living torch by napalm. She'd spent years with her father and sister in a refugee camp in Hong Kong before being allowed to immigrate to the States. A woman who'd been through that kind of horror wouldn't crumble easily.

Tobie wasn't so sure about herself.

The redhead jerked his chin toward the bowline. "You untie the ropes," he told Tobie. "Front first."

She didn't see any point in arguing. The marina was deserted. It might be safer for these men to shoot her and Dr. Vu out on the lake and quietly slip their bodies overboard, but she had no doubt they were willing to kill here and now, if they needed to.

She crawled out the molded bow pulpit, her fist sweaty on a steel rail burning hot in the fierce afternoon sun. Around her, the water in the basin shimmered. She looked toward the feathery leaves of the hurricane-battered trees on West End Park, drooping now in the sun. To get to open water they would need to cruise up the channel, past the park and what was left of the Southern Yacht Club and the Municipal Marina, to where the old lighthouse and Coast Guard station once guarded the breakwater and the West End boat launch. The marina itself might be deserted, but there was always a handful of old black men fishing for mullet and catfish from the breakwater. If Dr. Vu could run the cruiser into the rocks, maybe—

Redhead's voice cut through Tobie's racing thoughts. "What the fuck you doin' up there? Untie that rope and get back here. Now."

Tobie eased the line off the steel cleat and headed aft.

36

Jax pulled his rented G6 into the marina's narrow strip of parking lot, found an empty space near Pier 2, and killed the engine. The sun glinting off the water hurt his eyes, and he slipped on a pair of sunglasses before opening the car door.

Halfway down the pier he could see two men, one of them big and redheaded and unfamiliar. But Jax recognized the dark, good-looking one: his name was Stuart Ross, and six months ago he'd been in Colombia with the Army's Special Forces.

"Sonofabitch," Jax whispered, and headed for the steps.

The two men were on board now. Elizabeth Vu was at the wheel and Jax could see the girl, October Guinness, out on the bow. As he watched, she cast off the bowlines and started working her way aft.

Trotting down the pier, he called out cheerfully, "Hey, Elizabeth. Heading out? Mind if I come along?"

Without waiting for an answer, he leaped nimbly

aboard. The redhead with the freckles and sunburned arms turned a Glock on Jax and growled, "Go sit over there, shut up, and don't do anything stupid. Who the fuck are you?"

Jax glanced toward Ross. The guy was studying Jax with a frown. But Jax had worn a full dark beard in Colombia, and it was obvious that Ross's memory of him wouldn't gel.

The redhead growled again. "I said, who are you?"

Jax spread his arms wide and sat down on the aft bench. "You told me to shut up."

"A smartass."

Jax was aware of October Guinness, a silent watchful presence on the far bench. He glanced at Elizabeth Vu. Her face was pale, her dark eyes huge, but she seemed to have herself under control. She said, "He's a friend of mine."

Ross grunted. "He picked a bad time to come for a visit." Leaving Redhead to cover the other two, Ross turned his back on Jax and moved in close to Vu. "Back up slow and take us out on the lake. We need some privacy."

Jax could feel the deck vibrate, hear the swell of the water as Vu eased the cruiser out of its slip. For the first time, he swung his head and looked directly at October Guinness.

Her honey-colored hair fluttered loose around her face in the breeze, and the golden tone of her skin seemed to glow with health and vigor in the sun. He was surprised by how small she was, and by how young she looked. She had the body of a fifteen-year-old gymnast, with small high breasts and no hips. It made her look younger than he knew she was, and oddly more vulnerable.

She was staring straight ahead. He could feel the tension in her. She was wound tight inside, so tight he wondered how she was managing to hold herself together. He knew only the faintest outlines of the hell she'd been through in the last eighteen hours.

The last time she'd been through hell, in Iraq, she had not coped well.

The cruiser lurched forward, the engines racing. Jax glanced to where Elizabeth Vu sat tall and stiff at the wheel.

Ross said to her, "You're going too fast. Just take it slow and don't do anything stupid. No wake."

Wordlessly, Elizabeth Vu throttled back and the cruiser eased up.

They were out in the channel now, a long narrow line of wind-ruffled blue water cutting between grassy banks baking in the heat. Jax could see the point, opposite the ruins of an old lighthouse. As long as they were in the channel, Stuart Ross and his redheaded friend were unlikely to do anything. But once they were out on open water, Jax had no doubt he'd be the first one over the side with a bullet in the back of his head. If he was going to act, he needed to do it quickly.

He was aware of the hard outline of his own gun pressing against the small of his back, and casually leaned forward. The odds definitely were not good: two men with drawn guns against himself, a middle-aged math professor, and a woman certified as missing some of her marbles.

He looked again at Elizabeth Vu. She kept casting furtive glances at the console, her gaze drifting between the channel, Ross, and a built-in open shelf to the right of the helm. Jax shifted his position, trying to see what she might be looking at, but her body blocked his view.

He cleared his throat and raised his voice over the drone of the engines. "What's going on here, Elizabeth? Who are these guys?"

"I told you to shut up," snarled Redhead.

They were clearing the channel, the cruiser keeling gently to the right. Ross said to Vu, "Okay. Now bring up the speed and head out into the middle of the lake."

The boat began to pick up speed. Jax shifted his weight, giving himself lots of space around his right arm. Redhead leaned toward him, the Glock waving threateningly in the air. "Goddamn it, I told you to sit still!"

His shout jerked Ross's attention away from Dr. Elizabeth Vu. And in that instant she reached into the open compartment on the console and swung around, a heavy knife in one hand.

She lurched toward Ross, the knife clutched in her fist. Jax yanked his Cougar from his waistband, threw himself forward in a roll and came up firing. But Ross was already turning back toward Elizabeth Vu. He pulled the trigger, and an oozing red hole opened up in her chest as Jax's bullet slammed into Ross's face.

Jax swung back toward Redhead just in time to see October Guinness launch a well-aimed kick that knocked the gun flying out of Redhead's hand. Her second kick caught the man in the face. He toppled backward over the handrail, his body hitting the water with a heavy splash.

"You bastard," she shouted after the man in the water.

The helm abandoned, the cruiser swung in a tight, fast circle, the engines racing, the wheel spinning wildly. Jax leaped for the helm. He eased up on the throttle and steadied the helm, then went to make damn sure that Ross was dead. He was.

Slipping his gun into his waistband holster, Jax laid his fingertips against the pulse point on Elizabeth Vu's neck. "Shit," he whispered.

He heard October Guinness ask, "Is she dead?"

Jax sat back on his heels and swiped a forearm across his sweaty face. "Yes."

"What about him?"

"They're both dead." He glanced over at her.

She was standing in the middle of the deck. At some point when he wasn't watching, she had picked up the redhead's heavy Glock. Now, she was holding it out in front of her in a steady, two-handed grip, pointed at him.

37

"You can put that thing away," said Jax, keeping his voice soft and easy. But he was very, very careful not to move.

She kept the Glock on him, her body swaying gently with the lifting of the deck, her hair flying loose around her face in the salty breeze. "I don't think so. Who are you?"

He held up his hands where she could see them. "Calm down."

"Do I look hysterical?"

He had to admit she didn't. But then, he'd been in this business long enough to know that looks could be deceiving.

"Stand up slowly and turn the boat back toward shore. Do it!" she said, when he simply stared at her.

He eased to his feet and took the helm.

"Keep it slow and turn in a wide arc. I don't want to run into the redheaded gorilla we left swimming back there."

Jax did as he was told. "And if he can't swim?"

"Then he drowns." She shook her hair out of her eyes. "Who are you?"

"I work for the federal government."

She laughed. She actually *laughed*. Then her face hardened and she said, "If that's meant to reassure me, it doesn't. The jerks who tried to kill me last night said they were from the FBI."

"They're not FBI."

"Yeah? So who are they?"

Jax squinted off across the sparkling expanse of the lake, toward the grassy levee that rose in a high swell beyond the seawall. "Look, I'm on your side. I just killed one of the bad guys, remember?"

"I don't see anything altruistic in that. It looked to me like you did it to save your own ass."

"At least it means we have the same enemies."

"Maybe, maybe not. How do I know you wouldn't have killed me next?"

"What reason would I have to kill you?"

"What reason do they have to kill me?"

She was starting to sound a bit too emotional for his taste; Jax decided to keep quiet for a while.

She said, "How did you know Dr. Vu?"

"I just met her. I've been trying to find you. She called and told me you were coming out here to talk to her."

"And how did the bad guys find out I was here?"

"That, I don't know."

He glanced back at her. She was studying him through narrowed eyes. "Why did you want to find me?"

"I'm trying to figure out what happened to Henry

Youngblood—who killed him, and why. I thought it might be useful to talk to you."

She kept the gun on him. He remembered reading that she was a lousy shot, but a person could be blind and still not miss at that range. "Who do you work for?" she said. "And don't give me that federal government crap."

"That's all I can tell you." He glanced toward the shore. They were about a hundred yards out. "Where'd you learn to kick like that?" He didn't remember reading anything about martial arts in her file.

"Throttle back all the way," she said. "But keep your hands on the wheel."

He throttled back. The cruiser rolled heavily in the swell. He was suddenly aware of the sound of sea gulls wheeling overhead, of the pungent smell of fish and sun-baked mud in the air.

"All right. Now over the side."

He swung around to look at her. *"What?"*

"You heard me. Over the side."

"And if I can't swim?"

"I'll throw you a life preserver." She motioned with the Glock.

He backed toward the rail. "You need to think about this."

"I have." She lowered the muzzle of the gun until it pointed at his leg. "You can go over the side or I can put a hole in your knee and drop you over. Only then I don't think you'd find it very easy to swim."

Jax swung a leg over the side, then paused. "Listen to me. You're in danger. Everyone close to you is in danger. And the longer you play around with this, the more people are going to get hurt."

"Jump."

"If you change your mind, my name is Jax Alexander." He paused. "Although, I'm registered at the Hilton under the name Jason Aldrich. Room 520."

"I'm not going to say it a third time. I may be a lousy shot, but it'd be damn hard to miss at this distance."

He wasn't going to argue with a woman with a gun and a psycho discharge. He jumped.

He made sure he jumped feet first, so he wouldn't lose his Beretta. The water closed over his head and he plunged deep. Kicking up, he broke the surface—and caught a mouthful of spray as a life preserver hit the water beside him.

"Thanks," he called.

She hit the throttle and left him in a surging expanse of sun-shimmering waves.

38

Hadley rolled the Suburban to a stop in the shade of an ancient oak and nodded toward the house across the street. "That's it."

Lance studied the stately Victorian with its curving porch and wide steps. The place reminded him of the big old houses in the exclusive neighborhoods of his hometown of Lawton, Oklahoma. When he was a kid, he used to dream of owning a place like this someday. He let his gaze drift over the ornate gables and the stained-glass bay window, and knew an echo of the combination of envy and longing he used to feel every day when he'd walk past those beautiful old places on his way to school.

"The nurse took the old lady for a walk about five minutes ago," said Hadley, glancing at his watch.

Lance nodded. "Let's do it."

He had his hand on the car door when his phone began to vibrate. He frowned. The call was from Buck O'Meara, who had gone with Stuart Ross to the marina.

As the senior partner, Ross should have been the one checking in. Lance flipped open the phone and settled back in his seat. "What is it?"

O'Meara's voice was tight. "Ross is dead."

Lance's gaze met Hadley's. "What happened?"

"The girl was here."

"Guinness?"

"Yes."

"Did you get her?"

"No."

Lance slammed his hand against the car door in frustration. "Why not?"

"Some smartass came up. Driving a Pontiac G6."

The G6 again. Who the hell was this guy? "Tell me about him."

"Late twenties. Slim. Medium height. He didn't give his name and I forgot to ask for his business card. He shot Ross. Vu's dead, too. Ross killed her."

"And the Guinness woman?"

"She took off in the cruiser with the smartass."

"She knows him?"

"He acted like he knew the professor, but I'm not so sure he really did. The guy's a pro."

"Have the local police been brought into this yet?"

"Not that I know of."

"Where's Ross's body?"

"In the boat, with the girl and the smartass."

Shit, thought Lance. Aloud, he said, "Where are you now?"

"I swam back to the marina."

"Swam back?"

There was a short pause. "You need to send a car to

pick me up. Ross had the keys in his pocket. And you might consider sending someone to stake out the ass-hole's G6. It's still here."

"What about the girl's car?"

"I don't see it, but it must be around somewhere."

"Find it. I'll send Barello."

There was a short pause. "Can you tell him to step on it? I'm wet."

Lance grunted and put the phone away.

"I thought Ross was good," said Hadley.

"He was. One of the best. We've obviously got another player in the game." Lance tapped his phone against his lips for a moment, then put in a call to Fitzgerald.

"We got any Semtex left?"

"Yes. Why?"

"The girl's car is somewhere near the marina at the West End. Send Reggie to wire it to blow when she opens the door."

Lance snapped his phone closed and stood up, his shirt sticking to his back in the humid heat. They'd already checked out the girl's next door neighbor, Ambrose King; the guy was a clueless lowlife. "Let's go talk to this colonel. The last thing we need is one more loose end."

Tobie ran the cabin cruiser parallel to the shore. She wanted to put as much distance as she could between herself and the men she'd left swimming in the lake behind her. But she was shaking so badly she finally had to throttle back and simply let the boat idle in the water.

Unwanted memories crowded in on her, of a desert

night filled with tracers and bomb blasts; the ugly thump of bullets striking flesh; the sobbing screams of a frightened, hurting child. Letting go of the helm, Tobie slid to the floor, her arms hugging her bent knees tight against her chest.

Eyes wide and vacant, Dr. Elizabeth Vu stared at her.

Tobie tightened her jaw. She was not crazy and she wasn't going to start acting like it. If she wanted to stay alive, she needed to *think*.

She sucked in a deep, steadying breath, then another. She was on a boat in the middle of Lake Pontchartrain with two dead bodies. She couldn't simply pull back into the marina and tie up at the dock. Even if Lance Palmer or his men weren't there, waiting, she couldn't risk being seen leaving the scene of another crime.

A fly buzzed her face. She brushed it away, but it was back again in an instant. The smell of blood hung thick in the air, mingling with the briny fresh breeze coming off the lake. Beneath her, the cruiser rocked gently with the waves. Pushing to her feet, she stared off across the sun-sparkled water, her gaze scanning the shoreline.

A stepped concrete seawall formed the edge of the lake here, with the grassy slope of the levee and a cluster of tall buildings marking the University of New Orleans rising up beyond that. In the distance she could see the sprawl of the Industrial Canal. There'd be a dock there, she thought, then realized she couldn't risk heading into it. Even in this post-Katrina world, there would be too many people around. She needed to find someplace else, someplace like . . .

Pontchartrain Beach.

Her gaze focused on the small cove below the university. She'd heard that at one time the people of the city used to come here to swim and picnic. There'd been a pier and a restaurant, even an amusement park with a Ferris wheel, before the beach had to be abandoned with the rise of the pollution levels in the lake. Now there was only a deserted strip of weed-grown sand and the remnant of a storm-shattered pier that stretched out to nowhere.

Squinting against the late afternoon sun, Tobie scanned the levee and the copse of oaks that grew on the small point just beyond the beach. No one was in sight. But she still didn't like the idea of pulling into the cove with two bloody bodies sprawled across the deck in plain view. She went looking for a tarp.

The only one she could find wasn't big, which meant she had to drag Dr. Vu's body closer to her killer in order to get the tarp to cover them both. She threw a quick glance at the dead man's face and felt her stomach tighten. The bullet that killed him had taken out one of his eyes. She'd seen worse—much worse—in Iraq, but she'd never gotten used to it.

That done, she rummaged around until she found an old T-shirt that she used to wipe down every surface on the boat she could possibly have touched, including the bow. Then she took the helm again and eased the throttle forward. Turning the bow toward shore, she ran the cruiser straight into the beach.

The cruiser's hull screeched along the bottom, then caught fast to lurch sideways at a drunken angle, the engines racing. She quickly killed the engine. In the sudden silence, she became aware of the sounds of the lake, the lapping of the waves against the cruiser's hull, the cries of the gulls. She started to take off her sandals, then reconsidered. Surely footprints were as dangerous as fingerprints?

She wiped off the helm again and slung her messenger bag over her shoulder. She had one leg over the side, ready to jump, when her gaze fell on the redhead's Glock—the one that hadn't been fired. Scooping it up, she shoved the gun into her bag.

It was uncomfortably heavy, whacking against her hip as she eased herself over the cruiser's side into the shallow water. But she was glad to have it as she splashed ashore, the sand sticking to her wet feet and legs as she crossed the narrow beach to climb the levee beyond.

39

Barid Hafezi was in his office at the University of New Orleans, checking the footnotes to a paper on the effects of corporate ownership of the news media that he was preparing for an upcoming journalism conference, when the phone on his desk rang.

He stared at the phone for a moment. These days, every time the phone rang, he felt a twist of fear bloom in his gut. But he knew better than to ignore it.

"Hello?"

The voice on the other end was smooth, faintly mocking. "You know who this is?"

Barid squeezed his eyes shut. "Yes."

"Good," said the Scorpion. "I want you to do something for me tonight."

"I have other commitments."

"Cancel them. There's a bar at the corner of St. Charles and Lee Circle. The Circle Bar. You know it?"

"Yes."

"I want you to go there. Have a few drinks."

"I am a Muslim. I don't drink."

"You're going to drink tonight. You have a credit card, don't you?"

"Yes."

"Good. Pay for the drinks with a credit card. Leave the receipt on the table."

Barid felt a rush of helpless rage. "What is this about?"

"That's one of those questions you're not supposed to ask, remember? You still have the package I sent you?"

"Yes."

"Good. I want you to take it with you to the Circle Bar. Leave it there, on the table with your credit card receipt."

"That makes no sense. No one takes a Koran to a bar."

The voice at the other end of the phone laughed. "Mohammed Atta did."

"And then he died. Along with nearly three thousand other people. Did you set him up, too?"

The man on the other end of the phone was no longer laughing. "The Circle Bar, tonight. Or do I need to remind you what I'll do to your children? Your little girl is very pretty, you know. While your son—"

Barid bolted up from his chair. *"You bastard. You stay away from my—"*

But the line was dead in his hand.

Lance Palmer took the steps to Colonel F. Scott McClintock's porch two at a time.

Their background check on the Colonel had turned

up some nasty surprises. Yes, the man was October Guinness's VA shrink. But Lance didn't like the fact that the psychologist's time in the Army had been spent in intelligence. There were even hints that he'd been involved with the Army's old remote viewing projects back in the seventies and eighties. Lance supposed it was possible McClintock was the original link between the Guinness woman and Youngblood's program. But the fact that she'd called the Colonel this morning worried him. It worried him a lot.

"Colonel McClintock?" said Lance when the old man answered the door. "Lance Palmer, FBI."

Colonel McClintock was a good six feet four inches tall, and still upright and solidly built despite his silver hair and lined face. He subjected Lance's FBI credentials to a slow scrutiny before nodding pleasantly. "Gentlemen. How may I help you?"

"We have some questions we need to ask you. May we come in?"

The Colonel's expression was professionally blank. "Actually, I was just on my way out."

Lance gave the man a tight smile. "I'm afraid it's important. We won't take long."

McClintock hesitated, then opened the door wide. "Glad to help in any way I can. What's up?"

They followed him into a book-lined study with a worn, tapestry covered sofa and a wide antique partner's desk. "We're investigating the murder of Dr. Henry Youngblood and the disappearance of October Guinness. We understand you've been treating her through the VA."

McClintock settled himself in a leather armchair and

motioned for them to sit. "What do you mean, Tobie's 'disappearance'? Has something happened to her?"

"We don't know. She's mentally unstable, isn't she?"

"No."

Lance leaned forward, his forearms resting on his knees. "Really? It was our understanding she's suffering from post-traumatic stress syndrome."

"That doesn't mean she's unstable."

"She thinks she has 'visions,' doesn't she?"

McClintock reached out to fiddle with the heavy bronze statue of a man on a horse that stood on the round oak table beside his chair. It was a moment before he spoke. "Are you familiar with remote viewing?"

Lance had a flicker of surprise. It was the last thing he'd expected the Colonel to bring up. Lance settled back in his seat. "That's the project Youngblood was working on, wasn't it?"

"Yes."

"Did Miss Guinness ever talk to you about the various sessions she did with Youngblood?"

"No. She never talked to anyone about them. I think the entire program made her uncomfortable."

Lance nodded. It was good news. He didn't want to have to kill Colonel F. Scott McClintock. There were already too many bodies piling up down here as it was.

"Then why did she participate in it?" asked Hadley.

The Colonel shrugged. "She needed the money, among other things."

"Has she by any chance contacted you since last night?"

"No. But I wish she had. With all that's been going on, I've been worried about her."

Lance and Hadley exchanged a quick glance. Lance cleared his throat. "According to our records, Colonel, Miss Guinness called you this morning."

McClintock's poker face never faltered. "Tobie is my patient. I'm afraid that means her call to me this morning is protected by doctor/patient privilege."

"Did she tell you where she is?"

"No."

It was a lie, of course, and they all knew it. The silence in the room stretched out, tense and brittle. Then the phone on the desk began to ring.

Thrusting up from his chair, McClintock had taken two steps toward the desk before Hadley moved to block his path. "Leave it," said Palmer.

The phone rang one last time, then an answering machine somewhere at the back of the house kicked in. McClintock glanced from one man to the other. "I think you'd better leave now."

Hadley took another step forward, getting right in the Colonel's face. "You're lying, old man, and we know it. Where is she?"

Reaching out, Hadley thumped the old man's shoulder, shoving him back toward his chair. Only, rather than staggering backward, the Colonel pivoted with Hadley's push and reached up to grasp Hadley's arm and pull him forward.

Caught off balance, Hadley stumbled into the chair, knocking it over and going down with it in an awkward tumble.

Lance started to reach for his gun, but had to duck

when the Colonel grabbed the bronze statuette from the side table and hurled it right at his head. "*Stop him!*" Lance shouted as McClintock bolted for the door.

Still only half to his feet, Hadley managed to grab one of the man's legs. Yanking out his Glock, Lance brought the heavy butt down on the back of the old man's head.

The blow dropped McClintock to his knees. Lance hit him again, the dull *thwunk* of the impact echoing through the silent old house.

"The son of a bitch," said Hadley, and kicked the man in the face.

The sound of a woman's voice from the sidewalk outside brought Lance's head around. "Let's get out of here."

40

Back at the Hilton, Jax took a long shower and changed into a dry pair of khakis and a polo shirt. He tried one last time to call Sibel Montana, but when she didn't pick up, he figured he was about to cross the line from sincere to a nuisance and gave it up. He hesitated, then punched in the number for Clare's Florist on King Street.

"What do you want on the card?" asked the girl who took his order for a dozen white roses.

"Just . . . just, 'Thanks for the good times, Jax.'"

He went to stand beside the window overlooking the crippled city. Here and there tattered blue FEMA tarps still showed amid the scattering of new roofs and gaping demolition sites. New Orleans had turned into a strange hybrid, half bustling port and tourist city, half Apocalyptic ghost town. He couldn't figure out if the place was depressing or inspiring. Maybe it was both.

It occurred to him that in the past twenty-four hours, two of the people in his life had questioned his career choice. He wondered if maybe he was just being obstinate, staying with the Agency. He'd always had a habit of going against what people told him to do. At times that could be noble, something to be proud of. But sometimes it was just plain hardheadedness. Maybe this was one of those times. Except . . .

Except that whenever he thought about quitting, he felt diminished. He felt as if he would be giving up or selling out. So much of the time, he knew, he was just beating his head against a wall of bureaucracy and corruption and stupidity. But every once in a while he really did achieve something—something he could walk away from knowing he'd made a difference. He couldn't imagine anything else he could be doing that would make him feel so alive. He supposed it was the same instinct that drove other men to become priests or teachers. Perhaps at its heart that instinct wasn't even altruistic. Maybe it was just another form of arrogance and pride. But he didn't like to think so.

He pushed away from the window and put in a call to Matt.

"The girl's still alive," he told Matt, giving him a quick rundown of the afternoon's events—although he left out the bit about the swim in the lake. "She's badly spooked. She's not going to be easy to bring in."

"Any idea yet who we're dealing with here?"

"I recognized the cowboy I shot. His name is Stuart Ross. Last I saw him, he was with Special Forces down in Colombia. If you can find out what he's been doing for the last few months, it might tell us who we're dealing with here."

"You think these guys are Special Forces?" Matt asked.

"Maybe. Maybe not. Special Forces can't keep their people any better than the CIA can. Everyone makes more money working for the big mercenary companies."

"Did you get the feeling the girl was the target, or was she just unlucky enough to stumble on a hit on Vu?"

"I don't know." Jax hesitated, then added casually, "By the way, I'm going to need to rent another car."

Matt groaned. "What'd you do to the G6?"

"Relax. It's fine. It's still at the marina. But I'm going to need to let it cool off for a while. Some of Ross's friends might be on it."

"What are you leaving out, Jax?"

"Leaving out?"

"Yeah. After you shot Ross and Guinness kicked the other guy into the lake, what happened?"

Jax stared out the window at a heavy belt of clouds building on the horizon. "She got the drop on me and made me jump overboard."

"She what?"

"You heard me." Jax held the phone away from his ear until Matt had finished laughing his ass off.

"The lady sounds like maybe she's smarter than anyone's giving her credit for," said Matt, when he caught his breath.

"Smart? She's crazy."

Tobie tried calling Colonel McClintock from a pay phone on the UNO campus, but hung up when his answering machine kicked in. She glanced at her watch.

She felt a rising spiral of fear, as if her options were

narrowing down. She thought about catching a taxi back to where she'd left her car by the marina, then decided to go see the Colonel instead. It was after five. If he'd gone for a walk with Mary and LaToya, he should be home soon. Maybe he'd learned something from his friends in Washington, something she could use to make sense of this mess. She clung to that hope as she waited for the taxi outside the Union building.

But when her taxi finally drew close to the Colonel's house, she could see the flashing red and blue lights of emergency vehicles from more than a block away.

"Pull up here," she told the taxi driver.

"But Soniat's not for another—"

"That's okay. Just pull over." She thrust a twenty at him and tumbled out of the taxi.

A police car and an ambulance filled the street in front of the Colonel's house. Tobie could see the broad back and close-cropped head of Mary McClintock's nurse, LaToya. The Colonel was nowhere in sight.

Clutching her bag to her side, Tobie ventured across the street and up about half a block, to where a knot of three women and two men huddled together at the end of a driveway. Neighbors, drawn out of their homes and into the street by the sound of sirens.

"What happened?" she asked.

"It sounds like it must have been one of those home invasions or whatever they're calling them these days," said a plump, middle-aged woman with carefully coiffed platinum hair and a red boat-neck T-shirt decorated with an American flag appliqué. "LaToya came back from taking Mary for her walk and found Dr.

McClintock unconscious in his library."

"He's still alive?"

"Yes. Although Laura heard someone say he's been badly hurt. There's just not enough police in this town, ever since Katrina. That's the problem, you know. Not enough police and too many punks coming in from all over the country. New Orleans was bad enough before, but ever since the storm . . . "

Tobie wasn't paying attention anymore. She was watching the policeman who had just walked out of the Colonel's house. He glanced up the street, and Tobie swung her head away, her heart thumping wildly.

It had been a mistake to venture this close, she realized. Keeping her head down, she turned and forced herself to walk slowly back down the street. She kept her face averted until she rounded the corner. Then she broke into a run.

She'd covered about two blocks, heading toward St. Charles, before the pain shooting up from her bad knee became so unbearable she had to drop down to a trot. But she kept moving.

She'd thought she could fight these men, make them pay for what they'd done to Henry Youngblood and for what they'd tried to do to her. But she'd been wrong. You can't fight a corporation whose tentacles reach from the CIA to the Pentagon, all the way to the White House.

She was going to go back to the marina, she decided, get her car, and just get on the I-10 and head west. It's what she should have done when Colonel McClintock first suggested it that morning. Now Elizabeth Vu was dead and McClintock himself was in an ambulance on the way to the emergency room.

She still didn't know where she was going to go, once she got out of New Orleans. All she knew was that she had to get out of the city and stay away from anyone she knew.

Before she got someone else killed.

41

"How you doing, Jason?" said Clark Westlake to the man who occupied the desk outside President Randolph's office.

"Just fine, thank you, sir." The President's special assistant nodded toward the Oval Office. "He's expecting you."

Reaching for the door handle, Clark felt a familiar rush of adrenaline mixed with a cocky kind of pleasure. He'd been coming here to the White House for the better part of ten years now, yet he still felt a thrill of excitement every time he entered the Oval Office. *This* was the summit of all power. *This* was the center of the universe.

"You wanted to see me, sir?"

Bob Randolph stood at the window overlooking the rose garden. Clark could tell by the set of the man's shoulders that he was in a petulant mood. "I had a troubling talk with the Vice President this afternoon," said Randolph, not bothering to look around. "I'm afraid he's not proving to be much of a team player. I don't think we can rely on him to stay on message. He's going down to New Orleans tomorrow to give this keynote address at the American Legion Conference, and I can just hear him making some crack about needless sacrifices and wasted lives. Or worse."

"Mr. President, I can assure you that's not going to happen."

Randolph glanced at him over one shoulder. Clark could see the President's brows arc suggestively.

It was classic Randolph style. The President told his subordinates in vague terms what he wanted to happen, then left it to them to turn his wishes into realities. He neither specified nor wanted to know the details. He simply surrounded himself with people ruthless enough to do whatever was necessary to achieve his visions. That was enough.

"You can assure me of that?" said Randolph.

"Yes, sir."

Randolph swung to face the window again. From where he stood, Clark could see the barricades that kept the public well back from the White House's perimeter. It seemed hard to remember that there'd once been a time when tourists lined that fence and no one thought anything of it. A faint smile curled the President's lips.

"That will be all, Clark."

Clark smiled and bowed himself out like a courtier groveling before a king.

Someday, it would be his turn.

42

Homicide detective William P. Ahearn stood at the water's edge, his hands thrust into his pants pockets. The breeze fluttering up from the surface of the lake felt fresh against his face but the sun's heat was still fierce.

The two murder victims probably hadn't been dead for more than an hour or two, but already the sickly sweet stench of death filled the hot evening air. It would be easier being a cop someplace like Fargo, North Dakota, Ahearn found himself thinking. It might be damned cold, but at least the crime scenes wouldn't smell so godawful.

"You say she's a professor at Tulane?" he asked.

The uniformed cop, a guy by the name of Crouch, wiped the sweat off his forehead with the back of his hand and squinted into the evening sun. "Yes, sir. Dr. Elizabeth Vu. She was in the math department."

Ahearn stared down at the second body on the cruiser's deck. Someone had shot out the man's right eye. It wasn't a pretty sight. "Who's the guy?"

"According to his wallet, his name's Ross. Stuart Ross. He's from Texas."

Ahearn grunted. New Orleans was full of Texans, most of them contractors and construction workers who'd arrived after the storm. Only this guy didn't look like a construction worker.

"You want me to have the boat dusted for prints?" asked Sergeant Trish Pullman.

Ahearn glanced over at her. "What's the point? We couldn't process them even if there are any." Katrina had essentially wiped out the NOPD facilities. All they had was a bunch of bodies lying all over the place.

"I'll call it in," said Trish. "This doesn't look like another drug deal gone bad."

Ahearn grunted again. "Didn't someone in the psych department say something about Henry Youngblood working with a statistician from the math department?"

Trish squinted up at him. "You think the two murders are connected?"

"When was the last time we had two Tulane professors murdered in twenty-four hours? Of course they're connected." He squatted down to study the cruiser's bow, where it had been driven hard into the sand. "We've got two bodies, two bullet holes, and one gun that's fired one bullet. I'm guessing it's a pretty good bet neither one of our two vics drove this boat up on this beach." He pushed to his feet and heard his knees crack. "Any witnesses?"

"A jogger," said the uniform. "He was too far away

to see much, but he says one person got out of the boat after it rammed ashore."

"Man or woman?"

"A woman. A young woman. He says she ran toward the campus."

"What's she look like?"

"He couldn't say. The guy's nearsighted."

Ahearn stared off across the weed-grown sand toward the UNO campus. "All right. Let's get some more people out here. I want them to talk to everyone they can find. Let's see if we can get some kind of description of this girl."

43

The target was easy enough to find: an old yellow 1970s VW Super Beetle with a factory sunroof, parked on the street just outside the marina.

Reggie Williams ran a connoisseur's hand over one flawless fender. The car was a classic. It seemed a shame to blow up something this beautiful. There should be an easier way to kill the girl, he thought. But orders were orders.

He cast a quick glance up and down the street, then hunkered down on the sidewalk beside the passenger door. Reggie Williams had two loves in his life: cars and explosives. He'd always loved cars, but it wasn't until the Army sent him to Iraq that he discovered explosives.

In Iraq, Reggie had learned how to disarm Improvised Explosive Devices and how to make them, too. Sometimes at night he had dreams. Dreams of an exploding bus filled with Iraqi schoolgirls. Of burned-out Humvees and endless expanses of sand filled with mounded graves. When his eight years were up, he'd gotten out of the Army. He quickly found another market for his talents. A market that paid a whole hell of a lot better.

He had to lay flat out on the sidewalk to fix the package to the VW's chassis. Then he rigged up a mercury switch. The switch was so delicately balanced that the slightest shift in the level of the car would make it go off. He doubted she'd even be able to open the door without blowing herself to perdition.

He checked to make sure the switch was precisely adjusted, then he armed it. All he—

"What you doin' there, son?"

Reggie swung his head to find himself staring at a pair of black cop boots. His gaze traveled up the cop's blue pant legs, past his gun-slung hips and ponderous belly, to a red, full-jowled face. *Shit.*

Reggie was from New Jersey. But he'd been around enough Southern boys in the Army that he could lay it on when he wanted to. "Just fixin' my car, officer. Is there a problem?"

"Funny, but this don't exactly look like your kind of car."

"Well . . . actually, it's my sister's car."

"That a fact? She lives around here, does she?"

Reggie hesitated. There didn't seem to be a lot of people with dark skin in this part of the city.

The cop's hand rested, suggestively, on the holster at his hip. "Stand up and move away from the car."

Reggie scrambled to his feet and backed away. He wanted nothing more than to put as much distance as possible between himself and that VW. But then the cop said, "That's far enough. Now just stand there. Don't move."

Reggie watched as the cop unhooked the flashlight from his belt and knelt down on the sidewalk to peer underneath the car. But the man's balance was wobbly. He put out one hand to steady himself against the side of the VW.

Hideously aware of the delicately balanced mercury switch, Reggie saw the car begin to shift.

"No!" he screamed, *"Don't lean against the c—"*

It was déjà vu all over again. Climbing out of her taxi, Tobie stared at the column of thick smoke billowing up toward the evening sky. The street outside the marina was filled with fire trucks and police cars, two ambulances, and a Durango from the coroner's office.

Nearby, a TV camera with WWL CHANNEL 4 emblazoned across the side focused on a perky news reporter with a blond bob who stood with her head tilted as if listening for a cue. Then she looked into the camera and said, "This is Tracy Jacobs coming to you from the Orleans Marina. There are unconfirmed reports that an NOPD officer and an unidentified male were killed here this evening when what eyewitnesses describe as a car bomb exploded on Lake Marina Drive . . . "

Tobie swung away, her throat closing so painfully she could barely swallow. Skirting the gathering crowd, she managed to work her way around until she was close enough to catch a glimpse of the smoldering wreckage of what had been her car. As she watched, someone leaned over to zip a black body bag closed. Another body bag lay a few feet away.

It hadn't even occurred to her that the bad guys would search the area around the marina for her car. It was just sheer dumb luck that the blast hadn't killed her. Except how could she feel lucky about escaping the blast when two people were dead?

She'd left her flight away from New Orleans until too late, she realized with a sudden wash of panic. Now she was trapped here, without a car, without Colonel McClintock to advise her on what to do, where to go. She had no one left to turn to except a man she didn't know and had no reason to trust.

She began to back away, her gaze fixed on the black, twisted skeleton of her car. For a moment it was as if the hushed voices around her fell away. She was back in Baghdad listening to the wailing grief of women and smelling the acrid stench of burned flesh. A car door slammed somewhere close and she jumped, bumping into a guy behind her. Jerking around, she saw a big man with short-cropped sandy hair and a bony face who sent a frisson of fear through her. "Sorry," she said quickly, and turned to run.

44

Jax was cleaning his gun at the table by the window overlooking the city when the call came through on the
hotel telephone.

Setting aside the newly oiled Beretta, he hit the Mute
button on the remote, silencing the perky blond Channel 4 reporter standing in front of what was left of October Guinness's yellow VW Bug. He reached for the
receiver. "Hello?"

The woman's voice at the other end of the line was so
tight it cracked. "Why should I trust you?"

Jax's gaze focused on the television screen, where
paramedics were loading a zipped black body bag into
a waiting ambulance. The car bomb had obviously been
intended for her. So what had gone wrong for the guys
in the body bags?

"You need to meet me," he said. "This is something
we really can't talk about on the phone."

"Why should I trust you?" she said again.

"My guess is you've just about run out of options."

There was a long silence.

He said, "Listen to me. I can help you."

"Or you could kill me yourself."

"I could have killed you this afternoon."

There was another pause. He could feel the tension crackling over the line. Then she said, "Meet me at Joe's Crab Shack, on Lakeshore Drive at the West End. Can you be there in half an hour?"

"Yes."

"Come alone."

Jax reached for his Beretta. "I'll be there."

The Circle Bar at the corner of St. Charles and Lee Circle was a disreputable dive that reeked of spilled beer and urine and decay. Barid Hafezi had never been in such a place. Once a grand, three-story house with a turret and wraparound balcony, it had long ago degenerated into a haunt for winos and addicts and washed-up hookers.

Glancing around nervously, Barid chose a table in a dark corner and ordered two drinks. The first he dumped in the pot of a nearby dead palm. But the second one he drank. It might have offered him a form of false courage, but he'd take any kind of courage he could get at the moment.

He'd spent the afternoon taking care of some pesky tasks he'd let slide and assembling all the papers his wife, Nadia, would need in a file he'd labeled *Death* and left in the bottom drawer of his desk at home for her to find. Then he took her and the kids out to dinner,

and there'd even been time to stop by the old snowball
stand on Metairie Road.

Jasmina's snowball had turned her mouth blue, and
she opened her eyes wide and stuck out her tongue in
fun, and Barid laughed so hard he'd cried.

"What is it?" Nadia had asked him, her soft brown eyes
anxious as she searched his face. "What's wrong?"

"Nothing," he'd said, looping an arm around her
shoulders to draw her to him. "I just realize how blessed
I am."

Before he left the house that night, he'd hugged and
kissed each of them in turn—Nadia, Jasmina, and
Faraj—and he'd told them he loved them. Draining his
second glass, now, he found some solace in the thought.
They would have that to remember.

He left the credit card receipt on the table as instructed
and dropped the book Fitzgerald had sent him on the
bench. He'd often thought about that improbable string
of Korans that Mohammed Atta had left behind him
in the bar he'd patronized so noisily the Friday before
September 11, on the dashboard of his rental car, and
in his apartment. It reminded Barid of that European
fairy tale about Hansel and Gretel, stringing a trail of
bread crumbs to be followed. Now, he wondered where
his own false trail would lead.

Nadia would know he hadn't done it, whatever it was.
She would remember the way he had hugged and kissed
his children. And she would understand why he had co-
operated, so that they might live, even if he could not.

———————

days of the drawing. All winners, tickets and transactions subject to
Maryland State Lottery Agency Regulations and State Law.
TO CLAIM A PRIZE: Present this ticket to any Maryland State
Lottery ticket agent. Validated winning tickets valued to $600 are
eligible for INSTANT PAYOFF. Validated winning tickets higher than
$600 will be paid by check after claim is filed. Void if torn or altered.

Buddy W. Roogow
Buddy W. Roogow
MD Lottery Director

For Winning Numbers
Please call 410-230-8830

The Maryland Lottery
encourages responsible play

NAME

ADDRESS

CITY _____ STATE _____ ZIP

SIGNATURE

Ticket(s) are heat sensitive. Do not expose to prolonged periods of excessive heat or light.
Visit the Lottery website at mdlottery.com.®

PF

0581335371

IMPORTANT INFORMATION: This ticket is a bearer
instrument. Anyone possessing a winning ticket may claim the
prize. Valid only for date(s) shown. Winner must claim prize within 182
days of the drawing. All winners, tickets and transactions subject to
Maryland State Lottery Agency Regulations and State Law.
TO CLAIM A PRIZE: Present this ticket to any Maryland State
Lottery ticket agent. Validated winning tickets valued to $600 are
eligible for INSTANT PAYOFF. Validated winning tickets higher than
$600 will be paid by check after claim is filed. Void if torn or altered.

Buddy W. Roogow
Buddy W. Roogow
MD Lottery Director

For Winning Numbers
Please call 410-230-8830

The Maryland Lottery
encourages responsible play

NAME

Term: 17804101   18 Sep 2008 07:50
8297001251392O-84   363090

COMING SOON!!!! DOUBLE PAY ON BOX
PLAY PICK 3 PROMOTION!

Pick 4

$5.00 - 5 Draws
09/18 - 09/22
MIDDAY

3496   Straight $1.00

8297001251392O-84

The crowds were already beginning to disperse by the time Homicide Detective William P. Ahearn and his sergeant reached the Orleans Marina.

Ahearn stood on a patch of scorched grass, his arms folded at his chest, and studied the blackened, twisted skeleton of what had once been a classic VW Beetle. According to their records, October Guinness drove a 1979 VW Beetle.

"Jesus Christ," said Trish. "What did this? A car bomb? We turning into Baghdad or something?"

Ahearn nodded to the detective, Eddie Jackson, a slim, wiry man with gleaming ebony skin and a neat goatee. "Whatcha got so far?"

"It took us a while," said Jackson, "but we finally got the car's VIN number."

"You're kidding? Off of what?"

"One of the doors blew over to the other side of the seawall."

"And?"

"It's registered to October Guinness."

"But she's not one of the bodies?"

"We don't think so. They're in such bad shape it's impossible to be sure yet, but according to witnesses, there were two men near the car when it blew. A tall young black guy and a cop."

"Who's the cop?"

"Martie Driscole."

"Martie?" Trish's forehead puckered with distress. "Aw, hell." Martie Driscole had three kids under five.

"So who's the black dude?" asked Ahearn.

"That's anybody's guess. We haven't found anyone

yet who recognized him, and whatever ID he was carrying probably beat him to hell. Maybe the autopsy will come up with something."

Ahearn nodded, his gaze lifting to stare across the top of the seawall to where the masts of the sailboats in the marina stood out stark against the darkening sky. "I've got two Tulane professors dead in less than twenty-four hours. I've got the first prof's house trashed. I've got his research assistant's house trashed. And now I've got her car blown to bits right next to the marina where the second prof parked her friggin' boat. You think I'm going out on a limb here if I suspect the girl seen running away from the floating morgue we found at Pontchartrain Beach was October Guinness?"

Trish and Jackson exchanged looks, but neither said a word.

Ahearn hunched his shoulders, trying to ease a worsening kink in his neck. "I want her picture in the hands of every cop on the street. I want it on the ten o'clock news. And I want it on the front page of tomorrow morning's *Times-Picayune*."

Trish nodded. "You think she's doing all this?"

"Hell. I don't know. But I'd bet the pot of gold at the end of the rainbow that she knows a heckuva lot more about what's going on around here than I do. The woman's a goddamn walking crime wave. I want her off the streets."

45

Joe's Crab Shack was basically a long, covered pier with a tin roof and glass walls that looked out over the wide silver expanse of the lake. Tobie hung up the pay phone in the lobby and went to take a seat at a table facing the entrance.

She spent the next half hour sipping a bottle of water and scrutinizing everyone who walked in the door. But there was no way she could keep an eye on what was happening outside in the parking lot or on the perimeter of the building. She knew she was taking a huge risk, meeting with this guy. But she couldn't see that she had many other options at this point.

He walked in a few minutes before seven o'clock. He hesitated just inside the door, waiting for his eyes to adjust to the light and giving her a chance to study him unobserved. He had an air about him that spoke of prep schools and the Ivy League and weekends in the Hamptons. But there was something else there, too; an unexpected edge of irreverence and danger that didn't quite fit with the rest.

His gaze settled on her and he came to slip into the seat opposite hers. "I saw the news," he said. "I assume that was your car?"

"Yes."

"So why weren't you in it when it blew?"

"I don't know." She picked up one of the menus and handed it to him. "I recommend the shrimp étouffe."

He met her gaze and held it. "Sounds good."

A waiter came up to take their order. She waited until he'd gone, then said, "Henry once told me that if someone says he works for the federal government, it usually means he's with the CIA."

Amusement crinkled the skin beside his eyes. "You're the second person who's said that to me today. This guy must have told that to everyone he knew."

"Who was the first?"

"Dr. Vu." The faint smile was gone.

She leaned forward. "He said it's always a giveaway because people like to talk about themselves. If a guy's an accountant with the Department of Agriculture, he'll say, " 'I'm an accountant with the Department of Agriculture.' But no one goes around saying, 'I'm a spy for the CIA.' "

"Most people who work for the CIA aren't spies or even field operatives. They're analysts. Paper pushers. They get to spend a few days down at the Farm playing James Bond, but they're really just very boring people who spend all day sitting at a desk doing very boring jobs."

"Yeah? Well, you're not at a desk, are you?"

He reached for his glass of water and took a slow sip.

She said, "Did you kill Henry Youngblood?"

He set the glass down again. "Me, personally? No. But I can't speak for the entire Agency."

His candor caught her off guard. But then, maybe that's what it was supposed to do. He reminded her of the sunstruck shimmers on the surface of an uncharted stretch of water, all flash and sparkle hiding the deadly depths beneath.

She said, "Why would the CIA want to kill Henry Youngblood?"

"If this is a CIA operation, then it's a black op that's so secret even the Director doesn't know about it, and I find that hard to believe. I think you're tangling with somebody else here."

She paused while the waiter served their salads, then said, "Who?"

"I don't know. I recognized the guy I shot. Last time I saw him, he was in Special Forces, but he could be working for anyone by now. One thing I do know: men like him are expensive."

"Why should I believe anything you're saying?"

He looked up at her, his gaze uncomfortably direct. "Don't believe me. Don't believe anyone. Just keep going it alone the way you've been doing. But you need to recognize that eventually they're going to get lucky or you're going to make a mistake. And then you're going to be dead."

She looked away. He was right and she knew it. There was something to be said for that old Middle Eastern adage, "My enemy's enemy is my friend." The men on Elizabeth Vu's cabin cruiser had tried to kill him, too.

She drew in a deep breath and said, "You're familiar with remote viewing?"

"Yes."

That surprised her. She picked up her fork, looked at her salad, and put the fork down again. "Dr. Young-blood and I did a remote viewing session as part of a funding proposal Henry had in with someone. I don't know who. The target was a building, a modern office building. On one of the desks was a maroon folder with the Keefe Corporation logo. The men who came to my house last night were asking questions about that viewing."

He glanced up from eating his salad with an appetite she envied. "You're familiar with the Keefe logo?"

"Are you kidding? I spent ten months in Iraq. I would recognize that logo in my sleep."

"So what was in the folder?"

"Some kind of report. Maps. Diagrams. Photographs."

"Of what?"

"Only one photo sticks in my mind, of an old World War II plane. I think it was a kind of transport called a Skytrooper."

"That's it?"

"Yes. The only other thing I remember is the title of the report: the Archangel Project. Does that mean anything to you?"

"No."

She blew out a long breath in disappointment.

"So where was this office building?" he asked.

"I don't know. The target was given to me by its geographical coordinates." She studied his fine-boned face, with its patrician nose and hooded eyes. She knew that Look. The Look that said someone thought remote viewing belonged in the same class as séances and horoscopes.

"You don't believe in remote viewing, do you?" She sat back with a sharp laugh. "God. How can you possibly help me if you think I'm making this up?"

"I didn't say I thought you were making it up."

"You don't have to." She leaned forward again, her hands coming up together. "Whoever is doing this—whoever killed Henry, and Dr. Vu, and came to my house last night claiming to be the FBI—they knew about the viewing session Henry and I had done. They knew about the office building, and the folder, and the photograph of the Skytrooper. You might find it hard to believe in remote viewing, but that doesn't alter the fact that whatever I 'saw' was important enough that five people are now dead and another one is in the hospital."

She saw a flicker of confusion cross his face. "Who's in the hospital?"

"Colonel F. Scott McClintock. He's a therapist at the VA. They got him this afternoon."

He hesitated while the waiter set their dinner plates in front of them. "So do you remember the coordinates?"

"No. They were just numbers. I never paid any attention to them."

He reached for a roll of bread and carefully tore off a chunk. "Would you be willing to be hypnotized?"

She stared at him. "What? You don't believe in remote viewing but you believe in hypnotism?"

He met her gaze and held it. "Hypnotism might have

started out as a carnival act, but it was grounded in scientific fact a long time ago. Everything you've ever seen, heard, or done is stored in your subconscious; you just can't access it all. It's as if it's behind closed doors. Hypnotism opens those doors."

Tobie remembered Henry Youngblood telling her once that the CIA—in fact, all the intelligence branches—used hypnotism to debrief their agents. They'd discovered that particularly when he'd been given a previous hypnotic suggestion, a man under hypnosis could remember startlingly accurate details of things he hadn't even been aware of at the time he'd seen them. Of course Jax Alexander believed in hypnosis, she realized; he'd probably used it.

She pushed the food around on her plate. "Remote viewing opens mental doors, too. Different doors, maybe, but the concept is basically the same. It's just another way of accessing layers of the mind we're not normally aware of." When he continued to stare at her impassively, she pushed her plate away in disgust. "The CIA has poured millions into remote viewing, which means they obviously have people who believe in it. So why did they send you?"

He laughed. "Because the new head of the Agency decided this assignment had my name written all over it."

She thought she was beginning to understand. "I gather he's not one of your fans. What did you do to him?"

"Punched him in the face in the middle of an embassy dinner party."

"You're kidding. Why?"

"It's a long story." He signaled the waiter for their check. "Now, where can we find a hypnotist?"

Tobie stayed where she was. "Why would you want to help me?"

He rested his hands on the table. "I was sent down here to find out what happened to Henry Youngblood, and it looks to me like whoever killed the professor is now trying to kill you."

"So what am I? Bait?"

There was a long pause during which he simply looked at her.

Tobie let out a quick laugh that broke at the end. "Okay. So I'm bait."

"You're bait whether I'm here or not. But with me around, you've at least got a chance to survive."

It stung her pride, but she knew it was true. If he hadn't shown up that afternoon, she'd be dead by now.

She saw the glint of amusement in his eyes and knew he was following her every thought. But all he said was, "Now do we find that hypnotist?"

46

Lance Palmer stood in the center of their suite at the Sheraton, his hands on his hips, his gaze fixed on the television. The news media had been in a frenzy at first, convinced the West End car bombing was the work of al-Qa'ida or something. But that kind of crazy speculation seemed to have died down now.

The death of Reggie Williams weighed heavily on Lance's shoulders. He hated to lose men, and he'd recruited the kid himself. Williams was good at what he did. Lance still couldn't understand exactly what had gone wrong, why it was Williams and some cop who'd ended up in those body bags rather than October Guinness.

"Shit," said Hadley, looking up from his computer. "The police have put out an APB on Guinness."

Lance huffed a bitter, mirthless laugh. "It just keeps getting better and better, doesn't it? I've got two of my men dead. One car in a bayou and another crushed by a streetcar. And now I've got a dead cop. The boys in blue will be going nuts looking for Guinness. And they know this town and we don't."

"So why don't we just let the cops bring her in?" said Sal Lopez. The hospital had finally agreed to release him, although he wasn't going to be much use to them with one arm in a sling and a minor concussion. "They bring her in, and we take her away from them."

Lance wanted to laugh again. "They think she's mixed up in a cop killing, Lopez. They're not going to let her go that easily. We might eventually be able to make her disappear into the system, but it would take time. And time is the one thing we don't have."

"Maybe we'll get lucky and they'll kill her."

"Lucky? Why the hell would we suddenly start getting lucky?"

Hadley had left his computer now and was on the phone. Lance knew something was up by the look on his face.

"What is it?"

Hadley closed his phone, his lips stretching into a rare smile. "That was our friend in field support at Langley."

The guys in field support were what was known in the industry as backstop. They were the ones who provided the documentation for people in the field—the fake IDs, the credit cards with false names that actually worked. If an agent had a phone number on his business card and someone called that number, it was the guys in field support who answered the phone.

"So what's he got for us?"

"Jason Aldrich. It's an alias used by a guy named Jax Alexander. He's CIA."

Lance punched off the TV. "CIA? What the fuck? What's he doing down here?" He went to stand beside the window and stare out over the darkened city. But after a minute he swung back around, and he was smiling. "This might not be a bad thing. October Guinness keeps slipping through our fingers because she's unpredictable. She's a psycho case. But now she's with this guy Alexander, and he's a pro. That means we ought to be able to figure out what he's doing. We might not be able to find her, but maybe, just maybe, we can find *him*."

47

Every respectable hypnotist in New Orleans had long since locked his or her office and gone home. Which left only the unrespectable ones.

Using the phone book attached by a metal cord to the pay phone in the Crab Shack's lobby, Tobie found a woman named Sister Simone who worked out of a second floor walkup in the French Quarter. Her ad read: FORTUNES TOLD. PALMS READ. PAST LIFE REGRESSIONS. WALK-INS WELCOME.

"You can't be serious," said Jax, peering over her shoulder at the entry.

She glanced back at him. "If she does past life regressions, she must be a hypnotist."

"The woman's a charlatan."

"That doesn't mean she can't hypnotize people."

Jax was sipping a gin and tonic in a bar on Bourbon Street when Matt called him.

"Hey, Jax. I've got something for you."

Jax turned his back on the noisy, crowded room. "What is it?"

"Jax? I can hardly hear you. Where are you?"

Jax cupped his hand over the phone. "Where am I? I'm sitting at the window of a bar down in the French Quarter. From here I can look across the street at a ramshackle eighteenth-century building with a big pink neon eye in the window and a sign that says, 'Sister Simone's House of the All-Seeing Soul.'"

Matt laughed. "You're making that up."

"I wish I was. October Guinness is in there right now getting hypnotized so she can remember the coordinates that were used in some remote viewing session. My career is in the toilet, Matt."

Matt's voice sharpened. "You found her again?"

"She called me. Someone blew up her car and put her shrink in the hospital. I guess she ran out of options."

"McClintock? What happened to the Colonel?"

Jax set down his drink. "Matt, how do you know Colonel McClintock?"

"I've known him for years. What happened to him?"

"Someone beat him up this afternoon."

There was a pause, then Matt said, "What have you managed to get out of the girl?"

"Did you ever hear of something called the Archangel Project?"

"You're the second person who's asked me that today."

"Oh? So who's the first?"

Instead of answering, Matt said, "I can tell you the

same thing I told him: never heard of it. What else have you got?"

Jax gave him a quick rundown.

When he was finished, Matt said, "*Keefe?* Did you say Keefe?"

"Yeah."

There was another long silence, then Matt said, "This isn't good, Jax."

"No shit."

"What'd you say these coordinates are for?"

"The office where Guinness says she saw this Archangel file."

"So you're beginning to believe in this stuff?"

"Did I say that? All I know is that someone obviously believes in it. They're killing people all over town."

Matt grunted. "I looked into Ross. He was discharged three months ago."

"So what's he been doing since then?"

"I don't know. It's like he dropped off the face of the earth. Rumor has it he went to the Middle East."

The door across the street opened and October Guinness stepped out onto the narrow, crowded sidewalk. She was wearing a simple T-shirt and flippy cotton skirt, and her hair looked as if she'd recently been for a swim and let it dry in a breeze. As he watched, she brought up one hand to tuck a stray wisp behind her ear. The light from the wrought-iron street lamp slanted across her face as she turned her head, looking for him.

Jax pushed back his chair and stood. "The Middle East?"

"That's right. Listen, Jax: somebody tried to access your files."

"What?"

"They came at it through your identity documents. This wasn't by way of official channels. This was someone working the old boy network. Which means someone down there has contacts in the Company."

Jax stepped out of the bar into the street. The night smelled of the river and dank stone archways and spilled beer. "What are you saying to me, Matt?"

"I'm telling you to watch your back, buddy."

48

Just to the west of New Orleans and its suburbs of Metairie and Kenner lay a tract of uninhabited bayous and swamps known as the Bonnet Carré spillway. A bowl-shaped expanse that stretched from the Mississippi to the lake, the spillway served as a safety valve when the river reached flood stage. Locals knew it as a great place to fish and hunt and trap crabs. The area's less savory inhabitants knew it as the perfect spot to dump bodies.

Paul Fitzgerald turned his pickup off onto a narrow rutted track that wound down through ancient cedars and water oaks to a half-forgotten dirt boat launch. The pickup had been bought secondhand from a dealer out on Airline Highway who knew better than to ask questions. In a few days it would be found, torched, on the side of the road in some abandoned neighborhood in New Orleans East. No one would think anything about it.

Backing the pickup down to the water's edge, Fitzger-ald opened his door to a thick, hot night scented with the fecund smell of wet earth and green growing things. He stood for a moment, his well-trained senses alive to all the subtle nuances of the marsh. He was alone.

He closed the door with a quiet snap, then went to launch the small aluminum skiff from the back of the pickup truck. The rattle of metal against metal sounded unnaturally loud in the stillness as he piled the chains in the bottom of the boat. He hesitated, listening to the slap of murky water against the bank, the hum of a car engine somewhere in the distance. It faded quickly into the night.

Wiping his sleeve across his damp forehead, he went back to the pickup for the Iranian's body and dumped that in the skiff, too. The man had served his purpose. All the carefully arranged pieces of incriminating evidence were in place. Now the time had come for him to disappear. After tomorrow night, the authorities would assume he had fled the country. They wouldn't think to look for him here, in the back swamps of Louisiana.

Dipping his paddle with the effortless grace of a born outdoorsman, Fitzgerald eased out into the middle of the channel. At the other end of the skiff, Barid Hafezi's sightless eyes stared open and wide at the starry night sky above.

Belmont, Virginia: 5 June 10:20 P.M. Eastern time

Adelaide Meyer flashed her pass to the guards at the gates of Clark Westlake's sprawling country estate on the outskirts of Belmont and floored her Boxster up the long, winding drive. Like the Randolphs, the Westlakes were old New England money. They'd grown rich—like the Randolphs—on the slave trade of the eighteenth century. They'd grown richer on the ruined lives of hundreds of thousands of exploited immigrant workers in the nineteenth century, then richer again thanks to some nasty deals with European factories using slave labor during World War II. There was plenty of mud there, if anyone cared to dig for it. But what was the point? No one would ever be able to get it to stick.

"Adelaide," said Westlake, meeting her at the door. "I'm glad you're here." He led the way to his library and barely waited until the door closed behind them before he exploded. "What the fuck are your boys doing down there? Car bombs, for Christ's sake? You told me these guys are good."

"They're good."

"Are they? We've been planning this thing for months, Adelaide. There's too much at stake here to have the whole thing come unraveled at the last minute."

Adelaide tossed her Prada purse on the leather sofa and went to pour herself a drink from the wet bar. "It would all have been taken care of by now if you hadn't sent one of your field operatives down there to get in the way."

Clark shook his head. "What are you talking about?"

"Some turkey named Jax Alexander. He killed one of my men and now he's protecting the girl." Adelaide knocked back the shot of neat vodka and poured another. She'd learned to drink on the oil rigs, working with roughnecks and roustabouts. She could drink almost everyone in Washington under the table, and had.

Westlake came to pour himself a brandy. "How do you know he's one of my men?"

"Because the people I have on this have contacts. And those contacts are telling them this Jax Alexander is a real loose cannon. You've got to get him out of there."

"What are you suggesting? That I just head on over to Langley and order Chandler to pull this guy out? You don't think that's going to set off alarm bells someplace?"

"I don't care how you do it, Clark. Just get that guy out of New Orleans. I've spent a fortune setting this thing up. If it starts unraveling, all those threads are going to lead right back to me. Not you. Not your boss. Me. I did that so that you and your boss could keep your hands clean. But I should think the least you can do is avoid sabotaging me."

"Give me a break, Adelaide. You're not doing this out of the goodness of heart. You're doing it because it's a good investment. The contracts that are going to come out of this will make Iraq look like a boondoggle in a banana republic."

Adelaide threw down another shot. "No one's going to get any contracts if this thing blows up in our faces."

Clark took a sip of his own brandy and coughed. "I'll take care of the idiot from Langley. Just tell your guys to get this thing back on track and keep it there. We've got less than twenty-four hours."

49

"So did it work?" Jax asked, pushing through the drunken crowd of tourists and college students on Bourbon Street.

October turned toward him, a smile spilling across her tanned face as she waved a piece of paper through the air in triumph. "I got them."

"I can't believe it." It was true that hypnotism could unlock the secrets of memory, but it required specialized training to draw exact details from a subject's subconscious. When the CIA used the technique, its agents were always hypnotized before they went out into the field and given suggestions that primed them to remember everything they saw.

"Believe it," she said. "Sister Simone used to be a hypnotherapist in Jersey City. She says she got tired of only dealing with people who wanted to quit smoking or lose weight, so she gave up her practice and moved down here two weeks before Katrina hit."

"Great timing. I guess she forgot to read her own tea leaves."

October let out her breath in a little *huh.* "She was good. She not only helped me remember the coordinates, but I came up with something else, too. An address: 1214 Charbonnet Street."

"Where's that?"

"Charbonnet Street? It's here, in New Orleans. The Lower Ninth Ward."

"So are the coordinates in New Orleans, too?"

"You tell me." She handed him the paper with the coordinates. "You're CIA, right? Don't you guys all come with an On Star system or something?"

Jax blew out a long sigh. "Hang on," he said, and punched Matt's number on his speed dial. "Hey," he said when Matt picked up. "Me again."

Ten minutes later they were sitting in Jax Alexander's rented Monte Carlo, parked near the old Jax Brewery, when the call from the guy named "Matt" came through.

Tobie watched Jax talk on the phone. He kept going, "Mm-hmm." At one point he threw a sharp glance at her that made her go, "What?" But he just shook his head.

"The coordinates are in Dallas," he told her, closing his phone. "So what's this address here in New Orleans got to do with anything?"

"I don't know. I don't even remember seeing it in the file."

A group of drunken college kids staggered past, arms

around each other, voices raised in wild laughter. He watched them for a moment, then said: "Why don't you just do another one of your remote viewings and 'see' it all again?"

She'd wondered how long it would be before he asked her that. "I did try. But remote viewing doesn't work that way. It's not like a card trick you can repeat over and over. If the controls aren't in place, it's too easy to simply tap into your imagination. There's no way to know what is real and what isn't."

He turned his head to look at her, and she found herself wondering what he saw. If he saw her as crazy, too. "How do you ever know what's real and what's your imagination?" he asked.

"You don't. Which is why no remote viewer is ever one hundred percent accurate."

"How accurate are you?"

"Henry said I averaged around eighty percent."

"In other words, there's a one out of five chance that this Charbonnet address is just a figment of your imagination?"

"Yes."

"I guess there's only one way to find out." He turned the key in the ignition. "Let's go take a look at it."

She stared at him. "Now? You want to go to the Lower Ninth Ward *now*? At nine-thirty at night? Are you crazy? Do you have any idea what it's like down there?"

"My friend at Langley tells me there's an APB out on you. That means you don't just need to worry about the bad guys, whoever they may be. You also need to worry about the NOPD. They think you're involved in the death of one of their own. We need to find out what's going on here, and fast." He threw the car into gear. "So how do I get to this Ninth Ward?"

Lying just downriver from the Quarter, the Lower Ninth Ward had once been a vibrant community of mainly African-American, working-class homeowners. Now, since Katrina, it was a virtual ghost town. There were no trees. No cars that hadn't soaked in filthy brown water for weeks. No people. Some of the homes here had already been bulldozed; a very few of them were being renovated. Most were just empty husks, their yards overgrown, their windows boarded up or left as gaping holes with ragged dirty curtains that blew in the breeze like something out of a B-grade post-Apocalyptic film.

"The street signs are all gone," said Jax, driving slowly up St. Claude. He had his window down, the air rushing in warm and moist and faintly fetid. Not only were the street signs gone, but so were most of the streetlights and stoplights. No one in their right mind came down here after nightfall.

"I think Charbonnet Street is up there," Tobie told him. "Second on your left."

They turned down a broken street of dark, empty houses and weed-choked lots.

"That's it," she said. "The two-story frame house on the left." She put her finger against her window's glass as he drove right past the house. "Why didn't you stop?"

"Are you familiar with the Navaho culture?"

"No. Why?"

"The Navaho consider it rude to just pull up outside someone's house and go knock on their door. So when a Navaho goes to visit his acquaintance's hogan, he'll sit outside and wait for a while, to give the people inside a chance to get used to the idea of his being there. Basically to decide if they want to talk to him, or shoot him."

She turned sideways in her seat to stare at him. "I don't get it. What do the Navaho have to do with the Ninth Ward?"

"I don't want to get shot."

He crept around the corner, his gaze scanning the rows of empty houses.

"Why are you stopping here?" she asked when he suddenly braked.

He threw the car into reverse, backing into an empty driveway where a detached garage stood open to the night, its door long gone. He kept backing until the darkness of the garage swallowed them. "I don't think we want to leave the car anyplace visible. Not in a neighborhood as devastated as this one." He handed her one of the flashlights they'd picked up from a convenience store at the edge of the Quarter. "Here. Take this."

The click of the car door opening sounded unnaturally loud. Like most people in New Orleans, Tobie had periodically driven through the ruined neighborhoods of the city, looking for signs of progress that were pitifully slow in coming. "Misery tours" the locals called them. But she'd always stayed in her car. She'd never gotten out and walked the streets, never realized how silent a city without people could be. There was no hum of electricity, no swish of passing cars, no dogs barking in the hot sticky night. Only an endless, oppressive silence.

He touched her arm, startling her. "You all right?"

She nodded.

They cut through backyards, climbing over the weathered branches of fallen oaks and downed fences, skirting piles of rotting mattresses and water-warped furniture and smashed crockery that gleamed white in the night.

She hadn't thought to count the houses on the block, but he obviously had. Crawling through what was left of an old wooden fence, they reached the broken back steps of the two-story frame house she'd seen from Charbonnet. The door gaped half open before them.

"It looks deserted," he said. "You sure you have the right house?"

"It's what I wrote down."

Reaching one hand behind his back, he pulled out his Beretta before pushing the door open wider. It creaked on rusty hinges, then stilled.

Tobie stared into the moon-washed interior. The first floor of the house had been gutted to the ceiling: plaster, doors, door frames—all were gone, exposing the timber studs so that they could see right through what had once been walls. Even the floorboards and carpet had been ripped up, exposing an uneven pine subfloor.

"Doesn't look like you could hide much in here," he said, going to stand in the middle of what looked as if it had once been a kitchen.

One hand clutching the strap of her messenger bag against her side, Tobie walked over to peer through the doorway into an eerie, wall-less hall. "At least it shouldn't take us long to look around."

Neither one of them saw the motion sensor hidden at the top of the door frame. The sensor was set up to do two things: activate the various microphones scattered around the house, and put in an automatic call to one of the men who'd set up the system.

50

His name was Michael Crowley, and when the call came through, he was at his computer in the back room of a rented shotgun in that part of New Orleans known as the Irish Channel. All he had to do was glance at the number on the phone and he knew they had trouble.

He listened for a moment, then put in a call to Lance Palmer. "The Charbonnet Street house has been compromised. A man and a woman. They sound white."

"Fuck," said Lance. "It's Alexander and the girl. How the hell did they find the house?"

Crowley could hear Palmer shouting to Hadley in the background, "Where's Fitzgerald?" Hadley's reply was muffled by the slamming of doors, the slap of running feet.

Lance said, "He's closer to the Ninth than we are, if he's in Marigny. We'll meet him at the house. Let's go."

Crowley said, "You want me to head over there, too?"

"Negative. Keep monitoring the microphone feed. You can relay it to us when we get to the house. I don't care what it takes. I want those two dead."

The moonlight shining through the empty windows was bright enough that they didn't need the flashlights until they reached the stairwell, where the walls were only gutted to about halfway up. Jax Alexander slipped his Beretta back into the waistband of his khakis and flicked on his flashlight, holding the fingers of one hand splayed over the glass so the light came out diffused and tinted oddly red by his flesh. Tobie, following him up the stairs, did the same.

Nothing in the house seemed familiar to her, not even when they reached the second floor and found the walls there still intact. There were three bedrooms and a bathroom. The first two bedrooms were empty. But in the third bedroom, the largest, they found a stained mattress thrown on the floor in the corner. There was a folding table, too, set up near the curtained window.

Jax walked over to finger the heavy drape. "It's a blackout curtain. Someone obviously wanted to make sure no one knew they were in here."

Tobie let her gaze rove over the litter of items on the table: a pair of wire cutters and a couple of screwdrivers, a coil of wire, and a few snips of stripped wire. A canvas bag lay on the floor, next to the empty blister pack from a card of nine-volt batteries and the discarded packaging from a couple of cheap, throwaway cell phones.

"What's this?" she asked, hunkering down to look at a scattering of silver splatters on the floor.

"Someone's been soldering in here."

Straightening, she was reaching for a book she'd spotted on the edge of the table when he said, "We need to back out of here fast."

She swung around to look at him. "Why? What is it?"

"This place is a bomb factory. Did you touch anything?"

Tobie felt the hair rise on the back of her neck. "The book," she said, realizing she was still holding it.

"Bring it."

"I don't understand." She shoved the book into her bag as they headed back toward the stairs. "How does this fit in with any—"

He pressed a finger to her lips, silencing her as the distant creak of a board cut through the stillness of the night.

Her gaze flew to meet his. There was someone downstairs.

Rather than click off his flashlight, he carefully set it down on its face, reducing the light to a small, softly glowing ring. She did the same. Then, slipping the Beretta from its waistband holster again, he thrust out his left hand, his fingers splayed wide in a silent message. *Stay here.*

She expected him to creep down the stairs. Instead, she watched, bemused, as he laid down on his stomach at the top of the stairs and began to inch down the steps head first, his elbows splayed wide so he could hold his Beretta at the ready.

There hadn't been another hint of movement from the first floor. She was beginning to wonder if they'd simply been spooked by the sound of the ruined house settling when she heard another creak, this time from the stairwell directly below.

51

Jax slithered head first down the steps. He could feel the rough floorboards snagging his shirt, scraping his bare arms.

He had no way of knowing exactly who was downstairs. The last thing he wanted to do was get in a shootout with some Katrina-crazed homeowner, or maybe a cop. But then he saw the tall man at the base of the stairs, the shadow of his gun extended by the length of a suppressor, and Jax knew he wasn't dealing with either a cop or a homeowner.

The light filtering in through the uncurtained ground floor windows glinted on something shiny in the man's ear. Jax saw the gleam of a tiny blue LED and realized it was a Bluetooth earpiece. The guy was listening to a cell phone.

Then one of the steps groaned beneath Jax's weight.

The man jerked, his gun coming up to fire. But the sight of Jax upside down on the stairs must have confused him because he hesitated for a split second. Jax squeezed off two rounds, one right after the other, his ears ringing with the percussion in the confined space. The unsuppressed explosions bracketed the other gun's silenced *pop*.

The man in the hall jerked once, twice, then dropped to his knees. Jax was about to fire again when the man pitched forward onto his face. It was only when Jax felt the sting in one of his legs that he realized the sonofabitch had hit him.

Jax slithered the rest of the way down the stairs. Given the way he was hanging upside down, he figured it was easier than trying to get up. October Guinness came charging down the stairs behind him, a big Glock held in that professional grip she'd displayed on the cabin cruiser. She was so small and slim that he kept forgetting she was a vet who'd seen action in Iraq.

"Is he dead?" she asked in a hoarse whisper.

Jax held a finger to his lips in warning. Slipping the Bluetooth from the dead man's ear, he listened to the frantic voice at the other end of the connection.

"Christ! What the hell happened? Fitzgerald? Fitzgerald, talk to me. Lance says he's a few minutes away. I heard shots but now the microphones aren't picking up anything. Fitzgerald?"

Moving quickly, Jax went through the dead man's pockets, removing wallet, gun, keys. He found the guy's cell phone, turned it off, and took that, too. That's when he noticed the tattoo high on one of the guy's arms: a scorpion superimposed over two crossed arrows.

"Isn't that—"

Surging to his feet, Jax clamped his hand over her mouth. "The house is wired," he whispered, pushing her toward the back door. "They can hear everything we say."

He dashed back up the stairs to retrieve their flashlights, then pulled her out of the house. She waited until they were on the back porch, then said, "Who would bug an empty house?"

The sound of an engine pushed hard cut through the night. "Shit," he said. "Here they come."

Leaping off the back porch, they lunged across the overgrown, rubble-filled yard. From the street out front came a screech of brakes, the slamming of doors. A powerful searchlight lit up the darkness, wavering as running feet slapped around the side of the house.

"Shit," said Jax again. Grabbing her arm, he ducked through the broken fence separating that yard from the next. She snagged her foot on a branch buried deep in weeds and would have gone down if he hadn't caught her. The spotlight bounced over them.

"Keep low," Jax warned. They took off across the adjoining yard just as someone squeezed off a half-dozen suppressed shots that ripped through the pile of debris to their right and sprayed the air with splinters from the wooden fence.

"You all right?" he said, not missing a stride.

"God—I—hate—to—run," she said, her voice jagged as she leaped over an old bathtub and then what looked like a broken chair.

They had to cut across three more yards to get to where they'd left the car. By the time they reached the old garage, he could feel his shoe filling up with blood, and the wound in his calf was throbbing like hell. He threw Tobie Guinness the keys to his car. "Pull it out of the garage and open the passenger door for me."

She caught the keys. He could hear her yanking open the car door, gunning the engine. He crouched down in the shadow cast by the garage wall, took the silenced pistol he'd lifted off Fitzgerald and trained it on the fence.

The searchlight's powerful beam wavered as the man holding it stooped to duck through the storm-shattered wooden fence at the edge of the yard. Taking aim, Jax fired off three rounds. He couldn't be sure if he hit the guy, but at least the sonofabitch dropped the light and flattened. Someone shouted and two more searchlights split the night. "Jesus Christ," said Jax.

The Monte Carlo shot out of the garage and slammed to a halt beside him. Jax leaped for the open passenger door. "Floor it! Let's get out of here."

She hit the gas, lurching out of the driveway and laying down a trail of rubber the length of the street. Twisting around to look back, Jax saw two men burst into the street behind them. "Get down!" he shouted as both men opened fire. The back window shattered, showering them with broken glass.

"How am I supposed to get down when I'm driving?" she asked, careening around the corner.

Jax shook the broken glass off his lap. "Damn. There goes my good driver discount."

And then October Guinness did the most amazing thing. Her eyes were wide with fear, her grip on the steering wheel so tight her fingers showed white. But she looked over at him and laughed.

Lance was standing at the base of the staircase and looking down at Paul Fitzgerald's body when Hadley walked in the back door, a stream of dark red blood running down the side of his face. "You hurt?"

Hadley swiped the back of his hand across his cheek. "Nah. Scratched myself on the fucking fence. What's the damage?"

"Fitzgerald's dead."

"Shit." Hadley blew out his breath in a long sigh. "Has the operation been blown?"

Lance shook his head. "It's bad, but I don't think things have deteriorated to the point we need to abort. There's no one in the neighborhood to have heard the shots. The house is still intact. We take Fitzgerald's body and we get out of here."

"But they've seen everything."

"So? What have they learned? Right now, all this is meaningless to them."

"It won't be meaningless after tomorrow night."

"By then they'll be dead."

52

"**I don't think Neosporan is meant for gunshot wounds,**" said October Guinness.

Jax paused in the act of cleaning the jagged flesh of his calf with peroxide and a wad of gauze, and glanced up to find her watching him with a frown. "You think I should go to the hospital, do you?"

"Yes."

They'd pulled into the shadows of the parking lot of the Walgreens on the corner of St. Claude and Elysian Fields so he could load up on peroxide, Neosporan, and bandages. His khakis were beyond saving, but he could deal with his leg.

"And tell them—what? That I got shot by a guy I killed while I was breaking into a house in the Lower Ninth? Oh, and let me introduce Miss October Guinness, currently NOPD's most wanted."

Her eyes narrowed. "Are you always such an obnoxious smartass?"

Jax huffed a laugh and started winding a length of bandage around his leg. "Medical personnel are required by law to report all gunshot wounds to the police. That's something we really don't want to have to deal with right now. The NOPD has a bad reputation. A very bad reputation. And we have no friends here."

"What do you mean, we don't have any friends here? I thought you were with the CIA?"

"Yeah. And who was that back in the Ninth Ward?"

"You think they're CIA?"

"I don't know who they are. All I know is we seem to be dealing with an endless supply of bad guys here, with some seriously sophisticated equipment and resources out the ass. I don't know about you, but that worries me. That worries me a lot. The only reason we're still alive right now is that we've been damned lucky."

"And because they've underestimated us."

It was quietly said. He looked up, his gaze meeting hers. She was tired and she was scared, but she was holding it together remarkably well. He said, "You're right. They have underestimated us. But I don't think they're going to make that mistake again. And whatever it was we saw back in that house just upped the ante."

Perspiration had dampened her T-shirt so it was molded against her breasts. He could see her chest rise and fall with each breath she drew. "Are you sure it was a bomb factory?"

"Sure? No. But that's what all the evidence pointed to. The solder, the wire fragments, the cell phone and battery packs . . . it's textbook stuff."

"The book," she said suddenly, rummaging around in her bag. She came up with a small paperback, the intricate mosaic of its cover design nearly devoid of color in the parking lot's thin lights. "Hell," she whispered softly.

He frowned. "What is it?"

She held it out to him. "It's a Koran."

He took it in one outstretched hand, turning it over thoughtfully. "Looks new."

"Is that significant?"

"It could be, yes."

He was aware of her intense brown gaze upon him. "You said you recognized the guy you shot on the boat. Did you know the guy in the Charbonnet house?"

"No. But he was Special Forces, too."

"I know." He saw her eyes widen, if as she were seeing—or remembering—something horrible. "I recognized the tattoo."

She went to sit sideways in the Monte Carlo's passenger seat, the wallet he'd taken off the dead man in the Ninth Ward in her lap. While Jax tore off a strip of adhesive, she started thumbing through the guy's cards.

"So who was he?" Jax asked.

"Paul Fitzgerald. According to his driver's license, he's from Texas." She paused. "It's a Dallas address."

Jax tore off another strip. "Somehow, I don't think that's a coincidence."

"Look at this funny card," she said, holding it up. "It's the size of a regular credit card, but it's thicker. It's got his photograph on it and some numbers, but there's no magnetic strip, no company name. Nothing."

Straightening, Jax reached out to take the card in his hand. "It's for a proximity reader."

"A what?"

"A proximity reader. It's a kind of security system, usually for the doors of a high security office. This card is basically a key. You hold it up to a reader and it's like, 'Open Sesame.' It's part of a very expensive, state of the art system."

"So where's the office?"

Jax flipped the card over in his hand. "My guess? Dallas." He glanced down at her. "I think it'd be worth our while to fly over there. See exactly what's at those coordinates of yours."

"Are you kidding? I can't get on an airplane. NOPD's most wanted, remember?"

Jax tossed her the card and smiled. "Well now, that depends on the airplane."

Tobie leaned against the car and watched Jax Alexander make another phone call.

"Hey, Bubba," he said with all the exaggerated enthusiasm of the good old boy he wasn't. "Where you at?"

Tobie choked down a laugh and mouthed, *Bubba? His name is Bubba?*

Jax ignored her. Bubba's reply must have pleased him, because he said, "Good. I need you to pick me up from the New Orleans Lakefront Airport."

There was a pause. Jax said, "I don't need a taxi, Bubba. I need a plane." He waited for Bubba's reply, then said, "I know what time it is. This is important."

He held the phone away from his ear so that even

Tobie could hear the unseen Bubba bellow, "What? You guys don't have planes?"

Jax brought the phone back to his ear and said, "We got out of the Air America business a while ago. That's why we hire guys like you these days."

Tobie couldn't quite make out Bubba's response, but its drift was obvious when Jax said, "You'll get paid for this one, Bubba."

Bubba's response was so loud, even Tobie could hear. *"That's what you said last time, Jax."*

Jax looked affronted. "You got paid, didn't you? Come on, Bubba; how much?"

The figure Bubba named rocked Jax back on his heels. "Are you crazy? I don't want to buy the airplane. I just want to use it." There was a pause, then Jax said, "I don't need a pilot. I can fly."

Bubba's response was long and heated. When he finally ran out of steam, Jax said calmly, "That wasn't my fault, Bubba."

Bubba seemed to think it was. He ranted for another minute, until Jax said, "Okay, okay. You and the plane. Just meet me at Lakeside Airport."

Tobie watched, amused, as Jax snapped his phone closed. "Who is this guy?" she asked.

"A friend of mine with an airplane."

"What does he do for a living?"

"You really don't want to know." He tossed her the keys. "Here. You drive. I need to make another phone call."

Tobie got into the car as Jax slid into the passenger seat. "I remember hearing once that espionage is largely a matter of theft or assassination," she said. "Personally, I'd say it's degenerated into a series of phone calls. Don't you worry about someone picking up your calls?"

"They're secure."

She turned the key in the ignition. "Where are we going?"

"The Hilton. I need to get my stuff." He punched a number on his speed dial. "Hey, Matt." There was a pause, then he said, "Why does everyone keep asking me if I know what time it is? Listen, there's a house in the Ninth Ward, 1214 Charbonnet Street. I think it's a bomb factory. You might want to arrange for someone to call in an anonymous tip to the FBI. There's a dead body there, too . . . Yes, I shot him. What did you want me to do? Let him shoot me? His name is Paul Fitzgerald." He reached for the dead man's license and read off the address. "He's another Special Forces guy. See what you can find on him, would you?"

Tobie gave him a sharp look when he got off the phone. "You're calling the FBI? The guys who came to my house told me they were FBI."

Jax shook his head. "They're not FBI."

"You're so sure?"

"The FBI gets some ex–Special Forces people, but not many these days. They can make too much money working for outfits like Blackwater. Our government trains them, then they go work for private security companies who rent them back to the taxpayers for ten times what they'd cost if they'd stayed in the military."

"You think that's what we're dealing with here? Mercenaries? The CIA still gets ex–Special Forces guys, doesn't it?"

He swung his head to look at her and made an exasperated sound in the back of his throat. "I told you, this isn't a CIA operation. The Director himself sent me down here."

"So how did you know the guy in the boat?"

"Stuart Ross? I recognized him from when I was on an assignment down in South America."

"Why didn't he recognize you?"

"Because I looked different."

She huffed a soft laugh. "What do you mean you looked different?"

He said, "Just drive, okay?"

Jax stood with his arms crossed at his chest, his eyes narrowed as he stared off across the empty runway. The breeze lifting off the lake felt cool against his face and brought him the scent of honeysuckle and jasmine blooming someplace unseen in the night. He looked at his watch, then glanced over at October Guinness, curled up asleep on the backseat of the car.

So far she was holding up, but he knew she didn't have a good track record. He'd thought about asking Matt to send someone down to bring her in, then changed his mind. He didn't like the way Special Forces people kept turning up on the wrong side of this operation. Until he was sure who they were dealing with, he wasn't letting her out of his sight.

He still hadn't been able to accept the idea that she could "see" office buildings and secret project files simply by accessing the shadowy parts of her brain

through some spooky process. The very thought of it
went against the grain of a lifetime of hard, practical
thinking. But it was difficult to argue with what they'd
run into in the Ninth Ward . . . or with the dead bodies
that seemed to keep piling up around her.

The drone of an airplane brought his head around.
A sleek Gulfstream jet dropped down out of the
clouds building over the lake and cruised in to a landing. Jax opened the car door and reached in to touch
her shoulder.

She awoke with a start, her eyes wide with fear. At
the sight of him, she let out a soft sigh that made her
seem unexpectedly vulnerable and touched him in a
way he chose not to explore.

He gave her a lopsided grin. "Your ride is here."

53

Bubba Dupuis—as he introduced himself—was a great bear of a man with a walrus mustache and a shiny bald crown topping a fringe of salt and pepper hair he kept long enough to tie back in a ponytail. He wore torn denims tucked into biker boots and a faded white T-shirt with black lettering that read: I SURVIVED KATRINA AND ALL I GOT WAS THIS LOUSY T-SHIRT AND A PLASMA TV.

He didn't look like any pilot Tobie had ever seen. But then, she'd never been in a private jet with swivel leather seats and mahogany tables, a divan, and a bathroom complete with a shower.

"Dallas?" said Bubba, when Jax told him where they were going. "You couldn't just drive to Dallas?"

"We're in a hurry."

Flying time to Dallas in Bubba Dupuis's Gulfstream was forty-five minutes.

Tobie washed her face, then went to sit at the polished

table where Jax had spread out a bar cloth so he could clean his gun.

"How long have you been in the CIA?" she asked, watching him.

He glanced up at her. "Ever since I graduated from college. Why?"

She rested her elbows on the tabletop as he depressed the Beretta's release button and removed the magazine. "So what did you major in? Skulduggery?"

Amusement tugged at the corners of his mouth. "History. At Yale."

"Yale? I'm impressed."

He thumbed the disassembly latch and pulled forward the slide. "Don't be. The only reason they let me in was because the Winstons have been giving Yale money for something like ten generations."

"The Winstons? As in the Connecticut Winstons?"

"My mother's family."

"So what are you? The family black sheep?"

He gave a sharp laugh. "Something like that."

She watched him lift the recoil spring guide and take out the barrel. His fingers were long and lean, his movements quick and sure. He'd obviously cleaned this gun many, many times.

"Does it bother you, killing people?" she asked suddenly.

"Sometimes."

"Not this time?"

"Not when it's kill or be killed." He took a small piece of oil-soaked rag and pushed it through the barrel with what she realized was a cocktail stirrer from the bar. "You were in Iraq, weren't you?" he said.

"Yeah. But I never shot at anyone. I was a linguist."

"Somebody shot at you. You were wounded."

"Friendly fire." Then the implications of what he'd just said hit her and she leaned forward. "How did you know I was in Iraq?"

"I saw it in your file."

"My file? You saw my file?"

He wiped the barrel and put it back inside the slide.

She said, "So you know they gave me a psycho discharge."

He eased the spring back on the recoil guide.

She said, "I'm not crazy."

He pushed the slide back on the handgrip assembly and looked up at her. "Really? A lot of people would tell you that I am."

Startled, she met his gaze and gave a sudden laugh.

Through the window she could see the lights of Dallas on the horizon, and she went to settle in one of the swivel leather seats. As she fastened her seat belt, the lights of the city rushed toward them, millions of floodlights and streetlights lined up in neat rows that seemed to stretch on forever across the flat Texas plains. The contrast between the city they were approaching and the one they'd just left was profound.

Flying out of New Orleans, the lights had been dimmed, with great swaths of the city still as empty and black as the swampland that surrounded it. Even though she lived there and saw the lingering signs of destruction every day, it had still been a jolt to realize just how much of the city lay dark and abandoned all these years after the hurricane.

But Dallas was booming, flush with oil money and

the benevolent hand of a federal government run by politicians always eager to please that big block of Texas voters. As the small jet dropped lower, the lights separated into wide boulevards, shopping malls, row after row of tidy houses.

She swung her head to look at Jax. "Do you know what part of the city those coordinates were in?"

"Irving," he said, coming to buckle into the seat opposite her. "But I want to check out Fitzgerald's house first."

"Why?"

"Because if you're right about these coordinates, I have a feeling our appearance at this building of yours is going to stir up the natives."

"I thought you didn't believe in remote viewing?"

He grinned. "I don't."

He rented a Chevy Trailblazer from a sleepy clerk who threw in a map of the city. "Here," he said, handing Tobie the keys.

"What? Not another phone call?"

"No. There's something I want to try."

He navigated her onto the freeway headed south, then took out Paul Fitzgerald's phone and started flipping through the menus.

"What are you looking for?" she asked.

"Home." He hit the speed dial and listened as the call went through. On the fourth ring an answering machine picked up with a man's voice that said curtly, "Leave a name and number after the tone."

"Nobody home," said Jax, hitting End.

"Maybe his wife's in bed and just didn't answer the phone."

"With hubby out of town? I don't think so. He wasn't wearing a wedding ring."

It occurred to Tobie she hadn't even thought to notice. "A lot of men don't wear wedding rings," she said. "Why would he have his home number programmed into his phone if there's no one at home to answer it when he's gone?"

"The answering machine's probably set up so that he can remotely access his messages."

"Oh," she said, and shut up.

"You want the next exit," he warned her.

She turned off into a subdivision of hulking stucco houses with tiny yards of neatly trimmed box hedges and flickering gaslights. The dawn was still just a pale hint of lightness on the distant flat horizon. "Mr. Fitzgerald seems to have been doing quite well for himself," said Jax.

"What do we do when we get to the house? Break in?"

"We don't need to break in. I have his keys, remember?"

Paul Fitzgerald's house stood at the end of a gently curving cul-de-sac. She pulled in close to the curb and got out. The night air felt surprisingly cool compared to New Orleans, without the suffocating, wet-blanket humidity of the Crescent City. Somewhere in the distance a dog barked, but it sounded like the yappy complaint of something like a bichon frise or Chihuahua. People who lived in houses like these rarely kept big dogs that crapped on neatly manicured lawns and tracked mud onto white carpets and shed all over designer furniture.

They walked up the short path to the front door. On the porch, Jax paused to flip open Fitzgerald's cell and hit the speed dial for Home again. From the far side of the heavy leaded glass door came the peal of a phone, followed by the answering machine.

He tucked the phone away and drew out a black zippered case from which he selected a pair of gloves and a small black device about the size of a box of matches. He held it up to the door.

"What's that thing for?" she asked.

"It tells me if the door has an alarm system—" The box's green light suddenly started blinking red as he neared the corner of the door casing. "Which it does."

As Tobie watched, he took out another small box. This time he stuck the gadget up against the wall and left it there.

"And that?" she asked.

"The sensor on the door is wireless. This jams the frequency so we can open the door without setting off the alarm."

He tried a couple of the keys on Fitzgerald's ring in the door. The third one opened the lock.

He pushed the door in about a foot, then stopped. Holding the alarm detector in his hand, he moved it slowly up and down just inside the door, his gaze trained on the device's tiny LED. The green light stayed on.

Jax grunted. "Cheap sonofabitch doesn't have a motion detector. The only alarm is on the door."

Tobie cast a quick, nervous glance around. "Can we go in now?"

The house had travertine floors and thick moldings and an entry hall that soared two full stories high. When Tobie asked, "What are we looking for?" her voice echoed.

"Anything that catches our eye. You take the upstairs. I'll start downstairs. And here—" He handed her another pair of gloves.

She left him pulling out drawers in the living room, but most of them were empty. The house reminded her of a hotel—professionally decorated but impersonal, like a stage set. Or the home of a man who was rarely there.

There were four bedrooms upstairs, each with its own en suite. On the bedside table of the master bedroom she found a silver framed photograph of two boys. They looked about eight or ten years old, and were grinning into the camera. The boys' mother was nowhere to be seen.

Unsettled, she set the photograph back on the table and went quickly through the drawers, then the closet. Nothing.

She went back downstairs to find Jax Alexander dismantling the computer in the den.

"It's password protected," he said, yanking out the hard drive. "We'll have to take it with us."

"Where haven't you checked?"

"The kitchen."

The kitchen was all black granite and stainless steel industrial appliances that didn't look as if they'd ever been used. She found a scattering of opened mail on the counter, including a bank statement with an eye-opening balance of $250,000. She stuck it in her bag.

She was just turning back toward the den when her gaze fell on a book that lay at one end of the breakfast room's oval oak table. It was a Koran, the intricate blue and yellow mosaic pattern of its cover terribly familiar. She picked it up and headed back toward the den.

"Look what I found in the kitchen," she said. "A Koran. It's the same edition as the one from the Charbonnet Street house."

"Oh, yeah? Well, look at this." Jax pulled out a cardboard box from beneath the desk and flipped back the lid. Tobie found herself staring at stack after stack of Korans, with empty spaces where perhaps as many as a dozen copies had already been taken out.

54

"Why all the Korans?" asked Tobie as Jax pulled back onto the freeway and headed north. "What's going on?"

He glanced over at her. "Do you remember seeing any Korans in that vision of yours?"

"It wasn't a vision; it was a remote viewing session. But no, I don't remember any Korans."

He drove the Trailblazer as if it were a sports car, weaving nimbly in and out of traffic. "I'm beginning to think that house in the Ninth Ward was a setup."

"A setup?" She swung her head to look at him.

"That's right. Everything we saw—the snips of wire, the splattered solder—all of it was put there to lead the observer to one inescapable conclusion: Islamic terrorists. Right down to the Koran."

"Why would someone set up a house to look like a bunch of Islamic terrorists had manufactured a bomb there?"

"Presumably so it can be found after a bomb goes off.

A bomb that may or may not have been built by a bunch of Islamic terrorists."

"You think that's what this is all about? *A terrorist attack?* But . . . what could the Keefe Corporation have to do with something like that?"

He turned off the freeway onto Irving Boulevard. "Maybe we'll understand that a little better when we get to these coordinates of yours."

Tobie abruptly sat forward, her gaze on the soaring tower of glass and steel that rose before them. "That's it. That's the building I saw." She stared at the wide granite steps, the fountain, the small garden edged by a low wall. The street in front of the building was half obstructed by rubble from a building being demolished halfway down the block.

Jax pulled in next to the curb at the corner and killed the engine. In the pale light of early dawn, the city streets were eerily deserted. He thrust open the car door, and after a moment's hesitation, Tobie followed. She realized she was shivering, from cold, from exhaustion, from fear.

"Will the building be open this early?" she asked as they climbed the broad stone steps.

"The main door will be."

They found the building directory mounted high on the wall opposite a bank of elevators. Tobie ran through the names, but nothing leaped out at her. "What do we do now?" she asked.

"Get the access card out of Fitzgerald's wallet."

She dug the dead man's wallet out of her messenger bag while he hit the elevator button. One set of doors near the end snapped open immediately.

"We stop at every floor," he told her, pressing the button for the second floor, "and see what we find."

At each of the first three floors they came to, the elevator doors slid open to reveal halls lined with office doors. But on the next floor they found themselves staring at a darkened lobby sealed off behind heavy glass doors. Beyond the lobby lay another set of glass doors leading to a corridor of offices. A black sign with bold brass letters above the reception area read: GLOBAL TACTICAL SOLUTIONS.

"See that little box beside the first set of doors?" said Jax. "That's an access card reader."

Tobie jerked her gaze away from the sign to a flat white panel with a steady round red light. "Why don't I see any security cameras?"

"They're there. They're just hidden. They could be in the air vents, or the smoke detectors, or just about anywhere." The elevator doors started to slide shut, and he hit the button to hold them open. "I need you to stay in the elevator and keep it here. If you're right about this place, we're going to need to bail out of here in a hurry."

She put her hand on his arm, stopping him when he would have moved through the doors. "Should you even go out there? If there are cameras—"

He gave a soft laugh. "They've already seen us. An outfit like this will have cameras mounted on the outside of the building. Probably even in the elevators."

"And this is supposed to reassure me?" she said, pressing her thumb on the button to keep the doors open.

She watched him cross the reception area and hold

Fitzgerald's access card about an inch away from the remote reader. The steady light blinked from red to green. There was a loud click and the doors unlocked.

"Shit," he said, and ducked back in the elevator.

In quick succession he hit the buttons for the fourth, third, second, and first floors.

"I don't get it," she said.

"The surveillance cameras trained on that card reader feed somewhere—probably to a room in the basement where a very bored guard spends his life staring at a bank of monitors. When Fitzgerald's card popped that lock, the system would have flashed Fitzgerald's ID photo up on one of those screens for comparison. So whoever was looking at me through that security camera is, as we speak, on the phone with security saying, 'We've got an intruder.'"

The elevator doors popped open on the empty fourth floor corridor. He grabbed her hand and pulled her off. "Let's go."

They could see the fire stairs at the other end of the hall. They raced toward them, yanked open the heavy door. Breathing in stale, concrete-scented air, they pelted down the steps. By the time they reached the third floor, Tobie's knee was on fire, but she kept going, round and round, her hand slick on the banister, their clattering footfalls echoing up and down the enclosed stair shaft.

As they reached the ground floor, he held a finger to his lips, then carefully pushed the heavy fire door open about six inches.

From here, she could see the bank of elevators. Two uniformed guards with bulky black holsters on their belts stood in the corridor. Their gazes scanned up and down the line of doors. As Tobie watched, the elevator they'd sent down hit the ground floor and its doors flew open on the empty cage.

Jax slapped the fire door open wide. "Now."

The fire stairs emptied into the lobby just to the left of the entrance. They were halfway out the front doors before a shout went up behind them.

Skirting the fountain, they dashed across the narrow shrubbery and leaped the retaining wall. Sprinting across the sidewalk, Jax yanked the rental car's key out of his pocket and hit the remote, popping the locks on the doors. Tobie jerked open the passenger door and practically fell into the Trailblazer. She barely got the door slammed before Jax hit the gas.

They tore up the street, dodging orange construction cones and piles of sand. "Jesus. That was close," she said, just seconds before a white Crown Victoria with darkly tinted windows exploded up out of the parking garage and bore down on them.

55

A second Crown Victoria tore up the ramp from the underground parking garage. "Shit," said Jax, throwing a quick glance in the rearview mirror. "There's two of them."

He sped up the street, the first cruiser hard on his ass, the second darting out into the lane beside them and moving up fast. At the first intersection, he spun a quick right, flooring the accelerator as he straightened the wheel, the rear end fishtailing. Beside him, October flung out a quick hand to steady herself.

"Those are police interceptors," he said, the Trailblazer's engine racing as he tore up the street. "We're never going to outrun them."

She craned around to look back. "They're police?"

"No. No lights and sirens. But these guys have the same cars police drive. Which means they're fast." He hung another quick right, forcing the second car to fall back behind the first.

"So what do we do?" she asked. "We can't keep going around the block."

"I don't intend to."

They were almost at the next intersection. Jax geared down rapidly from fourth to third, then down to second, the engine revving way up as he kept his foot off the brake.

The cruiser behind him roared up on his back end. Jax geared down to first. Tobie watched his face harden.

"What are you doing?"

"Brace yourself." Halfway around the next corner, he slammed on the brakes and threw the Trailblazer into reverse.

"What the—"

He floored the accelerator, sending the Trailblazer screaming backward. The heavy SUV slammed into the cruiser's right front at an angle, crumpling the fender back into the wheel and setting off its air bags.

Jax threw the car into first and floored it again, disengaging a nanosecond before the second cruiser plowed into the back of the first.

"You all right?" he asked, throwing her a quick glance as he raced up the street.

"Yeah." She craned around to look behind them. "Oh, shit. Here comes the second guy."

Jax's eyes darted toward the rearview mirror. The pileup had immobilized the first cruiser, but not the second. Tires squealing, air bags still deflating, it whipped around the crippled first car and tore after them.

The light at the next corner was changing. Jax floored the accelerator, streaking through the intersection under a yellow light. The light turned red. The Crown Victoria barreled on through. An early morning commuter slammed on his brakes and went into a sideways skid, his horn blaring as the cruiser shot past.

Jax narrowed his eyes against the rising sun spilling golden light through the canyons of tall buildings. He could see a green space up ahead on his right, a small park of grass and low shrubs some two blocks before the street he was on merged with another street at a Y intersection.

He eased the SUV into the gutter, the right tires rubbing against the curb as he cut in close. There was a crosswalk with a handicap curb cut, just past a four-story building of glass and steel, where the park began. "Hang on," he yelled.

October grabbed for the armrest. He jerked the wheel to the right, just enough to send his right front tire into the curb cut, then straightened out with his right wheels on the sidewalk, his left wheels in the gutter. The Trailblazer tilted wildly as he ran that way for some thirty feet. He wiped out two parking meters, the impact jarring the wheel under his grip. A cross-walk sign tumbled off the front hood to skitter across the street.

She flinched. "What are you doing?"

"I'm going to cut across the park. But if I turn straight into the curb it'll flip the car."

"Uh . . . fire hydrant," she gasped, one hand braced against the Trailblazer's roof, the other still gripping the door's armrest.

"I see it." By now he'd eased his left tires against the curb. The friction pulled the heavy car up so that they literally climbed the curb. He felt the left tires grab the sidewalk's concrete and immediately spun the wheel to the right. The SUV skidded sideways, missing the fireplug with inches to spare.

"Holy shit."

He tore across the green strip, the Trailblazer's big tires ripping through soft earth and grass and smashing rosebushes. Careening through a line of low shrubs onto the far sidewalk, the Trailblazer rocked and bounced as it clattered down off the curb and onto the far street. He hit the gas, tires squealing as he spun the wheel to the right and tore back up the street.

"What are they doing?" he asked. "Can you see?"

She craned to look behind them. "They're going up to the intersection. There's no way they can follow you across the park in that car."

He made a quick left, then a right, then another left, weaving through the city streets, moderating his speed as the morning traffic increased and they left their pursuers far behind.

October released her death grip on the armrest and smoothed the skirt over her thighs with a hand that was not quite steady. "Well," she said, studying the Trailblazer's ravaged front and rear ends. "It's a good thing you don't rent these cars in your own name."

56

"I should have remembered that brass sign," said October, pushing a small serving of scrambled eggs around on her plate. "Global Tactical Solutions. God. I saw it in the viewing session. How could I have forgotten something like that?"

They had stopped for breakfast at a small old-fashioned diner just off Lemmon Avenue. Jax tried to put in a call to Division Thirteen, but all he got was Matt's voice mail. "You're familiar with Global Tactical Solutions?" he asked, looking up at her.

"Are you kidding? They're all over Iraq—almost as much as Blackwater. Those guys make more money in a day than most of our soldiers make in a month. They have better equipment, better armor, and they can kill, rape, and steal as much as they want, because the Iraqi officials can't touch them. And because they're civilians, the American military can't touch them either."

He grinned. "Not some of your favorite people, are they?"

"No. They're mercenaries. Their very existence perverts everything this country is supposed to stand for. It's like we're morphing into Imperial Rome."

"Did you know GTS is a wholly owned subsidiary of Keefe Corporation?"

She wrapped her hands around her coffee mug and shivered as if she were cold. "No. But that explains a lot, doesn't it? Henry Youngblood obviously got Keefe interested in the use of remote viewing for mineral exploration and put in a funding proposal to them. As part of the test viewing, they gave him the coordinates of GTS's headquarters in Dallas." She gave a soft, humorless laugh. "They probably thought I'd describe the fountain outside, maybe a vague impression of the building. Instead, I zeroed in on a file that was lying on some executive's desk. The Archangel Project."

Jax finished the last of his eggs and pushed the plate away. "In a sense, this complicates things. GTS has a lot of other clients besides Keefe. They could be working on this Archangel Project for anyone."

"Including the U.S. Government."

"Including the U.S. Government," Jax agreed. He reached for his coffee. "I think that bomb factory in the Lower Ninth may be the key. Right now, we don't know if GTS set it up or if they were just watching it. But I'm inclined to think it's theirs. After all, they're the ones who responded to our break-in."

She gave up all pretense of eating and pushed her own plate away. She'd barely touched it. "Bomb factories make bombs to blow things up. So what are these guys planning to hit?"

"They may not be planning to blow up anything. Sometimes the threat of a bomb can be nearly as effective as the real thing. Look at the hysteria that swept both Britain and the States when the Brits supposedly uncovered a terrorist cell that was about to blow up a bunch of airplanes with peroxide and acetone. It was actually impossible. Did it matter at that point? No. Anyone who wants to get on an airplane still needs to shove all their liquids into one of those silly little Ziploc bags. It's a lot easier to make people scared than it is to calm them down and get them to listen to reason."

"You think that's what this is about? Making people afraid?"

"The box of Korans sort of makes it look that way, doesn't it?"

"But what could that photograph of an old Skytrooper I saw have to do with this? Does anyone even still use them?"

"There must be hundreds of them still in service. Those planes are real workhorses. I know we used them in Vietnam. And I've heard some of the ones still flying in South America saw action during the Normandy invasion."

She pushed her coffee aside untouched. "There were other photographs in that file. If I could just remember some of them . . . " Her voice trailed off, her head turning away as she stared silently out the window at the street beyond, still largely empty in the pale light of dawn.

Jax studied the curve of her cheek, the stubborn tilt of her chin. He still thought remote viewing belonged in a carnival with card tricks and palm readers, and yet . . .

"You need to do another remote viewing session," he heard himself saying.

She swung her head to look at him, her splayed fingers raking the hair off her forehead. "I can't. I told you, I tried. The link between the tasker, the site, and the viewer is important. Otherwise there's no way of knowing what is real and what is simply imagination. It's hard enough as it is. Henry told me that's why all the intelligence branches finally dropped remote viewing. Sometimes it's amazingly accurate, but it's often just flat-out wrong, and there's no way of knowing which is which. I'm afraid that if I try to task myself, all I'll get is my imagination."

"So what we need is to get you to someone who knows how to do this tasking."

"Right. Like who?"

"You said it yourself: all the intelligence branches were dabbling in this at one time or another. There must be someone around here who knows how to do this. We just need to find him." He was reaching for his phone when it rang in his hand.

He flipped it open. "Hey, Matt. I've been trying to get ahold of you."

"I've been with the Big Man. How fast can you get here?"

"You mean, to D.C.?"

October looked up at him, one eyebrow raised in silent inquiry.

Matt said, "The DCI wants you in his office pronto."

"Chandler? What for?"

"He's one unhappy hombre. Someone on high has been sitting on him. You'd better be there."

Jax let out a long, particularly crude oath.

"By the way," said Matt, "I finally got a report on Fitzgerald. He works for Global Tactical Solutions."

"We kinda figured that out for ourselves, Matt. What else do you have on him?'

"He is—or rather, was—a Middle East specialist. Speaks Farsi."

"Farsi?"

"That's right. He had an Iranian wife, but they've been divorced for a couple of years now. She works here in D.C., at a think tank."

"Get her address. What about the house in the Lower Ninth Ward?"

"The FBI raided it early this morning. Everything was exactly as you described it, except there was no dead body."

"And the security system?"

"Fed to a house in the Irish Channel. It was rented by an Iranian named Barid Hafezi. The same guy who bought the Charbonnet house two months ago."

"Who is he?"

"A journalism professor at UNO. His wife's a bio-chemist at Loyola."

"That doesn't sound good."

"No. And get this: the guy's missing. They're grilling his wife right now. Her name is Nadia. She says she doesn't know anything, but they've got some guys from Gitmo they're bringing in to interrogate her."

"Ah, Jesus. What are they going to do? Waterboard her?"

Matt made an incoherent noise. "It's the classic scenario politicians and journos always use as a justification for torture, isn't it? If there's a terrorist attack about to go down and she knows about it—"

"And if she doesn't? Or if it's a setup?"

"You think it might be? There were traces of Semtex on that canvas bag they found."

"Well there would be, wouldn't there? What about the Archangel Project? Turn up anything on that yet?"

"Still nothing."

"Listen, Matt. I need you to do something for me. Find me someone who knows how to task a remote viewer. See if we can meet with him as soon as I finish with the DCI."

Matt gave a ringing laugh. "You're kidding me, right? I thought you didn't believe in this shit."

"I don't."

Jax snapped his phone closed and looked up to find October watching him. "What was that about?" she asked.

He downed the rest of his coffee in one gulp and stood up. "The DCI's got his tit in a wringer about something."

"The what?"

"The DCI. Director of Central Intelligence, Gordon Chandler."

"Is he the guy you said you punched at some embassy dinner party?"

"That's him." Jax paused to flip open his phone again and punch in a number. "Hey, Bubba. Got enough fuel to get us to D.C.?"

57

Lance stood at the window, his gaze on the heavy gray sky.
The day had dawned hot and sultry, with a thickening
bank of clouds that promised rain by the afternoon.

The report of the FBI raid on the Charbonnet Street
house had already reached him. It wasn't part of the plan
to have the house found first. But the development was
manageable, more a complication than a derailment.
The Feds had, naturally, traced the house's security
system to the Irish Channel, but Michael Crowley had
plenty of time to clear out. It's the way they'd planned
it, except that part of the operation was running about
twelve hours ahead of schedule.

His phone rang and he flipped it open without looking at the number. It was his six-year-old, Missy.

"Mommy told me you were coming home this morning," she said.

Lance closed his eyes. "I know, sweetheart. I'm sorry. It shouldn't be much longer now."

"Barney misses you."

Lance smiled. Barney was Missy's gray tabby. "I miss Barney, too. But not as much as I miss you. I love you, honey. I'll see you tonight."

Lance closed the phone and was staring out over the city when Hadley pushed up from his laptop. "Looks like they're in Dallas," he said, hitting the Print button.

"Dallas? How the hell did they get to Dallas?"

Hadley stood with his hand out, waiting to catch the paper feed. "I don't know, but they showed up at headquarters. Even used Fitzgerald's access card to pop the lobby door."

Lance swung around. "What the fuck? Did they get in?"

"Nope. They ran."

Lance stood, snapping his fingers. "Send a team out to Fitzgerald's house ASAP. They took his wallet and keys, remember? Maybe we can catch them there. And get somebody out to the airport. If they rented a plane, I want to know about it."

Hadley handed him a printout of a lean guy in a polo shirt standing outside headquarters. "At least we got a good picture."

Lance grunted. The security camera photo was grainy but sufficient. "So that's the son of a bitch."

"Our boys chased them, but they got away." Hadley waited a beat. "They also wrecked two more of our cars."

Lance studied the open elevator just visible in the

photograph's background, and smiled. "That's okay.
The asshole's been recalled to Langley, and he's still
got the girl with him. Tell our guys in D.C. to get ready.
I don't care what they do to him. But this girl better be
dead before seven o'clock tonight or we're all in trouble."

Jax Alexander was asleep before the Gulfstream taxied
down the runway. But Tobie was too wired to drop off.
She finally gave up and went to slip into the empty seat
beside Bubba Dupuis.

"Aren't you supposed to file a flight plan or something?" she asked.

Bubba looked up from adjusting his controls and
shrugged. "Nah. Even when I do, I usually lie about
where I'm going."

Tobie huffed a soft laugh. "What exactly do you do
for a living, Mr. Dupuis?"

"Call me Bubba." He shrugged. "I fly things for the
Company—and for other outfits. Things and people."

She felt a chill that stilled the laughter on her lips.
"You mean, as in the secret renditions the Administration has been doing?"

His brows drew together in a frown. "Nah. Not me. I
don't believe in kidnapping people and 'disappearing'
them into secret prisons. As far as I'm concerned, it's
that kind of shit that makes the bad guys bad guys."

She glanced back at the man asleep in one of the reclining leather seats. "How long have you known Jax
Alexander?"

"Let's see . . . it must be a good five or six years now.

First time I met him, he was running from a bunch of Samburu in Kenya. You should have heard the shit I caught when I landed in Nairobi with a damn spear sticking out of my fuselage." He leaned back in his seat and stretched. "I seem to spend half my time bailing Jax out of some tight spot or another. The last time was in Colombia."

Tobie smiled. "More spear-throwing natives?"

"Nah. Right-wing death squads and a pissed-off ambassador. Chandler. Jax coldcocked the son of a bitch."

"Why?"

Bubba went back to fiddling with his controls. "I think it might be better if you asked Jax to explain it to you."

Tobie stared at the man who still slept soundly, one tanned arm thrown up to shade his eyes from the dim light. She'd met a few CIA guys in the Green Zone in Baghdad; company men who never hesitated to suppress uncomfortable truths or twist the facts when the politicians in Washington let it be known that was what they wanted. This man was nothing like them.

"He'll tell you he only does this shit for the excitement," Bubba said, as if following the drift of her thoughts. "But it isn't true. Get him drunk enough, and he'll start talking about our obligation to make a difference in this world and to fight for the people who can't fight for themselves. And the need to keep the bastards honest."

"Even if the bastard in question is the American ambassador?"

"Especially then."

Tobie studied the big, hairy pilot beside her. "So why do you help him?"

"Me?" Bubba laughed. "Because Jax always manages to see that I get paid, one way or another."

"What do you mean, one way or another?"

"Well . . . let's just say a few times he had to get a bit creative." Bubba frowned and flicked his finger against one of his instruments. "I don't know what it is, but ever since you sat down here, it's like everything on the panel froze."

Tobie got up and quietly moved away.

58

"It probably wouldn't be a good idea for you to show up at Langley," said Jax Alexander as they walked away from the airport's valet parking window. "Not with that APB out on you." He glanced over at her. "How about if I drop you at Tysons Corner?"

The air outside the terminal was hot and breathless, and reeked of jet fuel and engine oil. Tobie lifted her hair off her sticky neck and arched her back. "What? Are you suggesting I need a change of clothes? I've only been wearing these for two days, and it's not like it's the middle of summer or anything."

He laughed. An attendant driving a black 650i BMW convertible with cream leather seats pulled up and got out to hand Jax the keys.

"This is yours?" She tossed her messenger bag in next to his garment bag. "What are you? A double agent passing secrets on the sly to the Russians or something?"

"Nah. The Chinese pay better." He started to close the trunk, then hesitated, his gaze sharpening on her face. "Are you all right?"

In point of fact, she felt like hell. She felt like she hadn't eaten or slept in a week, but she was too jittery to do either. She was scared and confused, and she'd never felt more alone in her life. All she wanted to do was crawl under the covers of her own bed and hug her cat—or maybe stroll down Magazine Street to Gunner and Pia's shop, and smile while she listened to Gunner rant about conspiracies and government corruption. She wanted her old life back, her old self back. And she wasn't sure she was ever going to have either again.

"Sure," she said. "I'm fine."

Gordon Chandler was at his broad cherry desk, his head bent over some papers, when Jax walked into the DCI's office in the Old Headquarters Building. From here he could look out over a stand of beech and maple in full leaf beneath a smog-smudged June sun.

"You wanted to see me?"

The DCI's head came up, his eyes narrowing. He was a tall man, with the pale coloring and long, thin bones of a New Englander. Like the President, he'd graduated from Andover and Harvard and moved comfortably between executive boardrooms, public office, and plum government appointments ever since.

He didn't wait for Jax to close the door before he exploded. "Jesus Christ. What the hell have you been doing, Alexander? We send you down to New Orleans to look into a suspicious death and the next thing I know, I've got a one man World War III on my hands."

Jax stood just inside the door, his hands clasped loosely behind his back. "According to the rules of engagement, we're allowed to use deadly force to preserve our own life or to protect the life of someone else."

Chandler swiped one hand through the air like someone brushing aside an annoying gnat. "I don't need you to quote me the rules of engagement. It's your job to keep yourself out of these kinds of situations. Instead, you seem to create them. I want you to go over to the armory and turn in your weapon. Then I want you to sit down and write up a detailed report on everything that's happened from the time you got off the plane in New Orleans until the minute you walked into my office this morning. Your report will be reviewed by the Office of Professional Standards. I suspect they'll come back with a recommendation for disciplinary action. In fact, I'll be surprised if you're still with the Agency at the end of all this."

His eyes remained hard, but a tight smile curved his lips. "Now get out of my office."

Jax went down to the armory and turned in his Beretta. Then he went over to Division Thirteen to leave Fitzgerald's hard drive with Matt.

"It's password protected," he told Matt. "See if one of our geeks can figure out a way into it, would you? And were you able to set up something with one of the guys from the old remote viewing programs?"

"Not until two-thirty," said Matt, handing him an address. "There never were that many of these guys, and most of them seem to have moved out to the land of fruits and nuts."

Jax grinned. Matt wasn't a fan of California. "So who's this guy?"

"His name's Ed Devereaux. He's a priest now. Lives in Silver Spring up in Maryland. He only agreed to do it because he used to work with Youngblood. I had to tell him everything we know about the prof's death." He handed Jax another address. "This is the information on Fitzgerald's ex. She's a scholar at the Foundation for a Freer Society on South Glebe Road." Matt gave Jax a hard look. "So what'd the Director want?"

Jax turned toward the door. "He said I'm doing a helluva job and to keep it up."

"You're shitting me."

Jax laid a splayed hand across his heart and opened his eyes wide in a parody of innocence. "Would I do that?"

"Yes."

59

October was clutching a big Nordstrom bag when Jax picked her up from Tysons Corner, then headed toward South Glebe Road. "We can't meet with the remote viewing guy until two-thirty," he told her, "which gives us time to talk to Sadira Gazsi first."

"Who?"

"Paul Fitzgerald's ex. She's a scholar at a local think tank."

October hugged the Nordstrom bag to her chest and stared longingly into the distance. "I found this great little pink sundress on sale. I was thinking I'd get a chance to change my clothes. Maybe even take a shower."

"You look fine," he said, although it was a lie. She looked like she'd spent the last thirty-six hours being chased through storm-wrecked neighborhoods and jetting around the country.

Amusement crinkled her eyes. "I look like shit." She

sighed and set the bag aside. "Why should this Sadira Gazsi talk to us?"

"Because we're going to tell her we're from the FBI and we're investigating her husband's disappearance."

"But he's dead."

The light at the intersection turned green and Jax hit the gas. "You think she knows that?"

The Foundation for a Freer Society stood near the intersection of Arlington Boulevard and South Glebe Road. Jax parked his BMW on the outer edge of the think tank's lot. He always liked to minimize the potential for contact with banging doors and bumping baby carriages.

"You didn't tell me she was Dr. Sadira Gazsi," said October when they were in the brass and teakwood elevator on their way up to the foundation's fourth floor. "What's her Ph.D. in?"

"Political science. Georgetown. She came here as a child after the fall of the Shah back in the late seventies. Her father was some bigwig in the SAVAK."

"Yikes," said October. The SAVAK was the Shah's secret police force. Set up by the CIA back in the fifties and trained by the Israeli Mossad, the SAVAK were modeled after Hitler's SS. Journalists, academics, and labor leaders were their favorite targets, although their spies were everywhere. No one was safe from the SAVAK's long, bloody reach. Their brutal, grisly torture of men, women, and children had continued unchecked for more than twenty years. "Sounds like a scary lady."

"She's not her father. She wrote her doctoral dissertation on U.S. funding of right-wing dictatorships and its contribution to radicalism and terrorism in the modern age."

"You're kidding. So what was she doing married to a guy like Fitzgerald?"

"She married him when she was working on her master's and he was in ROTC. She went back to graduate school after the divorce."

October regarded him with something close to horror. "My God. How do you know all this stuff?"

He bounced his eyebrows up and down and leaned toward her to say in a heavy fake accent, "Vee have our vays."

Dr. Sadira Gazsi was a tall, slim woman somewhere in her thirties, elegantly but quietly dressed in an unstructured silk jacket and straight skirt. She was typing at her computer when a secretary showed them in, but she paused and swung toward them with a smile that faltered at the sight of Jax's FBI credentials.

"Missing?" she said, looking from Jax to October when he explained the reason for their visit. "Paul?"

Jax tucked away his FBI badge and assumed a serious expression nicely blended with compassion and concern. "I'm afraid so, ma'am. When was the last time you heard from him?"

Dr. Gazsi put up one hand to her forehead and sucked in a breath that shook her chest. "Last Friday, I guess. He usually calls the boys every weekend." She hesitated, then added, "We have two sons."

Jax nodded in sympathy. "Any idea where your ex-husband might have gone?"

"Me? No. You'd have better luck with the people he works for."

"It was GTS who reported him missing. Although I'll be frank with you, Dr. Gazsi, I don't think they're telling us everything. Do you know what Paul has been doing for them?"

She shook her head, her shoulder-length hair dark and wispy against her pale cheeks. "Not exactly. He was in D.C. about a month or so ago, on business. He stayed over the weekend to visit with the kids and take them to the Air and Space Museum. It's one of the boys' favorite places."

Jax pulled out a notebook and made a show of writing the information down. "He never said what he was here for?"

"No." She went to stand beside the window overlooking Arlington Station. "That night, we all went out to dinner at Outback Steakhouse. It's the boys' favorite. I must admit, I found some of the things Paul said that night . . . worrisome."

"Worrisome? How is that, Dr. Gazsi?"

She swung to face them, her arms crossing at her chest as she leaned back against the windowsill. "Paul has always been extremely conservative in his political views, but since 9/11, he's become patriotic to the point of being jingoistic, even racist. That night, he talked a lot about how the people in the U.S. were being lulled— that they hadn't really learned their lesson after 9/11 and they were going to need to learn it all over again."

"What do you think he meant by that?"

"He was particularly infuriated by the growth of the antiwar movement. He said they needed to be shut up.

that the next time we go to war in the Middle East, we're not going to get bogged down the way we did in Iraq. He said next time we're going to hit the bastards with everything we've got." Her lips pressed together tightly for a moment before she went on. "I didn't put it all together at the time, but later I wondered if he was talking about the Armageddon Plan."

Jax looked up from his notepad. "The what?"

"It's a contingency plan that is to go into effect in response to another 9/11-type terrorist attack on the U.S. It was drawn up by the United States Strategic Command a few years ago under very explicit orders from the White House. The idea is for a large-scale assault on Iran using both conventional and tactical nuclear weapons. Hundreds of sites are to be targeted, and estimates for Iranian civilian deaths run in the millions. But the most disturbing part of the plan is that it is to go into effect whether or not Iran is even involved in the terrorist attack that triggers it. Basically, the plan sets Iran up for an unprovoked nuclear attack."

"You say it's called the Armageddon Plan?"

"That's not its official name," said Dr. Gazsi. "It's just what the military officers tasked with drawing it up call it. They were frankly appalled by what they were asked to do. The consequences have the potential to be horrific. No one has used nuclear weapons since 1945. Just drawing up a plan like this sends an ominous message to the world."

"But how many people know about it?"

"It's known in academic and diplomatic circles. The plan calls for the use of tactical nuclear weapons rather than strategic nukes, but the loss of life and environmental contamination would still be unimaginable. Plus, it's a line that once it's crossed, there's no going back. I don't think I want to live in a world where the use of nuclear weapons is an acceptable option."

"Unfortunately," said Jax, "a lot of people already see it as an acceptable option."

"That's because they never think it through. Even without the nuclear option, an attack on Iran would have horrific consequences. Look what's happened because of our invasion of Iraq. We've destabilized the entire region. An American attack on Iran could topple every pro-Western government from Egypt, Saudi Arabia, and Jordan, to Pakistan, Indonesia, and Malaysia. Plus, Iran would never simply absorb such a devastating attack and not retaliate. It's not in their nature. They'd hit back. They'd hit our troops in Iraq, they'd hit our allies in the Middle East, and they'd find a way to hit us here, in the States. Fifty years from now, our children would still be suffering the consequences. And think of the economic effects! An attack on Iran would send oil prices through the roof and devastate the world economy. And if China or Russia were to feel threatened by an attack on their back door and decided to step in . . . "

"Armageddon," said Jax softly.

Dr. Gazsi's lips pressed together in a grim smile. "Exactly."

Jax studied her pale, solemn face. "You said you found Paul's allusions to the Armageddon Plan worrisome; why is that, precisely?"

"Because he wasn't talking about it as if it were a possibility. He was talking about it as if it were something he knew was actually going to happen." She pushed away from the window. "After Paul left, Ben—he's our youngest—told me about something his dad said when they were in the Air and Space Museum. Paul was talking about how there's more than one way to serve your country and be a hero—ways that don't get made into movies or show up in museums."

"Black ops," said Jax.

Her eyelids flickered in surprise. "Yes. Except, Paul's not in the military anymore."

"No." Jax tucked away his notebook. "He's not. Tell me, Dr. Gazsi, have you ever heard of something called the Archangel Project?"

She thought a minute, then shook her head. "No. Sorry."

Jax handed her one of his cards. "Thank you for your help. If you think of anything else that might be useful, please give me a call."

She walked with them to the door. "You know, the scariest part of all of this is that there actually is a small group of fundamentalist, right-wing Christians in the Administration who I'd say are actively working to create a situation that could trigger Armageddon in the Middle East. They expect it to bring on the Rapture, and they're looking forward to it."

"You mean the Rapture as in *Revelation*?" said Tobie. "Where the saved Christians are all supposed to be gathered up by God?"

"I'm afraid so."

"You're kidding, right?"

"I wish I were. There's a huge movement out there of people who not only expect it to happen at any moment, but are more than willing to help hurry things along."

"You think fundamentalist Christians might be behind something?" said Jax.

She paused with one hand on the edge of her door frame. "I don't know. All I know is that religious fanatics of all kinds scare me, whether they wear robes and read the Koran, or quote the Bible and run teleministries."

"Do you think she'll cry when she finds out Paul Fitzgerald is dead?" October asked as they walked down the corridor toward the elevators. "She doesn't sound as if she likes him much anymore."

"She might not like him much anymore, but she loved him once." Jax punched the button. "She'll cry."

60

"If I came up with a scheme to trigger the implementation of the Armageddon Plan," said Jax as they crossed the lobby to push open the foundation's massive, brass-framed glass doors, "I think I might be tempted to call it the Archangel Project."

October paused at the top of the institute's broad granite steps to glance over at him, her eyes narrowing against the hazy sun. "Do you honestly believe that's what this is all about? A plan to launch a fake terrorist attack someplace in New Orleans and provoke the Armageddon Plan?"

"It fits, doesn't it?"

"But why New Orleans? Why not someplace bigger, more important. Someplace like New York or L.A.?"

"I can think of several reasons to pick New Orleans," Jax said. "What could be more despicable than terrorists hitting a city that's just beginning to pull itself back together after a devastating hurricane? Ever since Katrina, a lot of people in this country feel pretty emotional about New Orleans. They've given up their vacations to go down there and gut houses and help rebuild. It's like they've adopted the city as their own. An attack on New Orleans would hit this country hard."

"But I don't get it. You heard her. An attack on Iran has the potential to destroy the world as we know it. Why would anyone want to deliberately shatter the world economy and provoke World War III?"

"Because unless we're dealing with the nutcase Rapture crowd, the men behind this don't believe the consequences will be that severe." Jax stared across the parking lot, toward where he'd left the BMW. At some point in the last half hour, a blue commercial van had backed in right beside him.

"Remember all the hype that led us into Iraq?" he said, his gaze on the blue van as they cut across the lot. "I'm not talking about the mythical WMDs or the non-existent ties between Saddam and Osama. I'm talking about the fairy-tale assumptions that the Iraqi oil reserves would pay for the war, and that our troops would be greeted with flowers, and that a puppet government put in place by an invading army could somehow be called a democracy. Every analyst with any sense was warning that populations generally greet invading armies with bullets, not flowers, and that the destruction of Iraq's secular government would plunge the country into a brutal civil war and eventually bring the Shiites to power. But who listened? People believe what they want to believe, even generals and government leaders. You think Hitler expected what happened to him when he attacked Poland?"

October brought up one hand to lift the hair off the

back of her neck as heat and the stench of new tar roiled up at them from the blacktop. "Keefe," she said. "That's what this is all about, isn't it? Defense contracts and oil leases. And because the Iraq War has exhausted our military, a new war with Iran will require even more reliance on mercenary outfits like GTS. Talk about a win-win-win situation."

Jax nodded, still studying the van as they neared the edge of the parking lot. No one was at the wheel, but it was impossible to see into the paneled back. "It's inevitable that companies like Keefe and Halliburton will push for war," he said. "It's where they make their highest profits. The men on their boards know their sons won't be the ones going off to die or be maimed, and thanks to all the tax cuts for the rich that have been pushed through in the last few years, it's us poor suckers in the middle who'll be left holding the bill. And if Dr. Gazsi is right and oil prices go through the roof, well, that's also a good thing for the Keefes and Halliburtons of this world, isn't it?"

"There's a big difference between pushing for war and setting off a bomb in an American city to provoke one."

"It's a line that's been crossed before. Jewish terrorists blew up the King David Hotel in Jerusalem back in the forties, remember? And no one knows to this day who really set fire to the Reichstag in Berlin back in the thirties."

She paused while he pointed his remote at the BMW and punched the button. "So what are they going to hit in New Orleans? The Crescent City Connection? The Superdome?"

"That's the problem, isn't it? We don't have a clue what they're going to hit or when they're going to hit it," said Jax, reaching to open the passenger door for her. The passenger window was like a mirror, showing him the reflection of the haze-obscured sun and the image of the blue van that had pulled in beside him. "All we know is—" He broke off as he saw the van's panel door begin to slide open. *"Get down!"*

61

Jax spun around just as the barrel of a silenced pistol appeared in the opening door. But the guy in the van had miscalculated. He was right-handed, which made it awkward for him to open the door with his left hand and still be in the best position to shoot.

Lunging toward him, Jax grabbed the pistol barrel and twisted it straight up. He heard the man's hiss of pain, then the unmistakable crack of bone as the guy's finger caught in the trigger guard and snapped. Tightening his grip on the barrel, Jax jerked him out of the van.

The guy yelped. "What the—"

Jax swung him around and slammed him up against the side of the van. That's when he saw the second man crouched in the back. Bad Guy Number Two started to dive out, aiming for Jax. But October grabbed the man's arm and used his own momentum to smash him face first into the side of Jax's BMW. Blood poured from his broken nose. He sagged, stunned but not out, just as Jax wrested the gun away from the first guy.

Jax had to bring the pistol handle down three times on his head before he slumped, unconscious, to the blacktop. October kicked the second guy in the head and knocked him flying. He didn't get up.

"You're good," said Jax, moving quickly to relieve both men of their guns, cell phones, and keys—anything to slow them down.

He straightened to find her inspecting the side of his BMW. "I don't think I dented it," she said, a worried frown creasing her forehead.

Jax choked on a laugh and yanked open the door. "Let's get out of here."

As soon as they were out of the parking lot, he put a call through to Matt. "You need to send someone to pick up Dr. Gazsi," Jax said. "Fast. Some goons followed us here. They might decide to play it safe and silence her."

"I'll get on it right away," said Matt.

Jax glanced over to where October sat with her arms wrapped across her chest. "You okay?"

She nodded, turning her head to fix him with her frank brown-eyed stare. "Did you recognize either of those guys?"

"No. What do you think? That I know every hired thug in the country?"

"I don't really know anything about you, do I? You might have seen my file, but I haven't seen yours."

"Maybe that's a good thing."

She didn't crack a smile. "Is it? Tell me about the death squads in Colombia."

He shifted gears. "What do you know about Colombia?"

"Bubba mentioned it."

"Bubba has a big mouth."

"So what happened?"

He shrugged. "I was up in the mountains, recruiting agents. As part of gaining the mestizos' trust, we were training some of the villagers in self-defense. The idea was to help them fight back against the rebels."

"And?"

"One morning I was out working with a couple dozen men from a village when it was hit by a right-wing paramilitary death squad. They just swept in and started machine-gunning people. Men. Women. Kids. Everyone."

"Why?"

"Why? I don't know. Maybe one of the men from the village had the nerve to start a labor union at the local Coca-Cola bottling factory. Or maybe some general wanted to drive them off their land so he could grow coca on it. It happens all the time."

"So what did you do?"

"I had some old AK-47s I was teaching the men to shoot. I handed them out and we attacked, whooping and shouting like crazy. The death squad thought we were a rebel force and ran."

She kept her gaze on his face. "And this guy Ross?"

"He was with the death squad. I recognized him because I'd seem him before. He was one of the Special Forces people around the ambassador."

"You mean the American ambassador to Colombia?"

"That's right. Gordon Chandler. I went to the embassy and confronted him with the asshole's Special Forces beret."

"And?"

"And he told me it was none of my business."

"So you *punched him*?"

"I lost my temper."

A crooked smile touched her lips.

"What?" he said.

But she just shook her head and turned away to gaze out the window.

They drove in silence for some time.

She continued sitting ramrod straight, her arms wrapped across her chest. There was a coiled quality about her, and suddenly he understood what it was about.

"You're nervous about this remote viewing, aren't you?" he said.

She swung her head to look at him. The late afternoon sunlight streaming in through the car window fell across her face and brought out the warm highlights in her hair, honey-touched with strands of caramel and sun-streaked flaxen. "Yes."

"Are you usually nervous?"

"No. But I've never tried to do a viewing that was this important before. What if I can't do it? What if all I'm accessing is my imagination and it's all wrong?"

"Then we'll just have to figure out what's going on some other way."

"What other way?" she asked, her gaze hard on his face.

But he didn't have an answer, and she knew it.

New Orleans: 6 June 12:25 P.M. Central time

Tourak Rahmadad decided to stop by Mona's Café on Carrollton for lunch. Normally he loved eating the oyster po'boys and gumbo and crawfish étouffe that had made New Orleans cuisine famous. But not today. Today he wanted stewed lamb and baba ghanoush. Today he wanted comfort. He wanted to be reminded of home.

But the tendrils of nervousness in his gut made it hard to eat. He glanced at his watch. Six and a half more hours. He pushed his plate away and watched one of the old dull green streetcars clatter past on the grassy strip of the neutral ground.

He'd thought Dr. Hafezi might call to wish him luck, to tell him he'd do fine. But Hafezi hadn't called. Tourak had everything he needed. He had his press pass, his equipment. He knew what he had to do and how to do it. But Hafezi had always been so supportive, so encouraging. Tourak knew a vague sense of disappointment he tried to shake off.

He supposed it was possible Dr. Hafezi hadn't called because he knew he could trust Tourak, knew he would do a good job. Tourak sucked in a deep breath. He could do it. He just had to keep telling himself that.

He'd make his mother proud.

62

Once, Ed Devereaux had been a warrant officer in the Army. He'd spent his entire career in intel, running agents in Southeast Asia and monitoring Soviet troop movements from Germany. Then he caught an assignment as a remote viewer at Fort Meade.

This was back in the seventies, when the program had the support of people like General Stubblebine, commander of the Army Intelligence Command. According to Matt, Devereaux had never been one of the best viewers, although he'd done respectable work. His wife died of breast cancer six months before he retired in 1981. Six months after that, he'd gone to become a priest.

Devereaux lived now in a white frame rectory on a leafy street in Silver Spring. He met them at the door, a small man with thinning gray hair and a gentle smile.

"Come in, come in," he said, opening the door. "I have everything set up for you." He led them toward a room at the back of the house. "I hope you'll understand my need to keep quiet about this. Somehow, I doubt my parishioners would be comfortable with the knowledge that their priest once walked on fire and attended spoon bending parties."

"Henry told me about the spoon bending parties," said October as they followed the priest down a short hall. "He said he could never do it. Could you?"

"Not very well, I'm afraid. But I saw people do it." He put his hands together. "Now . . . there's a couch if you like to do your viewing lying down, or I've set up a table, if you prefer that."

"I'll sit at the table. Do you have a pencil and a pad?"

"Yes, yes."

She pulled out a chair and sat, while he scurried to assemble paper and a couple of pencils that he laid before her. "I also have Hemi-Sync tapes from the Monroe Institute, if you'd like to—"

"Thanks, but I don't need them."

"Really? I always did." He took the seat opposite her while Jax stood in the doorway, watching and listening.

She sat very straight, her eyes closing as she took a long breath. Jax could see her visibly relaxing, her breathing becoming deep and slow, her lashes resting thick and dusky against her golden cheeks.

"Good, Tobie," said Devereaux, watching her closely. "Relax. Focus your attention on the Skytrooper."

Her eyes flickered open. "You mean the photograph?"

"No. Not the photograph. The airplane in the photograph. That's the target."

She closed her eyes again, her breath flaring her nostrils. "I see it. The fuselage is dark. Not shiny. I think it's dark because it's painted. Except for the underbelly. That's light. I can see a row of windows, but they're . . . empty."

"Can you go into the plane?"

She nodded, her chest rising gently with each slow breath. "Curving walls. Cold. I'm not getting anything more. Just . . . fear."

"That's okay. Step back from the airplane and look at it again. Do you see any kind of insignia?"

"A star? A circle? I can't be sure."

"Good. Take another step back, Tobie. Tell me what you see around the airplane."

"I see a large flat expanse reflecting the light. It's a sheet of water, I think, behind the plane . . . " She paused. "Except that it has grids." Picking up the pencil, she began to sketch rapidly, barely looking at the paper, as if the images were simply flowing to her hand. "No. Not water. It's a window. A huge window, or maybe a modern building with glass sides. It's like the plane is flying in front of it."

Jax knew a frisson of alarm. Oh, God, he thought. Airplanes and skyscrapers.

"There's a big round tube," she said. "It runs up and across." She drew the tube running up, then across, as if it were dangling in the sky.

"A tube?"

"Just a tube. I'm not getting anything else."

"Okay, Tobie. Describe the surface you're standing on."

Jax watched as a quiver of concentration passed across her face. He couldn't understand what she was seeing, or how. But in that moment he had no doubt that what she was doing was real.

"Concrete," she said. "I'm standing on a semicircle of concrete. Hard. Gray. There's a railing in front of me, then it drops off. It's like I'm standing at the edge of a cliff."

"Turn around and tell me what you see."

"A black cylinder. A row of black cylinders." She sketched them, one above the other, their function unclear. "They're not guns, they're too big around and short. But they're pointed at the plane."

"What's behind the cylinders?"

"It's gray." She hesitated, then shook her head, the ends of her hair brushing across her slim shoulders. "I'm not getting anything."

"Okay. Turn around so you're facing the airplane again, then take a step closer to the edge and look down. What do you see?"

"Vehicles. Big green trucks. There are two of them . . . no, three. The first one is the biggest. It . . . it has only one wheel. A short, wide wheel. No, it's not a wheel, it's a tank tread. It's a tank. I can see the machine gun mounted on the top."

Jax's brows twitched together. Maybe they were off base completely. This was starting to sound more like Baghdad than New Orleans.

"Good, Tobie," said Devereaux. "What else?"

"The second vehicle is smaller, and the third one is even smaller than that. There's an anchor. But I don't think it's a boat. There's something big and boxy beside it. Gray." She shook her head. "I'm not getting anything else from it. Just . . . fear again. It's as if the fear has bled into it, become a part of it."

"Okay, Tobie. Now turn around and look behind you. What do you see?"

"Gray. It's all gray. It's like I'm in a big, gray, open space. I get the impression of concrete. More tubes. Girders. A building that isn't finished yet, or maybe a warehouse." Her pencil scratched quickly across the next page of the pad, sketching. "There's another gun, bigger than a machine gun. It's like an artillery field piece, but it's old. It's—"

She broke off, her chair skittering across the floor as she surged to her feet. "I know what it is. It's not a warehouse. It's a museum. I'm inside a museum." She snatched up one of the sketches. "These tubes are air-conditioning ducts." She laid the pad down on the table, her gaze lifting to Jax's, her face oddly pale. "It's the National World War II Museum in New Orleans. But they don't have a Skytrooper there. They have only two planes, one's a British Spitfire and the other's a naval torpedo bomber, an Avenger. They have them suspended from the ceiling on cables. But there's no Skytrooper."

Jax pushed away from the door frame. "Maybe they changed their display."

"Are you kidding? Those things weigh tons. They don't change them."

Jax was aware of Ed Devereaux, his gaze flicking from one to the other. "Isn't that the place they used to call the D-Day Museum?" asked the priest.

"Yes," said October. "They changed the name after Katrina." Her eyes suddenly widened. "What's the date today?"

"The sixth of June," said Jax. "D-Day."

63

"I was just reading something about the museum in my retired officer magazine," said Devereaux, turning to rummage through a stack of magazines on a nearby end table. "There's an American Legion convention in New Orleans this week and they're holding a reception for Medal of Honor winners in the World War II Museum."

October stared at him. "When?"

"Today, I think." He pulled a magazine out of the pile. "Here it is. At six. T. J. Beckham will be in town to deliver the convention's keynote address and he's scheduled to make an appearance at the reception tonight."

"Hell." Jax stared down at the printed schedule Devereaux had shoved into his hands. "They're not just going to blow up a bunch of war heroes. They're going to assassinate the Vice President of the United States."

"You need to phone this in right away," said October as they strode across the church parking lot toward his car. "Get them to cancel the reception and warn the Vice President—"

"Hold it, hold it," Jax said, swinging to face her. "You do realize, don't you, that we don't have one shred of evidence that any of this is going to happen?"

She turned toward him, her face shining with such determination and naiveté that it made his chest ache. "But if *you* tell them—"

He wanted to laugh. "You think this will have credibility because it comes from me? I'm supposed to be sitting at a desk right now composing a report on the error of my ways."

Her eyes narrowed with a quick flare of anger. "Okay, so I'll call it in myself."

"Oh, right. What are you going to say? 'Hi, I'm October Guinness. You may have heard of me. I'm going to be featured on next week's *America's Most Wanted*.'"

"I'll make an anonymous call!"

"That ought to increase your credibility. You'll be just one more crank caller phoning in a bomb threat. Believe me, they get them all the time. If Beckham is going to be at the museum tonight, that means they've already swept the place for bombs. They'll just ignore you."

"They must have missed it."

"How?"

"What are you suggesting we do?" She swiped her arm through the air in disgust. "Just sit around and watch it unfold on television? If no one's going to listen to us, then we need to go down there and try to stop this thing ourselves."

"And how exactly are we going to do that?"

"I don't know! But we need to do something." She sucked in a quick breath that shuddered her chest, the sunlight filtering down through the leaves of the maple trees at the edge of the drive casting shifting patterns of shadow across her face. "One time, when I was in college, I saw someone I knew—a good friend. I was just sitting in French Lit class and suddenly I could *see* her. It wasn't like you see someone who's right there in front of you. It was more an image I held in my mind. She was crawling out her dorm window, standing on the ledge. It was a sunny day in early spring and I could see the breeze ruffling the curls around her face. But of course I didn't believe I was really seeing her so I just sat there, listening to that lecture. She jumped."

Jax wanted to say something, but couldn't.

He watched the tendons of her throat work as she swallowed. "It happened again, when I was in Iraq. The outfit I was with became convinced this gathering in the western desert was a terrorist camp. I knew it wasn't. I could see children chasing each other and laughing, a young girl dancing. I tried to tell my CO, but he wouldn't listen to me. I had no evidence. There were no corroborating reports. He put me in his nutcase bag and called in an attack."

He studied her pale, set face. The heat of the afternoon had brought a sheen of perspiration to her cheeks and upper lip. "So you went out there to try to stop it," he said softly, "and got yourself shot."

She nodded, her lips pressed into a tight line. "It was a wedding. Two big tribes. We killed something like

150 people, most of them women and children. I got there too late."

"October—" He reached for her, but she swung away, her brown eyes wide and hurting.

"No. Don't you understand? I didn't believe in it then. I didn't know about remote viewing, or what Dr. Youngblood used to call spontaneous viewing experiences. But now I do know. This is something I've seen under controlled conditions. And this time—maybe this time I can make a difference."

"But we don't know where the bomb is."

"No. But everyone has hunches—some weird, inexplicable ability to pick up on what we can't see or know by what we call normal means. Some people have that ability more than others, maybe, but we all have it. It's like when you're looking for your keys and somehow you just know to pick up your brother's coat and look under it."

"I suspect finding a bomb in a museum is a lot more complicated than remembering where I left my keys."

A warm breeze feathered stray wisps of her sun-streaked hair across her cheek, but she made no move to brush it back. He watched the features of her face harden. She'd reached a decision and there was no way he was going to talk her out of it. "If you don't want to come with me, I'll go by myself."

Jax sighed. "I'm coming. And I'm going to phone it in." He reached for his cell and punched in Bubba's number. "I just wanted to make sure you understood what we're up against. This is why all the intel branches quit fooling with this shit. There's no way to verify any of it, short of sticking your neck out and hoping nobody lops your head off."

———

Jax waited until they were airborne before putting in a call to Matt.

He laid out the details of their conversation with Dr. Sadira Gazsi and the results of the remote viewing session. There was a long silence, then Matt blew out a hard sigh.

"You can't call this in, Jax. You got no evidence for any of it. Nobody's going to believe it. All you'll do is blow what's left of your credibility."

"How about another anonymous tip?"

"We can try it. The Secret Service is a bit jumpy because of that bomb factory the FBI found in the Ninth Ward. I hear they're tightening security. But they've swept the museum, Jax. How could there be a bomb in there?"

"What, Matt? You telling me now that *you* don't believe in remote viewing?"

"Sometimes it's right on the money," said Matt. "And sometimes it's just flat out wrong."

Jax glanced over to where October sat, her head half turned away as she stared out the window. "Everything has fit so far," he said.

Matt grunted. "We managed to get into Fitzgerald's computer. The password was his boys' names: benrichard. Right there on his desktop was a file called the Archangel Project."

"So what's in it?"

"Unfortunately, it's encrypted and we haven't been able to break it yet. But there are some subfiles that aren't encrypted, stuff that looks like it was imported from someplace else. E-mails and shit."

"And?"

"There's a list called 'Jamaat Noor Allah.' I'm told that means the Light of God, by the way. It contains the names of six Middle Eastern men. Tourak Rahmadad . . . Samir Haddad . . . any of this ring a bell?"

"No."

"We've been in contact with immigration. I'm sending you their files and visa photos. One of them is Lebanese but the rest are Iranian."

"I don't like the sound of that."

"I didn't think you would. There's also a flight itinerary. Our boy Fitzgerald flew into New Orleans yesterday morning. But this is kinda weird. He was scheduled to fly out of Baton Rouge early on June seventh. That's tomorrow."

"I don't understand," said October, when Jax gave her Matt's report. "Why would he be scheduled to fly out of Baton Rouge?"

"Because if someone blows up the Vice President tonight, the first thing they'll do is close the New Orleans airport." Jax opened his laptop. The files from Matt were already starting to come through. "Here come the photos. Maybe you'll recognize one of them."

She moved to stand behind him, and the screen instantly froze.

"Damn it," Jax swore, hitting the keys. "What the hell happened?"

She picked up her Nordstrom bag and headed toward the back of the jet. "I'm going to shower and change," she said.

Jax watched her walk away. Her skirt was short and

flippy enough that it swirled around her toned thighs as she maneuvered into the plane's bathroom and shut the door. Then he glanced back down at his laptop. And it was the strangest thing. As soon as she moved away from him, the computer unfroze.

64

A light drizzle was falling when the Gulfstream touched down at the Lakefront Airport. The day was overcast and sultry, the light flat and dull with the promise of more rain.

"What time is it?" October asked as they taxied toward the terminal.

Jax glanced at his watch. "Almost six. The reception starts in five minutes, but T. J. Beckham's not supposed to put in an appearance until seven."

"This last trip is gonna cost you extra, podna," said Bubba, bringing the plane to a halt. "I had a job down in Guadalajara I'm missing. We're talking five thousand an hour."

"Bubba," said Jax, unlatching the door. "We're trying to save the world here and you're talking about profit margins and overheads?"

"Hey, I'm a patriot. But I'm also a businessman. You see Halliburton and Keefe donating their services to the war effort? No."

"Oh? So you're going over to the dark side now, are you?"

"What are you talking about, dark side? Hold on there." Bubba unbuckled his seat belt and whipped off his earphones. "I'm coming with you."

Jax swung around to look back at him. "You're what?"

"Don't get the wrong idea. I'm just protecting my investment. You get yourself killed, I'm never going to collect."

The Monte Carlo was still parked where Jax had left it. He'd expected it to have attracted the attention of the local constabulary, since the back window was shot out and it had a few other stray bullet holes. But he guessed that was asking too much of the NOPD's post-Katrina force.

"I'll drive," said Bubba, lifting the keys from Jax's hand. "The last time I rode with you, you almost got me killed."

Jax laughed. "No I didn't."

"You did." Bubba eased his enormous frame behind the Monte Carlo's wheel. "So. How do I get there?"

"Turn left here, then head for the interstate," said October. She glanced back at Jax, who'd taken the rear seat. "I read someplace that they now regularly jam cell phones in an area where the president or the vice president is making an appearance."

"They do," said Jax.

"So how are they going to detonate this bomb?"

"They probably have an infrared sensor set up. Something that can receive a coded message from a transmitter rigged to a timer. You can jam an electronic frequency, but you can't jam light."

"Or they could be using a suicide bomber," said Bubba.

"I can't see some mercenary for GTS volunteering to blow himself up for the good of the company."

"No," said Bubba. "But what about the ragheads in those visa applications Matt sent you? Where you think they fit in all this?"

October twisted sideways in the seat to face him. "Tell me, Bubba: do you call Jews 'kikes'?"

He glanced over at her warily. "No. What you think I am? A neo-Nazi or something?"

"Do you call blacks 'niggers'?"

"No. My mama raised me better'n that."

"Then why did you just call those men ragheads?"

"Because they attacked us on 9/11. They—"

"No, they didn't. Nineteen young men did, and they're dead. I don't know about you, but I don't want to be held responsible for every sin committed by every American living or dead."

"Jax?" said Bubba, meeting Jax's gaze in the rearview mirror. "Help me out here, podna."

Jax grinned. "Sorry, Bubba, but you stepped in that one."

"He does have a point, though," said October. "GTS could have set up the assassination, then tricked one of those students into believing he was a martyr to a higher cause. I have a friend named Gunner who swears something like that happened on 9/11."

"The problem with that theory," said Jax, "is that no suicide bomber would ever get past the security at the door."

"So why did Paul Fitzgerald have that list of Middle Eastern men on his computer?"

"They're patsies. The ones who have been set up to take the fall."

"But why do they need patsies? You remember what Samira Gazsi said. The Armageddon Plan calls for an attack on Iran *even if* they're not linked to the next terrorist attack."

Jax shook his head. "That might have worked a few years ago. But things have changed. Iraq changed them. The American people have been lied to too many times and they're starting to get wary. It's easy to stir them up by talking about fighting to defend freedom and democracy, but they're not stupid. They see the national debt shooting into the stratosphere. They see young men and women coming home in body bags and wheelchairs from a useless war that has nothing to do with freedom or democracy, and everything to do with politics and oil and big profits for the defense industry. They're not going to go tripping down that primrose path so easily a second time. They're going to want to see proof."

"So the young Iranians have been set up to be the new version of yellow cake and WMD," said October.

"Exactly. Even if there's no link between the Iranian students and the Iranian government, people in this country will be too scared to be thinking straight. I suspect the Administration would find it easy to make the case for another war."

Bubba swept onto the interstate. "I don't want to rain on y'all's parade, but how you planning on getting into this reception? It's not a public event. I heard on the radio comin' in here that they've got the streets blocked off out front. There's some group of protesters that are pissed off because they're making them hold their rally a good block away."

"Gunner," said October, sitting forward.

Jax looked over at her. "What?"

"Gunner Eriksson. He's a friend of mine. No one holds a protest rally in New Orleans without Gunner's PA system." She turned toward him. "Let me use your phone."

Jax handed it over. She started to flip it open, then paused. "What if they've tapped Gunner's line?"

Jax met her worried gaze. "At this point, that's a risk you're just going to have to take."

65

"Hey, Gunner," said Tobie, when he answered his phone. "It's me."

"Tobie? Jesus. You okay? The police have your picture splattered all over the place."

"I'm okay. Where are you?"

He had to shout to be heard over the noise of traffic in the background. "We're set up at Lee Circle. They're not letting us get any closer."

"Listen, Gunner. You remember our conspiracy theory? Well, believe me, it's bigger than we imagined. Much bigger. I need to get into this reception at the World War II Museum. How can I do that?"

"Jeez. That's not going to be easy. It's not open to the public. Just Medal of Honor winners and a few select guests. One of our supporters has a cousin in the mayor's office and managed to get a couple of guest passes we thought we might use to sneak a few people inside. I'd let you use those but she said she'd meet us here at the Circle and she hasn't shown up yet."

"What time do you expect her to get there?"

"She was supposed to be here half an hour ago."

They came down off the interstate at the St. Charles exit. Mist clung to rooftops and the spreading branches of half-dead crepe myrtles dripping with old Mardi Gras beads. This part of the avenue had seen better days, the grand houses that once stood there having long ago been torn down and replaced by rows of dreary office buildings.

"Now where?" said Bubba.

"Left."

They swept under the interstate, past parking lots dark and sodden from a recent rain. Lee Circle stood just on the other side of the freeway, a broad circular mound planted with grass, dwarf yaupons, and wildly blooming pink rosebushes. In its center rose a sixty-foot column of white marble crowned at the top by a statue of Robert E. Lee.

The Circle had been on a downhill slide even before Katrina. Now most of its ugly 1950s-era buildings stood empty and boarded up. Of all the graceful old homes that had once fronted the green, only one remained, a decrepit pink turreted house at the corner that had been turned into a bar.

"There," she said, pointing to the small group of pro-testors in rain slickers who'd gathered on the right side of the mound. From here they could look up Andrew Higgins Drive, past the red stone towers of the old Confederate museum, to the concrete and glass ware-houselike bulk of the World War II Museum. There, a different kind of crowd had gathered, men in suits and women in jewel-toned silks and aging veterans in mothballed uniforms. The reception might be limited to Medal of Honor winners and select guests, but the guest list must be mighty long, Tobie thought. The streets in all directions were lined with parked cars.

Bubba pulled in close to the Circle's curb, the white pickup behind him honking as he stopped traffic. "It ain't gonna be easy to find someplace to park in this mess. I'll meet y'all outside the museum."

Tobie looked at her watch. "I'm not sure that's a good idea, Bubba. We don't find that bomb, this whole area could blow."

"You don't find that bomb," said Bubba, "and I'm never going to get paid."

She found Gunner fiddling with his PA system. He'd had to run an extension cord from the Circle Bar across the street to the steps in front of the statue, and the connection didn't seem to be working very well.

He flung up his hands when he saw her. "Oh, God; stay back, Tobie. You come any closer and I'll never get this thing to work."

"What's he mean by that?" Jax Alexander asked, giving her a hard look.

"I don't know," she lied as she stopped and let Gunner walk up to them.

"Leila got here a few minutes ago," he said, reaching under his rain slicker to pull out two gray cards embossed with the D-Day Museum emblem and encased in plastic sleeves suspended from black neck bands.

"Thank you, Gunner." She hung one of the black bands around her neck and handed the other to Jax.

"What exactly are you protesting, anyway?"

Gunner pointed at the damp white banner they'd stretched across the base of Robert E. Lee's column. From the size and shape of the cloth, she thought it might once have been someone's bed sheet before it was donated to the cause and stenciled in big black letters: MAKE LEVEES NOT WAR.

Lance Palmer had cast a final look around the museum's cavernous lobby and was heading for the exit when he got a call from one of his operatives.

"We just intercepted a conversation between the Guinness woman and that guy named Gunner Eriksson," said the operative. "She's on her way to the museum now."

"We'll pick her up," said Lance with a smile. He snapped his phone closed and nodded to Hadley. "We just got lucky."

66

Lance Palmer kept one hand inside his jacket, the handle of his small .380 Sig Sauer cool against his palm as he and Hadley worked their way through the press of sweating journalists and gawking tourists hoping for a glimpse of the Veep or maybe one of the Hollywood celebrities who were expected to put in an appearance.

The street in front of the museum had been closed to vehicular traffic, but they were letting pedestrians past the barricades. Only a scraggly bunch of unpatriotic lowlifes with a silly rain-drenched banner and a PA system that didn't work had been banished up a block to Lee's Circle. Which was a pity, Lance thought; he'd like them to have had a front row seat for the show that was about to take place.

"How much time we got?" Hadley asked, his eyes narrowing as he scanned the crowd. "We don't want to be standing here when that sucker blows."

Lance glanced at his watch. "Twenty minutes."

"There she is," said Lance, his gaze focusing on a

small woman in a pale pink sundress, with a guest pass slung around her neck. He studied the lean dude in chinos and a black polo shirt beside her. "And there's the sonofabitch who's been causing us so much trouble."

Hadley grunted. "How'd they figure it out, I wonder?"

"Does it matter?"

"It does if they told someone."

"If they did, it doesn't look like anyone believed them," said Lance as they cut through the press of onlookers. "I don't see the cavalry."

There was still a crowd of latecomers bunched at the door, held up by the bottleneck of security and metal detectors and X-ray machines. "You take the girl," said Lance, moving into position. "The asshole is mine."

Lance shoved his .380 into the small of Jax Alexander's back just as Hayden's fist closed around the girl's upper arm. "Put your hands in your pockets and keep them there," Lance said softly, leaning in close to Alexander's ear. "Your hands come out of your pockets and you're dead. It's that simple."

They walked down a street of painted old brick warehouses, through moist air heavy with the smell of wet pavement and machine oil. Tobie could hear the steady drone of traffic from the interstate that curled away toward their right and the rattling vibration of a helicopter hovering unseen somewhere in the distance.

She threw a quick glance at the man who held her, his fingers digging hard into the flesh of her bare left arm. He wasn't looking at her, and she had a pretty good idea why. She wanted to say something, but her mouth puckered with a bitter taste like old pennies and she knew there was nothing she could say that was going to change what was about to happen.

"This way," he said, jerking her around the corner into a street with brick gutters and a massive yellow Dumpster and construction crane that blocked the road, effectively turning it into a dead end. The warehouse beside them loomed some three stories tall, red brick framing old glass windows that showed wavy reflections of the day's fading flat light. They were maybe a quarter of the way down the block when Palmer said, "That'll do."

They paused beside an ancient portico of columns and an entrance door obscured by heavy bolted iron gates. "If you know who I am," said Jax, his hands still carefully kept in his pockets, "then you know that every last detail of this little project of yours has been turned over to the CIA and the FBI."

Lance Palmer laughed softly. "Right. That's why they've got every bomb squad in the South crawling all over the place even as we speak. You see, I know all about remote viewing. And I know why every intel agency in the country got out of the business more than a decade ago. Because a guy sitting in a darkened room 'seeing' things in some unexplained corner of his mind doesn't produce verifiable information. There's a difference between accurate and verifiable."

"Maybe. But the pieces are there. An idiot could put them together."

"Only an idiot would try. If you expect me to be scared, I'm not."

Tobie shifted her weight slowly, carefully, her heart

pounding so hard the blood surged painfully in her ears. No one was paying any attention as she slipped her right hand into her bag. She felt for the smooth handle of the Glock and found it, her finger curling around the trigger.

It was awkward aiming through the bag's canvas side, her elbow crooked out clumsily. She pointed the muzzle blindly at Lance Palmer's chest and squeezed off two rounds—*pop pop*—the air filling with the stench of cordite and burned canvas.

Both rounds hit, blooming red across the man's white shirt. His body jerked once, twice, his eyes widening in surprise and a desperate hope that was fading even as she swung the Glock's silenced muzzle toward the man beside her.

He'd had time to pull his gun out of its holster, but he was still bringing it up when she nailed him. She squeezed her finger over and over again, his body jerking, stumbling backward. This time she was careful not to look into his eyes. But she was close enough that she felt the warm spray of his blood on her bare arm.

"Holy shit," said Jax.

Tobie yanked the Glock out of her ruined bag and gripped the stock in both hands, ready to squeeze off another round if she needed to. She didn't. The men were dead.

Jax wiped the back of one hand across his sweat-dampened forehead. "You okay?"

"Yeah," she said, although she wasn't. She swallowed, breathing hard through her nostrils, her grip on the automatic so tight she realized her hands were starting to ache.

"How'd you think you were going to get that gun through the museum's security check?"

"I forgot I had it," she said, her voice cracking.

He put his strong hand over hers, loosening her grip. "Here. Give it to me."

She let him take the gun.

He wiped it down, which she would never have had the presence of mind to do. Then he tossed it into one of the construction Dumpsters and put a gentle hand on her arm. "Our fifteen minutes just narrowed down to five."

67

A crowd of latecomers still clogged the entrance to the museum. Tobie clenched her hand over the scorched hole in the front of her bag and hoped no one noticed the blood splatters on her arm and the skirt of her dress.

"Keep your head down," said Jax, leaning in close to her. "And whatever you do, don't turn around. Ever meet an NOPD homicide cop named Ahearn? Small, sandy hair, invisible eyelashes?"

The taste of copper pennies was back in Tobie's mouth. She was careful not to look around. "No. Why?"

"Because he's standing over there beside one of the uniforms at the barricades. I think he's made us."

"What do we do?"

One of the men guarding the doors said, "Excuse me, miss. You need to put your bag on the X-ray machine and move through the metal detector."

"Sorry," said Tobie. As she stepped toward the metal detector, she threw a quick glance over her shoulder and saw him: a plainclothes detective with sandy hair pushing purposefully through the crowd. "Shit," she whispered.

Jax grabbed her arm, pulling her up the stairs into the museum's huge main entrance hall.

It was a cavernous space that soared some four stories high. The main front wall was glass, but the rest of the structure was concrete and steel. Gray walls, gray ceiling, gray floors. The only color came from a row of allies' flags ranged along a shallow second story balcony at the rear and the three green Army vehicles parked in front of the windowed wall: a Sherman tank, a half-track, and what she now realized was an old amphibious jeep. She could see its anchor, still incongruously fastened near the rear.

Jax touched her arm. "There's your Skytrooper."

Tobie's head fell back. She found herself staring up at a huge C47. The last time she'd been here, not too long after she first moved to New Orleans, two small, single-engine planes were suspended by heavy cables from the ceiling of the museum's lofty main hall: a British Spitfire fighter and an old naval torpedo bomber called the Avenger.

The Spitfire was still there, in the far corner. But the Avenger had been replaced by a much larger C47. It hovered high over the center of the warehouse-like space, a lumbering transport with a white underbelly and rows of dark windows nearly lost in the dull sheen of its fuselage.

"Oh, God," she said, her gaze fixing on the encircled star that was the emblem of the old Army Air Corps. "That's it. They must have hidden the—"

"Don't say it," he warned her.

She lowered her voice. "They must have hidden the *package* in the plane when the museum made the switch."

"The problem is, how are they going to detonate it?"

Tobie scanned the laughing, chattering throng, their voices melding together into a dull roar. Clusters of men in suits and women in silken dresses balanced wine-glasses while selecting hors d'oeuvres from the trays of passing waiters. A wizened little man in a wheelchair sat looking out at nothing in particular, a proud grin on his face, the Medal of Honor on its blue ribbon around his neck nestling next to rows of other medals pinned to the chest of his faded uniform. Beyond him, Tobie could see the mayor's bald chocolate head thrown back as he laughed at something.

"What time is it?" she asked.

"Two minutes after seven. Beckham is already here. See him? By the podium."

Tobie followed his nod. A podium had been set up between the museum's two hulking Higgins boats.

"Every minute we stay here," said Jax, leaning in close to her, "brings us that much closer to dying."

She looked up at him. His voice was calm, but she could see the sweat glistening on his upper lip, see the rapid rise and fall of his chest. "What would happen if we yelled fire? Wouldn't that at least clear the place out?"

"No. We'd be tackled in an instant and hustled out of here."

"Then you leave," she said, frantically scanning the crowded hall. "There's no point in you staying."

"Right. I'll just clear out and let you and all these other people get blown to pieces."

She saw his eyes suddenly narrow. "What? What is it?"

She followed his gaze to where a young man with dark hair and a hawklike nose stood off to one side. He was lugging a huge video camera and had a press pass around his neck. What was it Jax had told her about the guy who owned the Charbonnet house? He was a UNO professor, wasn't he? A journalism professor.

"That's one of the guys in the visa photos Matt e-mailed me," said Jax. "He's Iranian."

As they watched, the Iranian raised the Canon camcorder. It was big and black, designed to take digital videos on tape. He panned slowly over the crowd, then swung to point it directly at the vintage airplane looming over them.

"Grab him!" yelled Jax, surging forward. *"There's a bomb!"*

"No, wait!" Tobie knew Jax had taken one look at that long black lens and remembered the cylinders she'd sketched during the remote viewing session. But it was all wrong. "That's not it!" she shouted. But Jax had already lunged.

Women screamed, their colorful skirts swirling as they scrambled out of the way. Jax knocked into a young waitress with a platter of shrimp that flew into the air, the waitress crashing back into a guy with a tray of drinks.

The young Iranian turned to stare, his green eyes wide with confusion, not understanding until the last minute that the guy in the khakis and the polo shirt was coming at *him*.

Jax slammed into him, bowling the kid over, the camcorder flying out of his hands to land with a shattering smack on the hard concrete floor.

Suddenly, something like a dozen guns erupted from beneath suit jackets and out of little purses, the *snick* of their hammers being drawn back loud in the hushed silence. "Get down, you son of a bitch," yelled a Secret Service agent with a big .357 Sig he stuck in Jax's ear. "Do it! Do it! On your face! Arms out to the side! Make a move and I blow your brains out!"

Jax lay facedown on the concrete, his arms spread-eagled, a Secret Service agent's foot in the small of his back and a dozen guns pointed at his head. "The camera," he said. "It's the triggering mechanism for a bomb."

One of the agents—a hulking guy with a blond crew cut—leaned over to pick up the Canon. "Doesn't look like a bomb to me."

"No, you don't understand . . . " Jax began.

But Tobie was looking beyond him, at the spotlights mounted on the wall behind him. *Big, black cylinders.*

"Shit," she whispered.

She swung around. The lights were everywhere, mounted high on the walls and on the exposed steel girders. Heart pounding wildly, she let her head fall back.

The hall had been built with a semicircular observation platform that jutted out into the air from the third floor balcony. It stood just about level with the Skytrooper hanging suspended from the center of the hall's ceiling. Two flights of concrete and steel stairs climbed toward it, wrapping around the elevator shaft.

Tobie stared at the platform's familiar gray metal railings. *Whoever took the photograph of the Skytrooper in the Archangel Project file had been standing on that platform.*

She looked beyond the platform, to the rear wall where a row of three black spotlights hung suspended from a pole, the last one positioned so it pointed straight through the side window of the C47's cockpit.

She raced toward the steps, taking them two at a time, just as the sandy-haired detective burst through the knot of security at the front entrance and shouted, "That woman in the pink sundress—*stop her!*"

68

Tobie sprinted up the stairs, her breath sawing in and out with terror and a surging rush of adrenaline. She hit the first floor balcony, nearly stumbling as her knee buckled for a moment, then held.

She was dodging the elevator shaft, headed for the second flight of stairs, when she spotted a fire extinguisher mounted on the wall near a restroom and some drinking fountains. A half-formed idea in her head, she swerved to yank open the small door and wrench out the canister. She was expecting it to set off an alarm. It didn't.

She turned back toward the second flight of stairs just as a man burst out the exit door ahead of her, a slim Latino with a pencil mustache. He came at her with his teeth barred. Clutching the fire extinguisher with both hands, she swung it at him. The end of the canister whacked against the side of his head. He stumbled back and landed on his rump. She dashed past him, up the second flight of stairs.

Careening around the elevator shaft, she darted out onto the viewing platform, then stopped, her chest jerking wildly with her breathing. She'd thought she would be able to spray fire retardant foam onto the face of the light canister, but she saw now that it was mounted too high. She'd never hit it.

She was aware of the sound of running feet, pounding up the stairs, slapping across the gallery. She spun around, her body pressing up against the railing as she frantically scrabbled with the extinguisher's safety pin. Pointing the hose, she squeezed the handle, a sulfurous powder shooting out the nozzle in an arc that filled the air with an acrid smell as it slapped against the cockpit window.

Rough hands grabbed her from behind, snatched her back from the railing, yanked the fire extinguisher from her hands. "Get down! Now!" someone screamed in her ear. They shoved her to her knees, the concrete scraping her bare skin.

And then, in the sudden, breathless silence, she heard it: an audible click. A small red beam of light appeared on the yellow powder obscuring the window of the C47's cockpit.

"What the hell is that?" said the big black agent with his Sig shoved against the base of her skull.

"It's an infrared signal," she said, sucking in a breath that shook her entire frame. "There's a bomb in the Skytrooper."

69

Adelaide Meyer sloshed a measure of Russian vodka into a glass and downed it in one long pull, her gaze on the fifty-inch plasma TV at the end of the room. The reports coming out of New Orleans were confused, the screen filled with flashing blue and red lights splashed across the World War II Museum's towering glass and concrete facade.

She didn't exactly understand what had happened or why. All she knew was that the Vice President was still alive and Lance Palmer, who should have been reporting to her right now, was dead.

She poured herself another drink. She wasn't the kind of woman to panic. She sucked in a deep breath, inhaling alcohol fumes and what smelled suspiciously like her own body odor. She was sweating. She knocked back the second drink and zapped off the TV.

Whatever the potential damage from this debacle,

it could be contained. She was certain of that. With enough money and power, anything could be contained.

She'd told Westlake that all the threads led back to her, but that wasn't exactly true. There was still one slender thread that ran to Clark Westlake and from there to the President himself. Oh, not that Randolph had ever come out and exactly said what he wanted done. That's not the way these things were handled in the Oval Office. He'd simply looked over at Westlake one frosty morning when they were doing their daily three mile run around the White House gardens and said, "The liberal press and the bleeding hearts on the Hill are becoming a serious threat to our agenda, Clark. Nine/eleven shut them up for a while, but they're back at it again, and too many of the good people of this country are starting to listen to them. They don't understand that America has a destiny. A destiny and a responsibility. Nine/eleven let this country go into Iraq and take care of Saddam, but without something similar, I'm afraid our plans for Iran are going to be derailed. I trust I make myself clear?"

And Westlake had blinked and said, "Yes, Mr. President."

Adelaide turned toward her library, to the safe she'd had built into the wall behind her desk. "Call Lopez," she told her maid, Maria. "I want the Learjet ready in an hour. I'll be flying to Dallas tonight."

"Yes, Meez Meyer."

Adelaide punched in the combination and yanked open the safe door, her fist closing around the small memo recorder she kept there. It wasn't enough to convict or impeach, but it could embarrass. And politicians didn't like to be embarrassed.

She shoved some papers into a soft-sided briefcase, but she didn't need to pack. She had another house in Dallas. It was where she'd been born. She was going home.

New Orleans: 7 June 2:00 A.M. Central time

Lieutenant William P. Ahearn stared at the young woman who sat at the end of the interrogation table, her crossed arms hugging her chest. He and Trish had been grilling her for six hours now, and she was still telling them the same story. It was the biggest crock of bullshit he had ever heard anyone spin. They'd had time to look into her background in the last few hours, and what they found was not good. The girl was a real psycho case.

"All right, Miss Guinness," he said, pulling out the chair opposite her and sitting down. "Let's try it again, shall we? Only, leave out the part about the crystal balls and Ouija boards, would you?"

She fixed him with a hard brown stare he found unexpectedly intelligent and lucid. "You people own a computer? Get on Wikipedia and look up remote viewing."

Ahearn met Trish's gaze.

She pushed up from her chair and stretched. "I'll go do it. I need a break anyway."

"And while you're out there," he called after her,

"check and see how Bullock is doing with the smartass. Last I heard, he was still claiming to be a CIA agent."

"He is a CIA agent," said Guinness calmly.

Ahearn glanced over at her. "Right. At the moment, we're still trying to figure out what the asshole's real name is."

70

Every morning of his life, T. J. Beckham rose at 5:00 A.M. He spent twenty minutes doing the series of push-ups and sit-ups they'd taught him in the Army when he was still a green kid from the hills of Kentucky. He shaved and showered, and then he liked to sit down to breakfast, usually orange juice, oatmeal, and blueberries, although on special occasions he allowed himself to splurge.

This was a special occasion. Besides, he was expecting company.

"They're here, sir," said one of his aides.

Beckham set aside his morning briefing papers and pushed to his feet. "Show them in, then leave us. All of you."

The young woman looked tired and apprehensive. Jax Alexander just looked tired.

"I understand I owe you my life," said Beckham. "Simply saying thank-you sounds so inadequate, but, well . . . thank you. I'm sorry if you spent an uncomfortable night in the local lockup. It took us longer than it should have to figure out what was going on."

"At least they drew the line at pulling out our fingernails," said Alexander.

"There was a time I might have laughed at that statement, Mr. Alexander. Not these days." He held out his hand toward a nearby cloth-covered table spread with domed silver serving plates and glistening pitchers of juice and milk. "Please join me. I don't know if they told you or not, but you were right. There were several pounds of plastic explosives in the cockpit of the C47, very carefully sealed and sanitized, and probably placed there months ago, which is why the security sweep didn't pick it up. I'm told the chemical signature they look for would have dissipated by now. However, I'm afraid some of the other information you gave us proved to be less accurate. There were no bodies in the street around the corner from the museum."

Miss Guinness looked up from scooting in her chair but said nothing.

"Please help yourself," said Beckham, handing her a plate of toast. He turned to Mr. Alexander. "You might be interested to know that the young gentleman with the camera you tackled—a Mr. Tourak Rahmadad—claims to have been ignorant of any bomb. It seems he's a journalism student and was there simply taking video footage for a documentary. It was his first such assignment, and I gather he was rather nervous. He admits to having been a member of something called Jamaat Noor Allah, but he claims their sole purpose was to study the Koran. Interestingly enough, his fingerprints were found on a Koran in Miss Guinness's bag."

"Interesting," said Mr. Alexander, giving nothing away.

"There was some talk of sending him down to Gitmo," Beckham continued smoothly, "but I've intervened. He'll be deported. It'll wreak havoc with his education, but at least he's alive. According to Matt von Moltke—you know Mr. von Moltke, I understand—his sole role in all this was probably to provide a dead Iranian at the scene of the explosion."

"What about the Iranian professor?" asked Alexander, helping himself to eggs. "Is he still missing?"

"Dr. Barid Hafezi? I'm afraid so. We suspect he may also have fallen victim to a scheme to discredit his nation of origin."

"And his wife?"

"Is being treated at one of the local hospitals. Unfortunately, she has no memory of how she came by her injuries."

Miss Guinness made an incoherent noise.

Beckham handed her a platter. "Some fruit, Miss Guinness?"

She took two slices of melon and passed the platter on to Alexander.

Beckham said, "I don't suppose you've heard about the accident last night? An executive jet flying the CEO of Keefe from D.C. to Dallas exploded in midair. Five casualties were reported: the pilot and Miss Adelaide Meyer, and three employees of Global Tactical Solutions—Paul Fitzgerald, Lance Palmer, and Michael Hadley."

Alexander met Beckham's gaze. "Matt told you we have Fitzgerald's computer hard drive at Langley?"

Beckham cleared his throat. "I'm afraid not. It seems to have disappeared from there."

"Son of a bitch," swore Alexander, leaning back in his chair. "There's no way to tie any of this back to Keefe, is there?"

"Keefe?" Beckham reached for the milk pitcher. "No."

"So who's going to be fed to the press? The finger's got to point at somebody."

"The President and I had some discussion about this. Under the circumstances, I convinced him that it would be in the best interests of all concerned that this be identified as a domestic problem. Right now, speculation centers on a disgruntled Iraq War vet." Beckham held the young man's gaze. "No foreign involvement. No conspiracy."

"A lone bomber instead of a lone gunman? Is that what you're saying? All we need now is a grassy knoll."

Beckham poured himself a glass of orange juice and glanced at the woman beside him. "You're very quiet, Miss Guinness."

She looked up, her eyes hooded, careful. "I'm a linguist, sir. When it comes to international intrigue and power politics, I'm afraid I'm out of my depth."

"You're also a very talented remote viewer."

A shadow of surprise flickered across her features. "You're familiar with the old programs?"

"Oh, yes. Which is why I've arranged to have you recalled to active duty."

"What?" The look of horror on her face was almost comical. "Can you do that?"

He hid a smile. "I'm afraid so."

"But—"

"You've been given a special, indefinite assignment to Division Thirteen in the Central Intelligence Agency."

"She what?" said Alexander.

"The CIA?" echoed Miss Guinness. "But no one there believes in remote viewing. Not anymore."

"That's not exactly true. No one knows better than the CIA the limitations of our spy satellites and the NSA's listening posts. A remote viewer has no limitations. He—or she—can send her mind anywhere in the world. It's cheap, and it's safe, and it works."

"But it isn't reliably accurate," she said. "Even an eighty percent accuracy rate means that twenty percent of the time I'm dead wrong."

"Considering the Company's track record lately," said Beckham dryly, "an eighty percent accuracy rate would be a big improvement." He swung his head to look at the man beside him. "As for you, Mr. Alexander—George Chandler wanted to have you cashiered for disobeying orders, but I convinced him to give you another chance. I hear you're something of a loose cannon. In my experience, there are times when loose canons can be valuable."

He picked up another serving platter and gave his guests a wide smile. "Now, who likes grits?"

Tobie waited until they were in the hall outside the Vice President's suite before she exploded. "They can't do this to me!" She swung to face Jax. "Can they do this to me?"

"I'd say so, yeah."

She ran the splayed fingers of one hand through

her tangled hair. "What in the hell is Division Thirteen?"

Jax's eyebrows drew together in a frown. "Obviously more than I've been told. I think Matt has some explaining to do."

Later that afternoon, Tobie bought a bouquet of daisies in the hospital gift shop and took the elevator up to visit Colonel McClintock.

She found him sitting up in bed, a massive bandage around the crown of his head and another on the side of his face. But his coloring looked good and he was reading a book that he set aside at her knock.

"Come in, Tobie. I've been wondering how you were doing."

She came to stand at his bedside. "I killed two men," she said.

His expression was professionally flat. "So I heard. Are you okay with that?"

"Not exactly. One of them had a couple of kids. A boy and a little six-year-old girl."

"He made bad choices, Tobie."

She nodded. When her throat opened up again, she said, "So, how are you?"

His features relaxed. "I've got a hard head. They're supposed to let me out of here tomorrow."

"I can't tell you how sorry I am that I involved you in this . . . that I got you hurt."

"What are you talking about, Tobie? I'm the one who involved you in remote viewing, remember?"

She laid the daisies on his bedside table. "I've been called up again. Had you heard?"

"Yes." An unexpected smile lit his eyes. "I'm sorry. I know you didn't enjoy your military experience."

"I've been given an indefinite assignment to the CIA. Something called Division Thirteen. You ever hear of them?"

Colonel McClintock shifted his weight, looking oddly discomfited. "As a matter of fact, yes. I hate to tell you this, Tobie, but I occasionally work for them myself."

CIA agent Jax Alexander and remote viewer Tobie Guinness team up once again in search of a missing World War II-era Nazi submarine and its dangerous cargo—a cargo that, decades later, threatens to kill millions and leave the fate of mankind hanging in the balance.

Don't miss this next heartstopping adventure

THE DEADLIGHT CONNECTION

Coming soon from HarperCollins

1

Engines throbbing, the salvage ship sailed into the secluded cove by the cold light of a misty Baltic dawn. Stefan Baklanov stood at the *Yalena's* prow, his hands clamped around the rusted rail, his gaze fixed on the rickety docks of the old shipyard before them. He was sixteen years old and just beginning his second season working on the *Yalena*, an early twentieth-century diesel-powered catamaran. He heard his uncle, the captain, bark an order from the bridge, then felt the deck of the old ship shudder beneath him as the engines slowed. A shiver of excitement tingled up Stefan's spine, mingled with a stir of unease. He threw a glance over his shoulder at the barge that wallowed in their wake like a dead whale. On the barge's deck rested the ghostly bulk of a Nazi-era IX class U-boat.

Even in the dim light of dawn, the submarine's long, low silhouette and conning tower were unmistakable, its steel hull dull and rusted and covered with accretions from the sixty-plus years it had lain beneath the waters of the Baltic Sea, a silent tomb to the scores of Germans who'd once sailed her. The sailors were still there—or at least, their bones were still there. Stefan knew because last night he'd taken one of the dive lights and squeezed in through the sub's popped hatch for a quick, furtive look.

His uncle and a couple of the men had already spent hours crawling through the U-boat's narrow passageways and cramped quarters. His uncle emerged unusually silent and grim faced, but that only piqued Stefan's curiosity more.

At first it had been a grand adventure, squeezing through silent portals, gazing in wonder at funny old glass and brass gauges in the engine room and at the cook pots still hanging over the galley range. But as the narrow golden beam of his light played over long-abandoned bunks and empty leather boots, Stefan grew more thoughtful.

He'd expected to crawl through a wet, rusted interior smelling of brine and the creatures of the sea. But nothing was wet. With a chill, he realized that for all these years the sub's hull had held. Then he saw the pair of eyeglasses lying on a table and the trumpet clutched against the desiccated rib cage of the man who'd once played it, and the awful truth of what he was seeing hit him. These men hadn't died quickly in a fiery explosion. They hadn't even drowned. They'd suffocated. Slowly.

Stefan had grown up hearing his grandmother's stories of the Great Patriotic War, of the siege of Stalingrad and the deadly winters of '42 and '43. He'd imagined the Nazis as demons, as somehow not quite human. He'd never thought of them as the kind of men who might set aside a pair of reading glasses to clutch a beloved musical instrument to their chest as they breathed in their last, dying gasps. Suddenly the narrow passageways and low ceilings seemed to press in on him, stealing his breath until he raced for the hatch again, not caring how much noise he made or who saw him.

Uncle Jasha had slapped his big hand against the side of Stefan's head for taking the dive light without asking. But when Stefan started ranting about how what they were doing was wrong—wrong and dangerous, for surely they were tempting the wrath of the ancient gods of the sea—Uncle Jasha had simply laughed and called him sentimental and superstitious. Yet the sense of foreboding lingered, even in the cold light of day.

Now, Stefan sucked in a deep breath of air tinged by the acrid stench of an old fire smoldering in the shipyard. A shout from one of the *Yalena's* crewmen drew his head around and he caught the sound of an outboard motor cutting through the stillness. He peered into the mist, past the rocky point where a scattering of stunted, wind-twisted pines grew. It took a moment before he could see the launch filled with six or eight men that skimmed across the flat pewter water toward the *Yalena*.

"Damn," muttered Uncle Jasha, coming to stand beside Stefan at the rail. A big, barrel-chested man with a salt-stiffened head of dark hair and a full beard, Jasha Baklanov still towered over Stefan by half a foot. For five years now, Uncle Jasha had been the closest thing to a father Stefan had.

Stefan glanced up at him. "Who is it? The men from the shipyard? Why are they coming out to meet us?"

Instead of answering, Uncle Jasha rubbed one work-worn hand across his mouth and down over his heavy beard, his nostrils flaring wide. "Get below."

"But I wanted to—"

"God damn it, boy. Do as you're told. For once."

Stefan threw a last look at the approaching launch, then pushed away from the rail.

But he didn't go below. Heading for the open stairwell, he ducked behind the tattered tarp that covered the life-boats and their davits and doubled back so that he was some ten or fifteen feet away from the landing where the men would come aboard. Through a slit in the tarp he watched his uncle station himself beside the rail.

The whine of the outboard motor drew close, then suddenly died as the launch bumped against the *Yalena*'s hull. Stefan watched the men come aboard—dark-haired, solemn-faced Slavs from the looks of them, with maybe a few Chechens. But the man who walked up to Uncle Jasha was subtly different. Dressed in a black sweater and loose overcoat, he was as dark-haired as the others, but tanned. When he spoke, his accent was strangely clipped, his phraseology awk-ward, like a man who'd learned his Russian as an adult or in school. "This wasn't the plan," said the man.

Uncle Jasha's face darkened, and Stefan realized this must be the man who'd hired the *Yalena*, the man Jasha referred to only as "the Major". "There were complica-tions," Uncle Jasha lied. "We needed to move early."

A tight smile split the Major's face. "And you didn't

notify us because . . . ?"

Rather than answer, Jasha Baklanov said, "You've been watching us."

"Did you think we wouldn't?"

From where he crouched behind the tarp, Stefan felt his heart begin to pound.

The Major glanced toward the barge and its long, silent burden. Jasha Baklanov said, "The sub's cargo is still there."

"Good. Then you won't mind if my men take a look." The Major nodded to the two Chechens. Stefan could hear the tramp of their feet as they headed aft. When Stefan brought his attention back to the Major, he understood why all the men were wearing loose overcoats. As the man stepped away from Uncle Jasha, the coat opened to reveal a MAC 10 machine pistol.

At a nod from the Major, all but one of the men spread out over the ship in a way that made Stefan nervous. The minutes crawled past. Then Stefan watched, terrified, as the Major flipped open a sleek cell phone. He said something Stefan couldn't hear before glancing over at Jasha Baklanov, his eyes narrowing. "The hatches on the sub have been blown."

The man beside the Major lifted his machine pistol so that the muzzle pointed at Uncle Jasha's chest. Jasha shrugged. "I was curious."

"I hope for your sake the cargo is still there."

"I told you, it's still there."

Again the Major said something into his cell phone. After a moment, he smiled. "You're right." He nodded to the man beside him. "Kill him. Kill them all."

Stefan sucked in a gasp of air, the betraying sound

lost in the rattle of submachine gun fire.

He heard another sharp, staccato burst of submachine gun fire from somewhere below, followed by another and another. He bit down hard on his lip to keep from crying out, his mouth filling with his own blood as the killing went on and on.

When the quiet finally came, it sounded eerie, unnatural. Stefan could hear the gentle slap of the waves against the *Yalena*'s sides and the surge of his own blood pulsing through his veins.

Uncle Jasha lay sprawled on the deck. As Stefan watched, the Major walked over to stand looking down at what was left of the *Yalena*'s captain. In a welling of near blinding grief and raw fury, Stefan willed himself to remember each detail of the man's full face, the thick lips that pulled into another tight smile. "Stupid greedy Russian," said the Major in his own language, a language that made Stefan shudder.

The Major glanced back at the man still cradling the extended stock of the machine pistol against his shoulder. "Search the ship. Make sure we have everyone."

Stefan flattened his hands against the cold steel behind him, not daring to breathe as the man brushed past. When they searched the ship they would find him.

He watched, shivering, as the Major headed aft, his footfalls echoing on the silent deck. Dropping to his belly, Stefan wiggled out from under the tarp, darted across the deck and climbed the rail in one frantic scramble. He heard a shout, but he was already pushing off, his body arching effortlessly into a long, flawless dive honed by years of practice.

The water was an icy cutting shock that drove the air

from his body and all thought from his brain. Gasping with agony and fear, he surfaced more by habit than by conscious volition, then heard a shout and dove again as bullets slapped into the water around him.

A pearlescent cave of icy soundless death, the sea cocooned him in crystalline suspension. He stayed down until his lungs burned and his vision dimmed and he knew he had to either risk being shot again or die. He thrust his head up into the air, his body aching and shuddering as he drew in breath. Swinging around, he realized with a new jolt of terror he'd become disoriented in the mist.

Behind him, the outboard motor coughed to life, the sound blurred and distorted by the softly drifting mist but unmistakably there. Kicking hard, Stefan struck out in the opposite direction, toward what he hoped was a rocky point crowned by the dark, twisted silhouettes of wind-tortured pines.

2

No one in the Central Intelligence Agency wanted to be transferred to Division Thirteen. Any project or assignment with the potential to be either personally embarrassing or a career-wrecker was handed down to the guys in the Division. Which is how the CIA file on the phantom Nazi sub ended up with Jax Alexander's name on it.

"A phantom Nazi sub?" said Jax when Matt von Moltke called him into the basement cubbyhole that served as the Division's offices. "This is a joke, right?"

"I'm afraid not," said Matt, coming from behind a row of filing cabinets with a sheaf of printouts in his hands. "We located it a couple of years ago, lying in about 300 feet of water off the east coast of Denmark. A British destroyer sank it with depth charges only a month or two before the Nazis surrendered." Matt paused. "It's a Monsoon, an IXD-2 class sub."

Jax leaned against the doorjamb, his hands on his hips. "That's significant?"

"Very." Matt limped over to start assembling the books and papers scattered across the battered chrome and Formica table that took up most of the floor space in his office. "They were some of Germany's biggest subs, designed for long-range operations. Only a few of the Monsoons were ever deployed, mainly carrying war material to the Japanese in the Pacific and bringing raw materials back to Germany."

"What was the sub that went down off Denmark carrying?" said Jax, pushing away from the doorframe.

Matt held out a black and white photo of a long, slim sub lying on a sandy seabed. "We're not sure, but we think it was gold."

"Nazi gold?" Jax took the photo with a soft laugh. "Somebody's been reading too many paperback thrillers."

Matt didn't even crack a smile. "It's no joke. The Nazis were sending all kinds of shit out of Germany near the end of the war. Some of it was jet engine plans and rocket research to help the Japanese. But some of it was just loot."

Jax came to perch on the edge of the sturdy old table. "So why is the CIA interested?"

"Because the NSA has been picking up chatter lately linking a Nazi sub to some sort of terrorist attack. It didn't make any sense until we realized the *Monsoon* off Denmark is missing."

Jax stared down at the grainy photo in his hand. "What do you mean, *missing*?"

"Just that. It's gone." Matt handed Jax another photo.

This one showed the same stretch of seabed, empty now except for a long depression in the sand and what looked like a few broken bits of rusting metal. "That image was shot this morning. Ever since we located the *Monsoon*, we've been keeping an eye on it. Given its cargo, our government wanted to raise it, but the Germans refused. Sixty-four men went down with that sub. They consider it a gravesite and they didn't want it disturbed."

"Looks like somebody disturbed it." Jax studied the two photos. "So who is this terrorist group the NSA is tracking?"

"We're not sure, although there's some indication we may be dealing with a homegrown outfit. Our guys think they're planning to use the gold from the Nazi sub to finance a major attack somewhere in the U.S."

Jax looked up from the photos. "No idea where?"

"Nope. Nor do we have a clue who these guys are. We're hoping the sub might lead us to them."

"Just how hard is it to raise one of these suckers, anyway?"

"That depends on how deep it is and how good a shape it's in. The Brits have started a salvage operation, raising the captured German subs they sank at the end of the war for their steel."

"Sounds like an expensive way to get steel."

"Yeah, but this isn't just any steel. This is pre-1945 steel. Steel production involves a lot of air, and we've exploded so many nuclear bombs in the atmosphere in the last sixty-odd years that the air is radioactive. Steel picks it up, which means all steel manufactured since 1945 is radioactive."

"Now that's a scary thought."

"No shit. The problem is, we need clean steel for certain kinds of sensitive instruments. The only place to get it is from old ships."

"And subs," said Jax. "Maybe terrorists didn't have anything to do with your missing U-boat. Maybe it was simply stolen by someone looking to make a quick buck salvaging the steel."

"You're forgetting the NSA's chatter."

Jax huffed a soft laugh. "Right. You know as well as I do that most of the linguists the NSA has translating their intercepts would have a hard time ordering a cup of coffee in Cairo."

"These guys were speaking English. Unaccented English. Which is why the thinking is, the operation is home grown."

"Shit." Jax reached again for the image of the empty seabed and frowned. "Our satellite photos of the area don't show anything?"

Matt shook his head. "It's open water. We had no reason to be targeting that area. We're running computer checks to see if we just happen to have picked something up, but it's gonna take time. And time is one thing we don't have."

Jax picked up the pile of files and books, and slid off the edge of the table. "I guess the first place to start would be to put together a list of every ship in the world capable of salvaging a sub of that size."

"I've got some people working on it. They should be

able to get you at least a preliminary tally by tomorrow morning. But it's going to be a long list." Matt glanced at the clock. "I'm hoping to have some more information in an hour or so."

There was something airy about Matt's tone that set off Jax's warning bells. "Some more information coming from where?"

Matt's gaze slid away.

"Out with it, Matt. What aren't you telling me?"

"I asked Colonel McClintock to task Tobie Guinness."

A couple of books skittered off the pile of files in Jax's arms and clattered to the floor.

"Good idea," said Jax, hunkering down to retrieve the dropped books. "A phantom Nazi sub loaded with stolen gold probably isn't quite enough to get Division Thirteen laughed out of the Company. Why not add a touch of woo-woo?"

"Remote viewing is not woo-woo. It's science. And you know it."

"Right." Just because Tobie had nailed Keefe Corporation's nasty little scheme last summer didn't mean Jax bought into the whole alternative states of perception business. With every passing month, he'd found himself growing increasingly skeptical, increasingly convinced there must be some other explanation for what had happened. He stood up. "Maybe we can find an astrologer and a tarot card reader to consult while we're at it."

"According to the last report I had from McClintock, Tobie's viewings have been running spot-on eighty percent of the time."

"Yeah?" Jax turned toward the door. "Well let's hope this isn't one of those twenty percent misses."